Time Funnels

Visit Two Worlds Media for titles from

Crosswater Books

Two Worlds Press

and

Max Features

www.twoworldsmedia.com

Time Funnels

The Accidental Journey

By Timothy Jones

Illustrations by
Lisa Hewitt

CROSSWATER BOOKS

TIME FUNNELS: THE ACCIDENTAL JOURNEY

© 2016 by Timothy Jones

Published by Crosswater Books

A division of Two Worlds Media

Brush Prairie, WA

Cover design by Lynnette Bonner of
Indie Cover Design - www.indiecoverdesign.com

ISBN-13: 978-1523732067
ISBN-10: 1523732067

Printed in the United States of America

Acknowledgements

This novel would likely never have been completed if not for my good friends Barry and Trish Dyck. After reading the first handful of chapters, which had been on hold for too long, their encouragement motivated me to revive the project and bring it to its conclusion.

To my daughter Anne Hollis, I owe the deepest gratitude. Her passion and enthusiasm for this story came to rival my own as we spent countless hours side by side raising the text to heights I never would have achieved on my own.

Also, I must thank Laura Petermeyer, TyAnn Hunt, Anne Cutone, Grace Klepec, Taylor Jones, and Lindsay Holmes for their extensive and insightful comments, questions, and suggestions, which proved so helpful.

A special thank-you is due to Dr. Keith Luria, Director of Graduate Programs at North Carolina State University. His expertise regarding early 17th-century Catholic observances was vital to the rendering of a historically realistic portrayal of French religious practices.

In addition, I wish to thank Travis Roth, Jared Grambihler, and Ben Howard, who after reading early drafts of this book endorsed the effort with their encouraging words.

And to my editor, Debbie Austin: the multitude of spot-on suggestions, comments, and new ideas was a remarkable boost to the manuscript I placed in your hands. It's been a lot of fun working with you. Thank you so very much for applying your talents to this project.

All of you played an integral part in the successful completion of this novel, and I appreciate every one of you for your invaluable contribution.

Contents

Prologue

Excerpts from

The Harleian Miscellany

A discourse of a strange and monstrous Serpent, &c.

True and wonderfull. A Discourse relating a strange and monstrous serpent (or dragon) lately discovered, and yet living, to the great Annoyance and divers Slaughters both of Men and Cattell, by his strong and violent Poyson: In Sussex, two miles from Horsam, in a Woode called St. Leonard's Forrest, and thirtie miles from London, this present Month of August, 1614. With a true Generation of Serpents.

Printed at London, by John Trundle, 1614.

In Sussex, there is a pretty market-towne, called Horsam, neare unto it a forrest, called St. Leonard's Forrest, and there, in a vast and unfrequented place, heathie, vaultie, full of unwholesome shades, and over-growne hollowes, where this serpent is thought to be bred; but, wheresoever bred, certaine and too true it is, that there it yet lives. Within three or four miles compasse, are its usual haunts, oftentimes at a place called Faygate, and it hath been seene within half a mile of Horsam; a

i

wonder, no doubt, most terrible and noisome to the inhabitants thereabouts. There is always in his tracke or path left a glutinous and slimie matter (as by a small similitude we may perceive in a snaile's) which is very corrupt and offensive to the scent; insomuch that they perceive the air to be putrified withall, which must needes be very dangerous. For though the corruption of it cannot strike the outward part of a man, unless heated into his blood; yet by receiving it at any of our breathing organs (the mouth or nose) it is by authoritie of all authors, writing in that kinde, mortall and deadly.

This serpent (or dragon, as some call it) is reputed to be nine feete, or rather more, in length, and shaped almost in the form of an axletree of a wagon; a quantity of thickness in the middest, and somewhat smaller at both endes. The former part, which he shootes forth as a necke, is supposed to be an elle long; with a white ring, as it were, of scales about it. The scales along his backe seem to be blackish, and so much as is discovered under his bellie, appears to be red; for I speak of no nearer description than of a reasonable ocular distance. For coming too neare it, hath already beene too dearly payd for, as you shall heare hereafter.

It is likewise discovered to have large feete, but the eye may be there deceived; for some suppose that serpents have no feete, but glide upon certain ribbes and scales, which both defend them from the upper part of their throat unto the lower part of their bellie, and also cause them to move much the faster. For so this doth, and rids away (as we call it) as fast as a man can run. He is of countenance very proud, and at the sight or hearing of men or cattel, will raise his necke upright, and seem to listen and looke about, with great arrogancy. There are likewise on either side of him discovered, two great bunches so big as a large foote-ball, and (as some think) will in time grow to wings; but God, I hope, will (to defend the poor people in the neighbourhood) that he shall be destroyed before he grow so fledge.

He will cast his venome about four rodde from him, as by woefull experience it was proved on the bodies of a man and woman coming that way, who afterwards were found dead, being poysoned and very much swelled, but not preyed upon. Likewise a man going to chase it, and as he imagined, to destroy it with two mastive dogs, as yet not knowing the great danger of it, his dogs were both killed, and he himselfe glad to returne with hast to preserve his own life. Yet this is to be noted, that the dogs were not preyed upon, but slaine and left whole: for his food is thought to be, for the most part, in a conie-warren, which he much frequents; and it is found much scanted and impaired in the increase it had wont to afford.

These persons, whose names are hereunder printed, have seene this serpent, beside diverse others, as the carrier of Horsam, who lieth at the White Horse in South warke, and who can certifie the truth of all that has been here related.

John Steele.
Christopher Holder.
And a Widow Woman
living near Faygate.

1
Garage Sale

Tyler lay on his back, eyes closed. His leg hurt, his arm hurt, but it was nothing compared to his headache. Every heartbeat sent throbbing pain through his head, creating nausea so intense his stomach threatened to push out his breakfast. He felt his left leg twisted underneath him, but as he started to straighten it out, a stabbing pain shot up into his back, so he stopped and slowly took inventory of himself. Keeping his eyes closed so he could concentrate, he gently wriggled his fingers, toes, and each limb to get a better idea what kind of shape he was in.

The nausea subsided, but he had to get his leg straightened out. Eyes still closed, he gingerly lifted himself up and slowly scooted backwards on his elbows. He had just freed his leg when the back of his head hit something hard. Opening his eyes, he looked behind him and saw he had bumped into a computer monitor. He surveyed the scene around him. He was in a small clearing in the woods, the ground littered with papers and what looked like the hardware from their workstations. *Wait! The ground?*

When he looked to his far right, he saw Jessi face down, her head on a rock, blood pooling onto the dirt beneath her cheek. Anxiously, he started to call out to her, but the nausea returned like a flood, and his stomach was soon empty. *Hmm, tasted better the first time*, he thought.

He took a deep breath of fresh air and slowly exhaled. He tried to make sense of it all, but the pounding in his head made it impossible to concentrate. All he could think was, *where are we?*

* * * * * *

1

April, Current Year

He stood at his locker loading his backpack. It was Friday, and he was making sure he had all the books and papers he and Jessi would need for the weekend's homework assignments. *Eighth grade almost over*, he thought. A locker door slammed, and he glanced over. She stood in front of her locker, shifting her weight from one foot to the other and jumping a little as she rocked back and forth.

"C'mon, Tyler. Let's go! I wanna get our work done," she called out.

"Hang on, I'm almost ready," he answered. "*Our* work?" he muttered under his breath. He zipped up his backpack and slung it over one shoulder.

I just should've said no, he thought as he headed her way. *But how do you tell your teacher you don't want to help a classmate with her math?*
"Okay, let's go."

They walked down the hall and turned left into the gym, heading for the opposite door that was their shortest way home. Parker Theissen was shooting hoops, as usual, and the ball bounced their way. Without breaking stride Jessi reached down and scooped up the ball, but she lost her balance as her backpack slipped off her left shoulder. She dropped to her knee before slowly getting back up.

"That wouldn't have happened if your boyfriend had been carrying your pack for you," Parker smirked.

Jessi stood up and handed her backpack to Tyler. "Hold this for me, would you please, Tyler?" Her voice was friendly, but fire was in her eyes. *This should be interesting, he thought.*

Her expression changed to a big smile as she turned towards Parker and casually walked over to him. "Thanks Parker, I'll keep that in mind," she said as she gently lofted the ball to him.

Parker's eyes followed the ball. It made contact with his hand—at the precise moment Jessi's fist made contact with his nose. He never saw it coming.

Tyler winced as he looked around the gym. No teachers in sight. *You really shouldn't have done that*, he thought.

The basketball rolled away as Parker was holding a bloody nose, and rubbing a sore butt.

"And *this* wouldn't have happened, Parker, if you didn't talk stupid," Jessi calmly responded.

Tyler shook his head as he helped her put her backpack on. "You know, that probably wasn't very—"

"Tyler," Jessi interrupted. "If you 'Pull a Parker,' I'll hit you too."

He stepped back beyond her reach and shrugged. "Fair enough."

Tyler and Jessi lived next door to each other about 10 blocks from the school. Jessi had moved from the East Coast last fall just as school was starting, and he had become her "first friend"—as she called him. Her mom had been a Second Team All-American in basketball, and her dad was a retired major-league third baseman. She was a naturally gifted athlete and fiercely competitive.

The warm afternoon sun shone through the large maple leaves as they walked down the sidewalk. It was a perfect spring day, and it was expected to last through the weekend. The warm weather was waking up everyone's yards, and the sound of a lawn mower buzzing in the distance reminded Tyler he had to mow this weekend. There were a couple other things on his chores list—a little longer now than during the winter, but not too much to handle. He was glad Jessi had agreed to do her math as soon as they got home—one more thing off his list.

They were just a few blocks from the school when Jessi called out, "Hey, Ty, let's check out this garage sale. Maybe I'll find another one of dad's rookie cards!" She ran on ahead. Everything was laid out on both sides of the driveway from the sidewalk clear into the garage. The owner stood in front of the garage just under the eave of the house, talking to a shopper that was holding an elementary grammar book. Tyler came up. "What's going on?" he asked.

"Don't know," Jessi replied quietly, "but they look a bit frustrated trying to communicate."

Tyler looked more closely at the two men "Oh hey, that's Uncle Jim!"

"You have an uncle?" Jessi asked.

"Nah, it's Mr. Foster. I call him that 'cause my aunt and him dated for several years when they were in college. After they broke up, he married my sixth grade teacher."

"Is that the teacher who disappeared all of a sudden?"

Tyler nodded. "She went home after school one day and never came back. Jim was in Los Angeles all week, so the police didn't suspect *him*. Her car was in the garage, but she was just gone! It was in the news and everything. We got a substitute to finish out the year, but it just wasn't the same." He took a deep breath and slowly let it out.

"I had heard something about that. Sorry, Tyler."

"Well, Jim developed a video game a few years ago, then turned it into an app for smart phones. It went totally viral."

Tyler's heart sank as he thought about it again. Mrs. Foster had been a great teacher and had gotten him hooked on reading. And now, thanks to her, he was always packing a book everywhere he went. Looking around at the things for sale, he saw a lot of ladies' stuff—*must be hers*. He swallowed hard.

"Let's go, Jessi," he said.

The other shopper said something to Jim. It caught Tyler's attention because it wasn't English, and he sounded frustrated.

"What country are you from?" Jim asked. "Where ..." He cut himself off and looked down at a box of books on the ground. Spying an atlas, he pulled out the large blue hardback book, opened to a page with a map of Europe, and gestured to the man to point out his country.

"Romania," the man answered. Jim nodded and smiled. "Stay here five minutes, please," he said as he pointed to his watch and then held up five fingers. "Five minutes." The man seemed to understand and nodded.

Without even seeing Tyler or Jessi, Jim disappeared into the house. Tyler knew he had to stay at least a few minutes now.

"Hey, look at this!" Jessi held up a video game.

"Star Commandos! That's the game he wrote! He must've had a few left over." Tyler looked around. There *was* some cool stuff to check out while he waited.

Jessi looked through the box in front of her. "Ty, come here," she said. "Look at this. He's got Star Commandos for Xbox®, PlayStation®, *and* PC. Did he really write the programs for all three platforms?"

"Yup, that's what Mrs. Foster said."

"By *himself*?"

"Yup."

"He must be a freakin' genius, *and* freakin' rich."

"Probably."

"So why doesn't he live in some big house somewhere? Doesn't make sense." Jessi continued to look through the disks, all priced at 50 cents each. She started reading the fine print on one to see if it was compatible with her computer.

Meanwhile, Tyler found a book about a kid whose family was among the original settlers of Virginia back in the mid-1600s. Anything about pioneer life always got his attention. He brushed his blond hair aside as he started reading, his green eyes darting back and forth across the lines of the opening pages.

A few minutes later Jim came out of the house, walking slowly. He looked a bit unsteady on his feet as he shielded his eyes from the sun.

He said something in what Tyler assumed was Romanian because the other man responded quickly and smiled, obviously pleased as they resumed talking. Jim kept squinting and rubbing his temples as they talked. He looked like he was sick.

Tyler watched as the Romanian gave Jim a five dollar bill for a box of English grammar books that had probably belonged to his teacher. He knew she would be happy that her books would be of use once again, but it was tough to watch.

Jim pocketed the money as he walked over to Tyler and Jessi. "So, you two see anything you want?" He smiled, but Tyler could tell he wasn't feeling so good.

"Kinda, but I might come back tomorrow once you've slashed your prices." Tyler smiled at him, hoping that his joke would be taken okay, and also hoping that maybe he could get a better deal right now on the book he was holding.

"It's too soon to haggle, but ..." He looked at Tyler with a sense of recognition. "Tyler, right?"

"Yeah."

"You probably don't remember me, but I used to, umm, be friends with your aunt."

"Yeah, I remember that."

"So how's she doing these days?"

"Good, I guess. She just got another degree. Art or history or something. And she got a cat."

"I'm a dog guy myself. So where are they living now?"

"Who? Her and her cat?" The conversation was feeling pretty awkward.

"Well ... yeah."

"She's still in California."

"Cool, cool," he said with a nod. "Sooo, tell ya what, for old time's sake, you can have that book for 50 cents. Deal?"

"Deal," said Tyler, as he pulled out a couple of quarters.

"And what about you?" he asked Jessi. "Find something you like?"

Jessi looked up at him. "Yeah, I *really* like that archery set over there, but ... will you take a dollar for these three games?"

Jim hesitated a moment. "Well, how about ... you help me move everything back in the garage, and we'll call it good, okay?"

"You bet!" Jessi exclaimed. "Give me a hand, will ya, Ty?"

"Sure, but you'll owe me." *In addition to the math tutoring*, he thought.

Together they carried everything into the garage. Jim still didn't look so good; he went inside and a minute later came out wearing sunglasses. He sunk into a lawn chair and watched.

"Be careful of the Beemer," he called. Tyler noticed it was a special edition; he took extra care not to bump it as he carried an armful into the garage.

"I'm opening the sale up at nine o'clock tomorrow morning," he said. "If you two get here at eight-thirty to help me set up, we'll see what other deals we can work out, okay?"

"Sure!" Jessi answered for them both.

As they walked down the sidewalk headed for home, Jessi blurted out, "That was *GREAT!*" She jumped and did a 360. She landed fine, but her backpack kept spinning and continued to pull her around. She regained her balance just in time to keep from falling into an azalea bush in someone's front yard.

"What's great?" Tyler asked.

"I'm getting an archery set tomorrow," she said mischievously.

Tyler shook his head.

"And besides that, I got three games for like, almost free!"

"Yeah, cool," Tyler replied. It *was* cool, but something was bugging him about Jim and the Romanian. He walked on in silence trying to sort it out.

"I don't get it," he said to himself.

"What?" Jessi asked.

Tyler didn't realize he had spoken out loud. "Umm, nothing." What he saw happen with the Romanian man kept his brain spinning in circles. "Hey, let's get on that math right away."

"Sure. Hang on, I just got a text." She pulled out her phone. "Oh wait, I can't. Mom says we're going to my aunt's for dinner, but I'll see ya tomorrow about eight-fifteen, okay?"

"Shoot. Yeah, okay," he replied.

Later that evening during dinner Tyler exclaimed, "Guess what? I saw Uncle Jim today!"

"You did?" his mother said. "He's such a nice guy. Where'd you see him?"

"Jessi and I stopped at his house on the way home from school today. He's having a garage sale."

"You went garage sale shopping on your way home? What's with that?"

Tyler twisted a little in his chair. "Jessi and I walked home together because I was gonna help her with her math. She ran ahead of me when she saw the stuff in his driveway; she's looking for her dad's rookie card."

His dad joined in. "I saw Jim at the hardware store Wednesday when I was getting the new light fixture for the study. He was picking up some garage sale signs and miscellaneous lumber. He said he was ready to let go of some of his wife's stuff, and he was doing some remodeling."

"Yeah, I saw a bunch of her stuff on the different tables. It was weird. I didn't want to stick around, but Jessi was looking at some video games, so we were there about ten minutes, and I *did* see some interesting books. Oh hey! He said he'd give us a deal on more of his stuff if Jessi and I would help him with his sale tomorrow. That's okay, isn't it?"

"What about the lawn? It needs to be mowed. And I was going to ask you to help me—" his dad began.

"But on the other hand," his mom interrupted. "It would be nice to help Jim. I'm sure this is a difficult weekend for him. I think it'd be okay. Don't you, Bill?"

Tyler knew his dad had only one possible answer—unless he wanted to sleep on the couch tonight. "Since you put it that way," he replied. "What time does he want you there, Ty?"

"About eight-thirty."

"Sounds good. Fix yourself something to eat before you go, since I won't be making our usual Saturday morning breakfast. I'm sleeping in tomorrow morning—I haven't had a chance to do that in quite a while."

"Thanks, Dad. Thanks, Mom. Can I stay there for a while?"

"Just be home by noon to mow the lawn," his dad said.

His mom rose from the table picking up her plate. "I wonder if Jim's going to move."

"No," his dad answered. "He told me he's staying. He said he'd knocked out a wall and is going to change one of his bedrooms into a computer lab. He's developed some software to teach foreign languages, in addition to his video game work."

"Still," she ventured, "it seems that new surroundings would be helpful."

"It doesn't sound like *that's* happening," his dad replied.

Software to teach foreign languages? That was it! Jim didn't speak anything other than English before he went in the house, and yet he was talking Romanian fluently when he came out. It was as if he learned the language in a few minutes—once he knew what language to learn. But that's impossible; a computer can't make you learn like that, no matter how good the program is.

"Mom," Tyler said. "Can we have Jim over for dinner some time? He may not be a good cook, and he might like something different than what he warms up in his microwave."

"I don't see why not. What do you think, Bill?" she asked her husband.

"Sure. He's a nice guy, and I *was* expecting he'd end up my brother-in-law. Besides, it might be good for him to have some adult friendships with reasonably normal people."

"*Normal?* I am *way* above normal." She glared at him playfully, a slight smile curling up one side of her mouth.

All right! Tyler thought. *The more time he spends here, the better my chance of checking out his computer setup and that foreign-language program.*

Besides that, he figured it might help him get the hardware upgrades his computer needed to make his World-at-War game run better.

2
𝕯iscovery

Jessi walked into Tyler's house without knocking. Some cold cereal was on the counter in front of him, and without bothering to ask, he got out another bowl.

"You about ready?" Jessi asked.

"Almost, but I haven't eaten yet. You *do* want some cereal, right?"

"Well, yeah!" Jessi got the milk out and poured it on the cereal while Tyler got two spoons.

"Did you notice anything weird yesterday at Jim's house?" Tyler asked.

"Nah, like what?" Jessi took the spoon from Tyler and plunged it into the bowl of cereal.

"Did you see what happened when he was talking to that foreign guy?"

"Uh uh. What?"

"He used a map to find out the shopper was from Romania, disappeared into his house for a few minutes, and came back speaking Romanian fluently."

"No one can learn Romonian in five minutes, Ty," Jessi said.

"It's *Romanian*, and he must have. He was using slow, loud English, and sign language until he came back out."

"You must have missed something," Jessi suggested.

"No, I didn't miss *anything*. You're the one who missed the whole thing."

"Relax, Ty," Jessi replied. She focused on her cereal.

"Anyway, last night my dad said that he talked to Jim a few days ago and learned that he was working on a foreign language software program," Tyler explained.

"Mr. Foster told your dad that?" Jessi asked.

"Yeah, and Dad also said he was getting some computer hardware to upgrade his system." Tyler was leaning forward and had forgotten about his breakfast. "I want to see his computer, so look for a chance to check it out today, okay?"

"All right, fine, but we'd better finish our breakfast and go. We've only got a few minutes, and I want to earn myself that archery set." Tyler saw she was on a track, and nothing was going to knock her off it.

* * * * * *

The garage door was closed and the house quiet as they walked up the driveway and knocked on the door. No answer. They rang the doorbell a couple of times before Jim finally opened the front door.

"Hey there, sorry about that. I was writing some code and wanted to finish my … umm … thought process." He looked distracted, but he seemed to be feeling better. Tyler immediately found himself in a tug-of-war between caution and curiosity.

"Mornin', Mr. Foster," Jessi jumped in with a smile.

"Call me Jim. People call my *dad* Mr. Foster, not me, okay?" He smiled with a wink and stepped back to let them in. "We'll go through here. The door to the garage is down the hall." Jim waved his hand ahead and to the right.

The house was orderly but obviously under construction. The way to the garage was on the backside of a wall that ran parallel with the front of the house, but an eight-foot section of the wall was removed right in the middle. A big piece of unpainted lumber was up against the ceiling—holding it up over the opening below.

Jim saw they were checking out his construction project. "I opened up the front and back of the house," he began, "and put up the header there to support the roof. Eventually I'll trim and paint it, but I haven't got to that part yet."

A perfectly circular custom-made desk was centered under the header where the wall used to be. Three complete workstations were set up, making it possible for a user to spin back and forth with ease between them—or three people to work simultaneously. The workstations sent out a quiet hum, and all three towers had water-cooled systems with neon blue tube lights that fit in perfectly with the soft jazz quietly playing out of a sweet set of speakers.

"This setup is great for my work," Jim said. "I work here on the inside of the circle and have access from the outside to all the connections. I call it The Bridge. Kinda fits with the Star Commandos theme. Know what I mean?"

He went on ahead of them and opened the door into the garage, then hit a button to raise the garage door. "Tell you what. I'd like to get back on this project, so if you two are up for it, you can run the garage sale. Everything is priced already, so just set it up kinda like yesterday, and have at it." He looked at them, waiting for a response. They just stared back at him. "All right. State your terms," he said with a smile.

Jessi pursed her lips and looked up at him. "How about your archery set?" she asked.

"If it doesn't sell, deal. How 'bout you?" Jim asked, looking at Tyler, eyebrows raised.

"Well," Tyler hesitated, "my dad said you were upgrading your computer. Can you upgrade mine with your old parts?"

Jim straightened up a little, surprised by the request. "Sure," he said. "I probably would've just tossed the old stuff anyway. Reduce. Reuse. Recycle—right?"

Jim headed back to his computer. "Go for it, guys. It's almost nine o'clock. I'll check on ya later."

* * * * * *

The next few hours flew by. A lot of people came through, some of them just browsing, not caring if they left empty-handed. Then there were those intent on finding something in particular. They'd swoop in, scout the place out, and leave in a hurry, like they had to rush to the next sale down the street before someone else beat them there for whatever-it-was they were looking for.

Around noon Tyler called his mom to see if they could stay the whole day, since they were so busy, and a little later she came by with some sandwiches for lunch. They thought they had the garage sale thing figured out, at least until the very end of the day.

A man in a big truck parked right in front of the driveway. He glanced at what was left on the tables, then looked at Tyler. "Are you in charge? I'll give you a hundred dollars for everything here."

Jessi looked questioningly at Tyler.

"I'll go check with Jim," Tyler said.

He went inside the house. Jim was at The Bridge, his back to the garage door. He sat wearing headphones and a mic and was speaking rapidly like the guys at the end of a commercial doing all the legal talk—real fast and pretty much impossible to understand. As Tyler got closer, he realized Jim was speaking lines of code. As he spoke, the code appeared on the screen, advancing from one line to the next, based on just the slightest hesitation. It was an impressive interaction of human and machine.

Tyler looked at the left monitor; it showed an empty street at night, from a camera apparently mounted over a sidewalk made of paving stones. He could tell it wasn't in the US—it looked old and very non-American. An unfamiliar car drove by. *Must be a live-cam from somewhere in …?* He shrugged and turned back to Jim.

"Jim?" he ventured.

Jim jumped slightly in his chair and abruptly stopped talking, and the code on the screen stopped. He reached forward and typed on the keyboard for a few seconds, hit the enter key, and looked up at Tyler with a smile.

"Always, *always*, save your work."

"Yeah, I learned that the hard way a couple years ago on a book report. I had the whole thing done, had some trouble printing it, and somehow deleted the whole thing. It was *bad*."

"Mmm hmm, I think everyone does that at least once," Jim replied. "So what do you need, and … hey, what time is it anyway?"

"About five o'clock. We're done, and there's a guy outside who wants to buy everything that's left for a hundred dollars. What do you want to do?" he asked.

Jim got up and started walking toward the garage. "Depends on what's left," he said over his shoulder.

Tyler followed him into the garage, keeping a bit of distance behind him. Jim looked around at what was left and sighed. Sadness, and pain, briefly flickered across his face. He sighed again and walked over to the man.

"Hey, what's up?" he asked.

"I want everything you've got here, and I'll give you a hundred dollars for the whole lot. I'll take it *all* off your hands," the stranger answered.

"Tell you what, I promised my help here," he pointed at Jessi, "my archery set as payment. Did it sell?" he asked Jessi.

"Nope."

"Okay. So after she pulls that, you can take the rest."

"I already pulled it," Jessi said with an impish smile.

Jim shook his head. "Let me guess. First thing this morning, right?"

Jessi looked away and started whistling.

Jim turned back to the man. "It's all yours," he said and took the two fifties the stranger handed him.

All three of them helped the man load up his truck, and they stood in the driveway and watched until the truck disappeared around the corner.

"Hey," Jim offered, "how does Burgerville sound? Call your folks and see if it's okay with them. I'll get take-out and bring it back. Meanwhile you two bring all the tables out of the driveway into the garage, and I'll put them away later."

* * * * * *

After a Tillamook Cheeseburger, fries, and the seasonal fresh strawberry milkshake, Tyler straightened up in his chair and a big burp surprised them all. After they stopped laughing, he leaned forward over the table. "Jim?"

"Yeah?"

"I got a couple questions for ya."

"Okaay, what?"

"My dad said you were writing a program to help people learn foreign languages."

"Yeah, that's right."

"Does it work real quick, like *instantly* or something?"

Jim looked intently at Tyler. "What do you mean?" he asked. *Uh oh. Here it comes.*

"Well, yesterday you couldn't talk to that guy from Romania until you went inside for a few minutes. Then you came out and started talking to him no problem. How'd you do it?"

Oh crap! He saw that! Jim thought. He looked down and stared at the table for a few moments. How could he acknowledge what Tyler saw without revealing just about everything that was going on here? He looked up. They were obviously waiting for an up-front explanation. He hesitated, but the silence was getting very loud. *I'm not a very convincing liar,* he thought.

"All right," he began. "What I'm going to tell you would be hard to believe, except you already saw proof that what I'm going to say is true. Can you two keep it to yourself, at least for now?"

Tyler and Jessi looked at each other, and back at him, suspiciously.

"Okay," Jessi finally said. Tyler nodded.

"I'm not saying you can't ever tell your parents, 'cause no adult should ever make someone promise *that*. Just don't blab this around, like, *at all*. Okay?" Jim looked from one to the other, unblinking.

"Ohh–kay," Tyler answered slowly.

Jim nodded toward The Bridge. "Picture this," he said. He formed a sphere with his hands in front of him, fingers and thumbs lightly touching each other. "This is the earth. Imagine there's a net above the atmosphere wrapping all around the planet. This net is the electromagnetic field generated by the earth's core, only it's not 'perfectly' formed. There are points all over the world—I don't know how many yet—where the field presses down like a funnel towards the earth's surface. It's not a hole, more like an indentation, and there's a tremendous concentration of magnetic energy all along this funnel, getting stronger and stronger as it approaches the earth's surface."

"So," Jessi said. "If you could *see* this funnel, it would look like a tornado?"

"Yes. Exactly!"

"Is your computer in a funnel?" Jessi asked, pointing at The Bridge.

"Yup."

"So what happens?"

"And how did you discover it?" Tyler added.

"I can answer those questions best by letting you experience it for yourself. You ready for that?"

They hesitated, and he saw apprehension in their eyes.

"Tell you what," he said. "I'll go first, then you go after me, okay?" He smiled, trying to reassure them. They didn't answer, but their eyes narrowed.

"Hmm, you're in eighth grade, right?" They slowly nodded their heads. "Were you in the band in grade school?" They slowly nodded again. "What instruments?"

"Clarinet," Jessi replied.

"I played alto sax," Tyler added.

Jim squinted one eye as he thought about the music concerts he had been to at the school the prior couple of years. "I'm gonna guess you played 'Jolly Old St. Nicholas.' Yes?"

"Yeah, we did," they responded together. Tyler looked sharply at Jessi.

"Hey, *everyone* plays that," she retorted good-naturedly.

"Since you're both familiar with *that* song, that's what you'll get to listen to."

He grabbed his phone off the counter, selected a track, put in his Bluetooth and tapped the play button. He walked into the center of The Bridge and stood there with his eyes closed, as a hint of a smile crossed his face. After a few moments, he opened his eyes and walked towards them. He took a deep breath and slowly exhaled as he left The Bridge.

"Your turn," he said, tapping the pause button as he handed his phone to Tyler.

Tyler's hands shook a little as he put the Bluetooth in his ear. Jim smiled—Tyler was about to experience something he'd *never* forget. "It's okay, really," he said reassuringly. "It's 'Jolly Old St. Nicholas,' played by the Oregon Symphonic Band, and you're gonna *love* this!"

Tyler tapped the play button and walked towards The Bridge as the music filled his head with sound. When he entered The Bridge, he momentarily lost his balance, steadying himself with his hand on a monitor. He closed his eyes and started nodding his head to the music.

Jim gave him about a minute and stood up to retrieve Tyler out of The Bridge.

"Tyler … Tyler … TYLER!" Jim shouted at him. He opened his eyes. He walked right by Jim, handed the phone and Bluetooth to Jessi, and sat down without saying a word. He closed his eyes and put his face in his hands.

Jim sat down as Jessi slowly walked towards The Bridge. She took a deep breath and touched the play button. She slowly turned around and faced them, her dark brown eyes wide open but obviously not really seeing them. "That's so cool," she kept repeating slowly.

Jim got out of his chair and, grasping Jessi by the shoulders, gently pulled her out from the center of The Bridge. He waited a few moments while she recovered from the experience.

"So what do you think?" he asked.

"It was so, so … so powerful," Tyler stammered. "I, I felt like I was in the middle of the band! And I could hear every instrument so good it was … it was like I was looking at the notes on their music stand along with them—everyone all at once. It was awesome!"

"And not just the notes," Jessi jumped in. "But it's like I now know *why* each instrument was playing each note! What my teacher called … umm … musical composition!"

"Well," Jim began, "it seems that just about anything electronic just 'takes off' in that spot. Thanks to that interaction, symbiosis, or whatever you want to call it, there seems to be no limit to what can happen there." He hooked his thumb towards The Bridge. "For example, I can write code—software—in an hour that would otherwise take days, and do it flawlessly."

He leaned forward. "Don't get me wrong. I don't think it *teaches* you anything; it just raises your capabilities, maybe by ramping up the electrical impulses in the brain, perhaps? Anyway, the result is you can then *understand* what you already know, or have been struggling with ..." His voice trailed off, unable to put into words what could only be experienced. He was sure they knew what he was grappling with, just from the few moments listening to the music. How *could* anyone explain this?

"If it doesn't teach you, then how did you learn Romonian so fast?" Jessi asked.

"Romanian!" Jim and Tyler said in unison, then laughed. Jim continued, "I've written a program that combines word lists, pictures, and grammatical rules that when processed here"—he nodded again towards The Bridge—"imprints the information directly into your brain. Then you just ... absorb it all. The tough part is that you get such a bad headache that it makes you sick."

"Yeah," Tyler broke in. "You didn't look so good when you talked to that guy yesterday. Is that why you wore sunglasses?"

"That's right. It made my eyes super sensitive to the light."

"So what I heard in the music with the different instruments, and music structure —I wouldn't have understood if I hadn't already studied it in school?"

"Well, you would have heard it; you just wouldn't have understood its relationship within the context of the entire piece."

"I watched you write programming by talking. How'd you do that?"

"I use speech recognition software, but because I'm using it within the funnel, I can write software as fast as I can think it or even speak it. Plus I can do it faster and without error within the circle, 'cause I'm partnering *with* the machine. There's actually been a few times where I've written code just by thinking it! There's virtually no limit to where I can go with this." He took in a deep breath and let it out slowly, looking up at the ceiling. "That's why I'll never move out of this house."

"But there are funnels in other places too?" Jessi asked. "Do you know where?" She had lifted herself out of her chair and was leaning over the table.

"Oh yeah, I've found over fifty so far. One in particular is stronger than most, and I've spent the last week writing code in this funnel to pinpoint the other's location. The progress I've made would probably have taken me at least two years of effort anywhere else. Now I can actually see out from that other funnel as if I was standing there myself, looking around."

"In a street in Europe?" Tyler asked.

Jim shot him a look. "You saw that?"

"Yeah, on the left monitor. Where exactly is it?"

"I don't know. At this point I have only one view. My next goal is to find a way to rotate my view so I can get a 360° of the location."

"Well, once you can look east, you could get the longitude of it pretty quick, couldn't you?" Jessi asked.

"And how, Ms. Geography, would he do that?" Tyler asked.

"By finding the exact moment of sunrise, you can figure out where it is!"

"Oh yeah." Tyler jumped in. "And by measuring the angle of a shadow at noon you can figure out the latitude!"

"Well," Jim laughed, "I think it *was* safe to fill you two in on this … discovery." He waved his hand once again towards The Bridge. "I've been so focused on using technology to determine its location, I forgot about using the old ways. So how do you know those old techniques of determining latitude and longitude anyway?"

"We studied geography a few months ago," Tyler answered, "and our teacher collects old maps. He explained why, and how, the maps of the continents kept changing and getting more accurate."

"Can we help you?" Jessi said. "There must be something we can do." Jessi rose from her seat, knocking her chair back. She spun around to catch it, but missed and the chair clattered to the floor. "Oops."

"Careful, Jessi," Tyler said and picked up her chair.

Jim nodded. "Yes, there *is* a way you can help. You can build my backup system."

"Backup system?"

"Everything needs to be backed up. I can't use any of the online services for that because I have too much data accumulating by the hour. Besides, if somebody hacked into my data and traced it to me here … well, this could all come to an end. This week I purchased new hard drives and all the equipment necessary for continuous drive mirroring." He pointed to the empty bedroom to the left of the front door. "It's all in there."

"Sounds good. We'll do it!" Jessi exclaimed.

"Absolutely!" Tyler added.

Neither of them knew what continuous drive mirroring was, but they weren't going to let that stop them.

* * * * * *

The next few weekends found Tyler and Jessi drilling holes in Jim's floor and running cables. They connected a complete backup system in the extra room: running the connecting cables down into the crawl space under the house then back up into the extra room, so no one would trip on them.

Within a month, Jim had become a regular at Tyler's house too. He had accepted their first invitation to dinner, and a pattern soon developed of Friday night dinner at Tyler's with a Saturday "workshop" for Tyler and Jessi at Jim's place.

Thanks to Tyler's help, Jessi began to think she actually *would* pass math. In just a couple weeks she'd know for sure.

3
Departure

May 25, Current Year

"Mom, tell me what to do!" Jessi begged.

Katie Hernandez looked up at her daughter with a playful grin. "Well, it's been a long time since I've heard that!"

"What?" Jessi answered, then grimaced. "No really, I don't know what to do about this," she continued. "I don't wanna be mean, or hurt his feelings, but ..."

"Just tell me what happened." Her mom stopped stirring the chili.

"For our research project, Mr G. put names of half the class in a jar and had the other half take turns drawing names for partners—and I drew Tyler's name! You should've heard the snickers. Tyler was nice about it, but the look on his face, for just a moment—well, it wasn't exactly a happy face."

"He *has* been a big help getting you caught up in math, honey, and it is pretty convenient he lives next door."

"I know, Mom. Thanks to him I'm totally acing math now. It's just that everybody's starting to act like he's my boyfriend, even though they know he's not. Besides, he's kinda—"

"Boring?"

"No, he's not boring, more like predictable. He's *real* smart, and nice, especially over this last month, but it's like he needs to loosen up a little. No, a lot. I don't know how to get out of this."

"Don't even try; this is your last big project before school's over, so just tuck it in and get it done. Summer vacation is around the corner, and then you can put as much space as you want between the two of you—and don't eat any more chips. Remember, we're all having dinner at the Duncan's tonight."

Jessi's family had joined Jim for a Friday night barbecue at the Duncan's, and just before dessert, their end-of-year project came up.

"So what exactly is the assignment?" Jessi's dad asked.

"A minimum fifteen-item list comparing and contrasting seventeenth-century England and France," Jessi explained.

"Just be glad you didn't get two countries you'd never heard of," he said as he took another mouthful of potato salad.

"Yeah, I guess," she grumbled.

"Sounds like a basic research project to me," Jim shrugged.

"That may be easy for you, with your monster computer lab, but not for us," Tyler said before turning to his mom. "Mom, do you care if Jessi and I do this at Jim's so we can get it done faster?"

"I didn't hear him offer that," she said. "Besides, it's not polite to invite yourself over to someone's house at the last minute."

"Hmm," Jim murmured and looked at Tyler's mom. "You know, Val, I'm heading down to Eugene later tonight. My cousin is moving to northern California next week, and I promised I'd help him pack. I'd rather have Tyler house-sit for me than leave it empty while I'm gone—if it's alright with you, of course."

Later that evening Jessi and Tyler were at Jim's kitchen table, planning their strategy for the weekend. "Ty," Jessi finally asked, "how about I just take England, and you do France? I'm going with my aunt to a midnight movie, and I gotta run."

"Fair enough," Tyler replied as they closed their notebooks and got up from the table.

As they approached The Bridge, Jim gave them a confident smile. It had taken him almost a week to figure out how to rotate their view from the target funnel. He then determined its location was in the French town of Amiens, about 70 miles north of Paris.

He raised his hand, index finger pointed high for effect, and slowly, dramatically, lowered his hand until his fingertip hit the enter key. "Watch the monitor," he said.

They turned to look at the familiar street scene. It was late evening here at home, but in France the early morning sun was just brightening the street. Two blocks away the street ended at a stop sign where cars had to turn either left or right because of a small cliff face of maybe 50 feet of vertical rock on the opposite side of the street.

"Look at the cliff!" Jessi exclaimed. "It looks like there's a giant face carved in the rock!"

"That's cool!" Tyler said. "It looks like the rock face on the back of the quarter from ..."

"Maine?" Jessi blurted out.

"No, New Hampshire," Tyler corrected. "But yeah, it looks the same."

As they looked on, a car died at the intersection, and the driver re-started it and drove on. Their mouths dropped open; they'd heard the driver start his engine!

"I applied the same technique that collects the light waves for our video to capture the sound waves. Now we have both." Jim beat his chest with his fists Tarzan style. "Me good, very good."

Jessi frowned as she leaned toward the speakers. "You're better than you think, Tarzan. The speakers are unplugged."

"What?" Jim jumped forward in his chair.

"And I smell car exhaust," Tyler added.

"But that's impossible!" Jim objected. "The only way we can smell that exhaust is if the air from over *there* is being brought over *here*." He slumped back in his chair, dropping his chin onto his chest.

"All right. Change of plans. I've gotta work some more on this, so you'll have to start your project in the morning, okay?"

The look on Jim's face was intense, and they were glad to get out of his way so he could figure out what was going on. Besides, just the thought of the two funnels being literally connected gave them a chill, and not just from the early morning air coming over from France.

After Jessi left, Tyler spread out his sleeping bag on the floor of the bedroom that now housed the backup drives. They had designed a layout, approved by Jim, and had set up an array of hard drives that continuously copied and updated each of the drives within The Bridge. The hum of the equipment surrounding him quickly lulled him to sleep.

* * * * * *

Jim worked feverishly at The Bridge for a couple of hours, then started a routine to collect ongoing data. He wrote a note to Tyler, grabbed his duffel bag, and headed for the garage. He backed his SUV into the driveway—his Beemer was too small to haul anything—hit the button on the remote to drop the door, and drove away. He hesitated at the corner.

Maybe I should go back and make sure that routine finishes before the kids get on the computer, he thought. No, they're smart kids and besides, he had left a note for Tyler on the computer. Still his gut told him something was about to go badly, but he shook it off and headed towards the Interstate. Eugene was two hours away, and he needed to get going.

* * * * * *

May 26, Current Year

Beep! Beep! Beep! Beep! Jessi groaned and slapped at the clock. After three tries she opened her eyes. *Where is it?* she asked herself. It was just beyond her reach, and on the fourth try she silenced it. Ten minutes later, with a fully loaded backpack, she was on her way to Jim's.

Tyler was rolling up his sleeping bag when she arrived. Jim had left the computer running, and they spotted the sticky note on the main screen.

Tyler dropped his backpack next to his chair as he grabbed the note. "Don't start your project until the program is complete," Tyler read out loud. "Make *sure* the left screen says 100% complete."

They looked at the screen. It said "Process 91% Complete."
They waited about 20 minutes, helping themselves to some cold
cereal. The screen read 92%.

"This is gonna take forever," Jessi groaned.

"Nah," Tyler said, "We'll just minimize his program and let it run."

Thirty minutes later, they had made a lot of progress. Jessi had a full e-clipboard of notes and had even found a Middle English database from Jim's language work. Tyler had done almost as well. "Read this," he said, as he hit the enter key.

"Yeah right, it's all in *French*," Jessi laughed.

"I know, I know, but watch this. Here's the text after Jim's language program reads it." Tyler hit a few more keys, and the text changed into English. "His program translates *everything*! It's so cool."

He switched his document back to French and started studying it more closely. Just for fun he started searching for words that looked familiar. His mom was fluent in French but had never taught him more than just a few simple phrases. He couldn't understand very much of it, but he saw a lot of words that were similar to English.

A block away a car turned and headed down the street in front of Jim's house. The driver pulled his coffee out of the cup holder and took a sip. Only then did he look up and see a jogger right in front of him. He panicked and swerved away, but pulled too hard on the steering wheel and crossed over to the opposite side of the street, running into a power pole. The bracket holding the transformer broke, and falling onto the power lines directly below, it exploded into a shower of sparks, sending a power surge through the nearby homes. The lines snapped and twisted together as the pole ended up leaning precariously over the street. The entire neighborhood went dark.

* * * * * *

Jim laid his head back on the red- and white-checkered picnic blanket. *This* was the way to spend an afternoon: a few lazy hours in the Mt. Hood National Forest with his wife, talking about everything and nothing. *This is so much better than being in front of a computer,* he thought, as the sun broke free of a thin cloud and shined brightly through the branches of the tree overhead.

A short distance away he heard a teenage boy and girl talking at a picnic table. They were talking English, but for some reason their voices were muddled, and he couldn't understand a word they were saying. The girl lit a sparkler, and the light seemed unusually bright. The boy lit a firecracker from the sparkler and tossed it aside.

The explosion sounded more like a bomb, and moments later the echo made everything shake. The sparkler grew even brighter.

He opened his eyes and saw that the morning sun was reflecting off his neighbor's window into his face. *A dream*, he thought. *It was a dream.* Then he realized the echoing vibration from the dream was *real*, and was from inside his house. He glanced at the alarm clock on his nightstand. It was dead; the power was out.

He closed his eyes and tried to organize his thoughts. He had obviously slept in but was still really tired. He brushed the cobwebs out of his mind as he finally remembered why. *Right, 'cause I'm an idiot.* Spencer needed him *next* weekend, not this weekend, and Spencer wasn't even home. He had headed back to Portland and got home at 5 a.m., saw the routine still running on the computer and Tyler asleep on the floor, and went straight to bed.

Jim got up, put on his bathrobe, and grabbed his watch. Nine o'clock. The kids should be here.

With the power out, the house was eerily quiet. In the hallway, he stopped and looked at where his computers were supposed to be. They were *gone*! His circular desk was there, but the chairs and all his computer hardware were missing. What he saw instead was a tree, about three inches in diameter, stretching from the floor up *through* the ceiling into the attic. At the outside edge, severed cables led out of the circle to the backup in the next room. In the middle stood a tall pile of dirt and rocks, some grass. He stared in silence as an earthworm came wriggling out at one end. A sense of panic was growing, and his heart sank. Where were they? What happened and *how*?

"Jessi! ... Tyler!" he called out uselessly, knowing he'd get no answer. He looked at the equipment in the backup room. Tyler's sleeping bag was rolled up, and Jessi's backpack was nearby. "Hey!" he called out desperately.

He felt instinctively that his only hope of determining what happened was in the backup room on the mirrored drives and CPUs. That would require a run to the supply house to get a couple new workstations. A couple of hours to restore from the backup and he'd be able to see exactly what was going on up to the moment everything ... just *went away?* He got dressed but couldn't even *begin* to shake off an overwhelming sense of dread.

* * * * * *

Jim turned off the water, grabbed a towel, and surveyed his front room as he dried his hands. He glanced at his palms. A few small blisters. Nothing too serious. There had been a hundred pounds or more of damp earth, besides the tree, that he'd dumped in the backyard—one bucket at a time.

Now that the circle was scrubbed clean, he could start unpacking all the hardware he had neatly stacked in the living room: two new workstations. The best he could get off the shelf. He could get his special-order hardware overnighted, which would be soon enough. Good thing the electricity was back on.

He pulled a box cutter out of his pocket and started opening the first box. His dad's antique clock chimed the top of the hour; he glanced up—noon. Then the clock's hammer began to strike the gong, and each stroke felt like a knife blade in his gut. His arms started shaking, and he felt weak. By the time the vibrations of the twelfth stroke died away, Jim lay on his side, the box cutter on the carpet next to his open hand.

4
𝔄𝔯𝔯𝔦𝔳𝔞𝔩

June 11, 1614

Jessi heard someone calling her name in the darkness, but it was muffled and distant. She tasted blood as her world slowly went from black to pale gray. She then heard a gurgling noise and lifted her head just in time to watch Tyler finish throwing up. *Well, that's special*, she thought.

She touched her finger to her lips and pulled it back bloody. "What happened?" she asked.

Tyler ignored her question. "I thought you were dead or something."

"Not yet." She looked past Tyler. "Umm ... where are we?"

"I dunno. The last thing I remember I was looking at the French document on the screen. You were turning back to look at your monitor ... and then I wake up in the woods with this wicked headache. Oh man, my leg hurts!"

Jessi pushed herself up on her elbows to look around her. Everything from The Bridge was there, including some pieces of the ceiling lying across the back of her legs. She spat out something bloody, and her tongue found a hole in her right cheek. *I must have bit it when I fell*, she thought. *Fell?*

"Where *are* we?" she asked again, her voice quivering. "Ty, what's goin' on?"

Tyler squinted his eyes as he looked around them once again. He rubbed the back of his head and groaned. "It looks like everything from The Bridge, including *us*, is here. But where is *here?*"

"That's what I just asked *you*."

"Take it easy, Jessi. We'll figure this out. How's your head?" he asked.

She slowly sat up before gently touching her head. She had an inch-long gash just above her hairline. "It's okay. Mom always says cuts on your head bleed more, and look worse, than they usually are."

Tyler stood to his feet, gingerly putting weight on his left leg as he straightened to his full height. He grimaced a bit as he extended his hand to help Jessi to her feet.

Upon standing up she wobbled a bit. "Whoa!"

"Your head hurt?"

"Nah, I'll be okay. Just a bit dizzy. How 'bout you?"

"I have a killer headache, making me nauseous. Anything broken?"

"Nope, you?"

"Don't think so. Let's take a look around. What d'ya think?" Tyler asked.

"Sure," Jessi shrugged.

They left the clearing and fought their way through the underbrush between the trees, Tyler leading the way. The trees were short, only about 30 or 40 feet high, not like the tall firs at home.

Glancing ahead through an opening in the forest Tyler stopped, his mouth dropping open. He grinned. "I know *exactly* where we are. Look!"

Jessi looked where Tyler was eagerly pointing, but her dizziness made everything a little fuzzy. "I don't see anything," she mumbled.

"Follow me."

A couple minutes later they were standing on a dirt road. On the opposite side were a few scraggly bushes with some kind of red berries, but they didn't notice them. They were looking at what was above.

"I see it," Tyler muttered. "Do you?"

"I see it, but I don't hardly believe it."

"Yeah, standing this close makes it look different, but that's for sure the face on the cliff we've been looking at back at Jim's."

"Okay, so we're in Amiens. I was wondering about that, but what's with all these trees? We're in a forest! And how did we get here?"

"Well, remember last night how we heard and smelled the streets of Amiens? The actual air must have been ... transporting over to us—"

"And now *we've* been transported?" Jessi said in alarm. The thought was more frightening than exciting. She leaned over and spat out some more blood.

Tyler put one hand on his knee to steady himself while he rubbed the back of his head with the other. "So the real question isn't *where* we are; it's *when*." He straightened up as a look of shock came over his face as the pieces came together. "We both had our CPUs working on seventeenth century documents. Something must have gone wrong and sent us to Amiens, only in the 1600s! Jessi, we need to go back."

"Why?" she asked.

"We don't know where we're going, and Jim will be looking for us."

"Ya think he's gonna follow us?"

"No, that's not what I mean," he frowned. "He's gonna be looking for us out of a funnel. Right there," he pointed back towards where they had started.

They retraced their steps and returned to the pile of computer hardware. "Oh no," Tyler groaned. "He *can't* be looking for us, The Bridge is *here*. All the equipment, databases, *everything*; he has nothing at home to work with."

"Oh, yeah." Her heart sank. "But wait! He's got backup. We made it!"

Tyler straightened up. "Yeah, that's right! He'll be able to figure out what happened and where we are!"

* * * * * *

Thankfully, Tyler's backpack was in the pile. Good thing he'd had it under his chair in The Bridge. He wrote a message to Jim on a yellow sticky note and stuck it on one of the monitors telling him they were fine and would be back the next morning; it'd be dark soon, and they didn't want to spend the night outside if they didn't have to.

They headed towards the cliff face. Once again, between the uneven ground, fallen trees, and dense underbrush, it took over five minutes to get the couple hundred feet to the base of the hill. Jessi looked both ways along the road. "Well, which way you think?" she asked. "You're better with directions."

"Well, Paris is behind us to the south, a *long* ways away, but Amiens has *got* to be real close."

To their right they could see a fork in the road. "That way."

They piled a stack of branches to mark where they were and started walking. They came to the fork in the road. The left branch curved gradually towards the north and disappeared into the trees.

"Ummm . . ." Jessi frowned.

"South," Tyler answered. "The funnel was in the north part of Amiens, so the town's gotta be that way."

They went to the right, quickening their pace as the eastern sky grew darker. Within a few minutes the trees opened up at a split in the road; in the distance to the right they saw the village of Amiens, while to the left, about half a mile away, they could see below them a group of four homes within a hundred yards of each other. The land leveled off, and they saw that the small valley had been entirely cleared for farming, except for hedges of low-growing trees and bushes that separated the properties. Somewhere a couple dogs were having a long-distance conversation. The valley oozed of peace and safety.

"So now what?" Tyler asked.

"We find out everything we can without getting in trouble," Jessi replied. "Your grandma is from Quebec, right? And your mom is fluent in French, so you know at least a little, don't ya?"

"Just a few words, not much more," he said dejectedly.

"Like me and Spanish. Dad never taught me much either."

Their shadows preceded them on the road, growing noticeably longer in proportion to their uneasiness. The first home was on their right, set back from the road about 50 feet.

Hunger and the desire to get some questions answered pushed them forward.

As they approached the door, a dog came charging around the corner of the house. "So much for not getting in trouble," Tyler muttered. It wasn't very big, but it was an ugly thing that seemed fearless, which was fine, because they had plenty of fear to give away.

"Socy, you stupid mutt, shut up!" a voice cried out. A woman rushed out the front door, broom in hand. She started to swing it at the dog but stopped when she saw them approaching. "Who are you?" she demanded. "What do you want?"

Tyler and Jessi stopped where they were as the growling dog circled around them.

"What'd she say?" Jessi asked out of the corner of her mouth.

"She asked us what we wanted," Tyler answered.

"Cool, your French is pretty good!"

"Yeah, but I don't know why."

"Please, ma'am," he began, and a cold chill shot down his back as the French effortlessly flowed out of his mouth. "We're lost and we need help."

The woman looked him up and down a couple of times. Jessi took a step back as the woman frowned in her direction, but then her gaze softened. *Maybe that cut on Jessi's head will get us some sympathy*, Tyler thought. After a few seconds the woman stepped forward. "Socy—go!" she commanded the dog, which dropped its head and slowly walked away. "Come on in," she finally offered. "I can't let you two spend the night outdoors." The woman turned back towards her open door, motioning for them to follow.

5
Working for Food

June 12, 1614

The weight of the firewood pressed the leather strap deep into the blisters on Tyler's hand, and the burn only slightly diminished as he let the firewood fall to the ground. *Last trip—finally*, he thought. Jessi came up behind him and dropped her final load.

"Almost done, Ty," she declared.

"Yeah, working for bed and breakfast isn't as exciting as it sounds," Tyler answered. His fingers tingled as he slowly opened and closed his hand several times. Exciting or not, moving the firewood from the woods on the other end of the pasture and stacking it behind the house was "paying" for their meal.

They finished stacking the wood and knocked on the back door. The woman came out to inspect their work. "Very good, just fine," she said approvingly. Without saying another word she walked up to Tyler, grabbed his arm, and turned his hand palm-side up. "Eh, looks like you've not done such work in a while, yes?" She laughed. "Both of you come with me. I have something for you to take with you—come!"

Tyler turned to Jessi. "She says she's got something for us but didn't say what it was."

Jessi smiled. "I can guess what she said about your hand!"

"From the look of your clothing," she began, "you're most certainly far from home. But you have worked hard and spoken respectfully, and not just so you may have food! So, here's something for you to take with you as we say good-bye. Blessings on you both." She handed Jessi an old cloth, with the four corners tied together. Inside was something firm but slightly squeezable.

37

She leaned over and kissed each of them on both cheeks. "Now go. Stay on the road, but if horses come by, give them lots of room," she advised.

They thanked her for her kindness and headed back towards the funnel. As soon as they were out of sight of the cottage, they stepped off to the side of the road and sat down on a patch of grass.

Jessi fumbled with the knot, her fingers sore from the morning's work.

"So what do you think is in there?" Tyler asked.

"Smells like bread," she said. The knot finally came loose and the cloth opened up, revealing its contents. It was an entire loaf of bread, maybe two pounds of a milky-yellow cheese, and six dried apples.

"Score!" Jessi shouted, pumping her fist. "I love apples and cheese!"

"Quiet, Jessi!" Tyler hissed. "We should keep this out of sight and not draw attention to ourselves. Getting food may not always be so easy!"

"You call this *easy*? We worked two *hours* for this!"

"No, we worked for breakfast. This is a freebie, and it may not be so easy to earn our next meal. Besides, haven't you seen the play, *Les Miserables*?"

Jessi curled her lip up on one side. "Lay Mizz ... what?"

"*Les Miserables*. It's a story that takes place here, in France, maybe sometime around now, I'm not sure exactly, but in it a guy goes to prison for stealing a loaf of bread! So we gotta be real careful about everything we do while we're here."

"Where'd you learn about Lay ... whatever?" she asked.

"My mom and dad saw the show. It's in town now—well, four hundred years from now—some kind of Broadway tour, and Mom was explaining the plot to me."

"Oh. Well, we probably won't be here for long, Ty. Look at it this way. A free trip to Europe! No adults required! This is gonna be fun. Check out the sights, go home, no problem!"

"Yeah, I'm sure you're right."

Soon they were back at the spot where they had made the pile of branches. Jessi looked up at the cliff face. "Huh, don't see it at all."

"See what?" Tyler was looking down the road.

"The face in the cliff."

He looked up. "Good thing we marked the spot, but hang on and don't leave the road yet. We gotta make sure no one sees us go into the trees, 'cause someone following us into the woods could be bad." They hadn't seen anyone on the road, but he didn't want to take any chances. They looked both directions, listening intently—nothing.

"Let's go," he said.

They plunged into the bushes and were quickly out of sight, but the silence of the woods made every step feel loud and clumsy, shouting out to anyone, or any animal, that they were coming through.

Within minutes they saw the pile of computer hardware ahead of them; nothing had changed but a few pieces of loose paper that had been blown, or dragged, a few feet away into a nearby bush. They slowed down as they approached the site.

"So what do we do now?" asked Jessi.

"Talk to me, that's what!" said a disembodied voice.

Jessi yelled and jumped back, bumping into Tyler, and both of them fell to the ground. The voice laughed.

"Good morning," Jim's voice sang out. It seemed to come out of the middle of the air.

"C'mon, you could've warned us before we got so close!" Jessi whined.

"Sorry, but only a little," Jim answered. "As I watched you come over, it just seemed like the thing to do! Oh, by the way, thanks for the note. That was good thinking."

"No problem," Jessi replied. "So are ya gonna bring us back now—hey, where are we anyway? No, I mean, *when* are we. We already figured out the *where*."

"June 12, 1614. It appears Amiens hasn't expanded to where you are yet, so I'm curious, is the town very far away? I can't tell, because all I can see from here are trees."

"Yeah, the town's about a mile to the south," Tyler explained. Talking to a voice coming out of thin air was disconcerting, like a video chat without a screen. "So are you gonna bring us back now?"

"Can't. At least not yet, but I'm working on it. I'll get you back, I promise. Listen to me, you *will* get back, you hear me? You *will* get back."

"How long are we gonna have to wait?" Jessi asked warily. "You're not exactly filling me with confidence here."

"Okay, just listen," Jim began. "I know for you it's just been one day, but for me it's been two *weeks*! Anyway, it took me four days to figure out what happened to you and another week to figure out how to talk to you. About an hour before you arrived just now, I saw a deer walk by and hit it with a loud 'hey'," Jim laughed. "It must've jumped three feet into the air! Anyway, you don't need to worry about how long it takes me, 'cause once I figure out how to bring you home, I'll reconnect with you and bring you back. Now sit down and let's talk."

They sat down, not needing to be told twice. Jim sounded really confident, but they were totally helpless, and the whole thing was overwhelming. The familiar smell of the warm grass was pleasant but not very comforting so impossibly far from home.

6
Traveling Orders

"Okay, Jim. It's ready," Jessi called out.

"Yeah, it looks good to me too. Now stand back." Jim's voice was clear and familiar, but hearing it come out of midair was still unnerving.

The equipment was packed together in a tight stack, and they moved back about 15 feet and waited. "Go ahead," Tyler called out.

There was a slight hissing sound that quickly grew louder, then a rush of air that blew outward from the funnel, blowing their hair off their foreheads. Then a sound like a balloon popping—inwards—and the pile disappeared.

"Awesome!" they jumped and yelled. Two high fives, then silence.

"Jessi?"

"Yeah?"

"We're *really* alone now."

She looked at the now-empty circle where the equipment had been and realized that Tyler's backpack and their clothes were the only 21st-century things left. She took a deep breath and let it out slowly—*don't panic.*

They waited; nothing happened.

"Jim?" Tyler called.

No answer, no nothing. Overhead some birds they didn't recognize flitted amongst the branches. Everything around them suddenly felt strange and threatening, making them feel very small.

After about 10 minutes a twig snapped in the dense bushes about 40 feet away. Their hearts jumped into their throats as they sucked in a breath and froze, looking in the direction of the sound. A soft breeze blew directly in their faces as their eyes searched every bit of scrub brush and shadow in between.

They saw some movement towards the left, and pulled together, tensing, ready to run if they had to. A brown animal slowly emerged between an old tree stump and the bush next to it—a young deer, so young it still had its spots.

Tyler whispered, "Looks like Bambi; maybe the one Jim mentioned."

"Quiet, its mom or dad is probably out here too."

Upon hearing them, the deer fixed its gaze on them and a moment later disappeared into the trees.

"It didn't know we were here," Tyler said. "I thought they had really good eyesight."

"I think they smell things better," Jessi answered.

"Right, and we were downwind from it, too."

They kept waiting, and after a while their fear of a dangerous animal showing up subsided, as they eased into an attitude of relaxed alertness. They didn't say much but quietly took in their surroundings as they sat down back to back. Eventually they got a better sense of the world around them more through their hearing than by sight.

"Ty?" Jessi asked.

"What?"

"I ... I gotta apologize about something."

"What for?"

"I've been calling you my 'first friend', and that's ... that's just dumb. I'm sorry."

"Hey, no problem," Tyler quietly answered. He reached behind him and put his hand on the ground palm side up. "Low five," he said.

She reached down and gently tapped his hand. "Thanks."

"Hey, guys," Jim's voice suddenly called out, startling them. "Sorry you had to wait so long." It was good to hear him again, but there was something in his voice that sounded ... not good.

"What took you so long? Is it our turn now to come home?" Jessi asked, as she and Tyler sprang to their feet.

"Do we go together or one at a time?" Tyler added.

"Hang on, you two. Have a seat." There really *was* something wrong; they could hear it in his voice. Without another word, they sat back down.

"First of all, I *am* going to get you back. I don't know exactly how yet, but you must believe me, okay? It's just gotten more complicated than I expected. Umm, a *lot* more complicated. Anyway, the reason you had to wait so long for me to get back to you is 'cause the most precise time I can connect to is about every 20 minutes. You know how some car radios have a little 'click' you can feel when you turn up the sound? It's kinda like that; every 'click' is about that long. By the way, it's been three days for me since I brought back the hardware, but only minutes for you. Weird, huh? Now stand back; I'm sending you some gear."

They moved back, and a few moments later there was a rushing of air *towards* the funnel, and then with a *shuunk* a backpack and two sleeping bags appeared. Tyler rushed forward and started to pick up the backpack but quickly let it back down—it was heavy.

"So what's in it?" Jessi asked.

"Hang on, let me open it first."

He kneeled in front of the backpack, pulled on the zipper, looked inside, and started pulling out the contents. On top was mostly food—energy bars and a couple of water bottles. In the bottom were a map, a compass, some camouflage rain gear, a knife, a tarp, a hatchet, some matches, and a ball of twine.

Watching Tyler unload the backpack, Jessi frowned. "This doesn't look good."

"What do you mean? This is great! Look at all this food!"

"Exactly, and the map! And a compass! Something tells me we're not going to be hanging around here waiting for Jim to take us home."

"Oh, yeah."

Jessi leaned over and picked up a piece of wood. "What's this?" she asked. It was a perfectly round piece of wood, about four inches long and a couple inches thick. It looked like it had been cut with a saw. There was no bark on the outside, although the core of it was dark and a little soft.

They waited.

"I see you got your supplies," Jim's voice finally called out. "I sent you a tarp instead of a tent so it'd draw less attention. Now let me see that piece of wood, Jessi. Hold it up so I can get a good look at it."

There was a long pause. "Shoot! Okay, that confirms it. To come back home you need to go to another site—another funnel."

"No way! Are you sure?" Tyler asked.

"Yeah, I'm sure. Now listen up. The stuff you sent back here arrived backwards, no ... more like inverted. Meaning everything on the outside is now on the inside, and vice versa. Look carefully at that wedge of wood. That's from a tree that used to be where you're standing right now. It came here into my house on the rebound after you went there. It looks like it's always and only a one-way trip between funnels. Things get twisted inside out on the return trip."

"Eeeww, like a transporter gone bad." Jessi grimaced.

"Exactly. So here's what you have to do: Follow the map. It's a *modern* map of France on one side, England on the other, so I'm guessing that some roads won't be there for you, but it's very accurate for direction and distance. You're going to go to a funnel in a town called Lille. The funnel is ten feet directly east of a very large tree in a park. From the funnel, looking south, you will see the large bell tower of a really big church about fifty yards away. Also, the tree itself is next to a little stream. You'll find it; don't worry."

"Jim?" Jessi jumped in. "I got something I gotta say before we go."

"Yeah, I'm so sorry about this," Jim began. "There's no way around this—"

"Couldn't ya have given us a couple of pillows?" Jessi finished with a smile.

A few minutes later, they were back on the road. With one last glance towards the face on the cliff, they went right and retraced their steps from the day before, stopping briefly at the fork in the road. Going right would take them back toward the little valley and Amiens, but this time they went left, heading north into the unknown wilderness.

7
𝔄 𝔚𝔦𝔫𝔡𝔦𝔫𝔤 ℜ𝔬𝔞𝔡

It was early afternoon when they finally got started, and there was hardly a cloud in the sky. After a few minutes they stopped, took off their sweatshirts, and stuffed them in their backpacks.

"All right, let's go," Tyler said confidently. He glanced back at Jessi, who was peering into the woods on the opposite side of the road, listening intently.

"What's up?"

Jessi put her index finger to her lips. After a few moments she spun around and quickly caught up with him, moving at a fast pace. After they were well away, she slowed a bit.

"Jessi?"

"Yeah, I thought I saw something, some kind of brownish-purple animal, way deep in the trees. It looked a little bigger than a deer, but moved ... different. We need to keep an eye out for animals ... predators, who knows?"

About a half hour went by. "How far have we gone, you think?" Tyler asked.

"Aw, come on, Ty. You sound like my little sister every time my parents take us anywhere."

"No, I mean it. Have we gone maybe two miles? It *will* help to know. After all, Jim said Lille is about seventy miles away. If we can make fifteen miles every day, that's five days, which gives us ... four energy bars each per day—right?"

Jessi spun around to face him. "Tyler, I'd eat four of these things for a *snack*, not a whole day's worth of meals! Come on! That means we're gonna hafta beg or work for food along the way, especially since we'll be walking all day." Suddenly she grabbed Tyler's shirt and pulled him off the road.

"Hey! Whatcha doing?"

"Quiet!" Jessi hissed, "Someone's coming."

They crouched in the bushes and waited; about a minute later they saw a man walking next to a donkey pulling a cart. There was a woman riding in the cart. The man had a thick walking stick in his hand, and he was talking just loud enough for the woman to hear him. The man was looking along the road, as if searching for something, and lightly whacked the donkey's butt when it slowed too much. Tyler and Jessi crouched in the shadows, waiting until they could no longer hear the cart on the road. Only then did they creep out from under the trees.

"Jessi, it's going to take us forever if we run and hide every time we see someone, and we sure can't hide when we get to a town."

"Yeah, but with our clothes looking so different and having *nothing* to protect ourselves with, we gotta be careful. What was that man saying when they went by?"

"He was telling her he thought he saw something on the road—it was probably us—and she was telling him about … some kind of snake, I think."

"Snake?"

"Well, I think 'serpent' was the actual word she used."

"Oh, great. Wild animals are bad enough, but we should be looking out for *snakes* too? Hey, wait a sec. If they're in a *road* looking around for a snake in the *woods*, that'd have to be an awfully big snake. And have you thought about how we're gonna sleep? We don't even have a tent!"

"I don't know, Jessi. We'll think of something."

They walked on, meeting no one on the empty road for at least an hour. The trees on either side grew close to the edge of the road, their upper branches sometimes touching each other overhead, casting shadows onto them, especially now that the sun was halfway to the horizon.

Tyler set his backpack down. "I think we need to swap packs for the rest of the day. I'm *sure* mine is heavier than yours. We definitely moved too many energy bars from yours to mine."

"Aww, quit complaining. You can handle it. Besides, it'll be getting lighter as we eat them."

"Yeah, in a *week!*"

"Look, it's *your* backpack, so why *shouldn't* you carry it?"

"I dunno," Tyler grumbled. "I'm just tired … and hungry." He opened the main compartment, and pulled out two energy bars. "Ya want one?"

They ate in silence on the side of the road. It didn't take long before their hands were holding empty wrappers. The sun was warm, but Jessi shivered anyway. "I think I know what's been bugging me."

"What's that?"

"It's the silence. At home there's always noise, at least traffic, even if it's from the main road, what? Five blocks away? You know, a dog barking, or a lawnmower running, always something making noise."

"We live in a city, Jessi."

"Yeah, I know. But this is so … quiet. Just birds and crickets, but it's like how the music in a movie stops just before the monster jumps out. Only the monster never shows up here."

"Ya want it to?"

"I just feel like I need to keep looking behind me."

* * * * * *

They kept heading north as Jim had told them. "Turn east after twenty miles," he said. But how far was that? They knew they lived about a half mile from school. After some practice, and a little arguing, they finally agreed on how far a mile probably was.

The sun was sinking in the west when they sat down to eat. Tyler pulled out the knife Jim had sent them; it was some kind of hunting knife, very sharp. He used it to slice the bread the lady had given them, putting half of it back in the cloth wrapping. They each had an apple and ate half the cheese. A good meal, but they weren't exactly full.

Tyler glanced down at their remaining food and quickly snatched it off the ground.

"What's the matter?" Jessi asked.

"Ants. I'm not sharing our food with them!"

"I'm with you on that. So, how far do you think we went today, anyway?"

"Don't know for sure, but I think about nine or ten miles, maybe more. At this rate, we'll be in Lille in what, five or six days! And we only walked for half a day—this is gonna be easy!"

"Not with so little food to eat. I'm still hungry."

They fell silent for a while, listening to the only constant sound around them—the droning and buzzing of unseen insects. Even the birds had quieted down for the evening.

"Ya know, I was thinking," Tyler began. "We went from the middle of May to the middle of June in like, no time at all!"

"Well, maybe four hundred years!" Jessi shot back with a smirk.

"So, we went forward while we went backward?"

The sun was now below the horizon, and it would be dark soon, so they started looking for a place to spend the night. They wandered along the side of the road, going into the trees, but never getting too far from the road, looking for a place to spend the night.

"That lady's cottage wasn't anything like our houses," Tyler began. "And I was kinda looking down on it, but now I'm thinking it was a whole lot better than sleeping in the open forest."

Finally, they found a place where four trees formed a half circle that opened towards the road about 30 yards away. It felt about as secure as they could hope for.

Tyler pulled out the camouflage tarp. It was the same pattern as their rain gear. He spread it out on the ground and put their packs on two of the corners. He then unrolled his sleeping bag and dropped down on top of it.

"Ow! There's a rock under my shoulder." He twisted around, reached under the tarp, and pulled it out. "These bags are really thin!" he grumbled.

"Yeah, but it *is* summer," Jessie answered.

She quickly grew silent when she thought about how hard the ground would be, and how soft her bed at home was; her bed that wouldn't even *exist* for another four hundred years. "Ty?"

"What?"

"If we don't do this, if ... if we don't connect back up with Jim, the only part of us that'll make it back to the 21st century is gonna be our bones."

Tyler propped himself up on his elbow. Jessi's eyes were filling with tears. "Aww c'mon, Jessi. We're gonna make it fine; both of us." He impulsively gave her a quick hug and flopped back onto his sleeping bag.

Jessi wiped her eyes. *Well, that was awkward*, she thought.

"Think happy thoughts, Jessi. Happy, happy, happy!"

A tight smile crossed her face. "Right. Well, we might as well try to get some sleep."

"Sleep? It's too early." Tyler clasped his hands behind his head and looked up at the branches that almost completely blocked out the sky overhead. "It's probably not even nine o'clock!"

"Yeah, but we walked a lot more than usual, and on this hard ground I don't think we'll sleep very good. Besides, we'll probably wake up early when the sun comes up."

Jessi noticed a fair amount of dead branches on the ground around them. If they weren't going to go to sleep right away, they could clear the dirt in front of them and make a fire to keep any animals away. "Hey, Ty. What d'ya think about making a fire?"

She hesitated when he didn't answer. A moment later she heard his relaxed breathing. He had fallen asleep. She sat up and took a long look at him, then to the forest beyond. Under the canopy of the trees it was getting too dark to see anything clearly as the crescent moon and a few of the brighter stars could now be seen in the gaps of the forest canopy above. A cool breeze carried the scent of dirt and grass.

Her gaze returned to her friend, and she smiled. She gently pulled the hood of his sweatshirt up to better cover his head and ears. He stirred, and she froze until she was certain he was still sleeping. "You're a good friend, Tyler Duncan," she whispered.

She looked apprehensively around them in the gathering gloom. "And no matter what happens, I'm glad we're in this together."

She pictured herself kissing him on the cheek, but the mere thought of it gave her a shock. Thoroughly confused, she quickly dropped down onto her sleeping bag. She closed her eyes and swallowed hard. "Where did *that* come from?" she muttered to herself.

8
Good Advice

June 13, 1614

Though she fell asleep quickly, Jessi was right about not sleeping well. The hard ground kept them both tossing and turning all night, but in the end exhaustion finally won out.

The early morning sun threw long shadows across the forest, completely missing them in the hollow of the trees. The birds started singing, getting noisier as the day brightened. Flies and other insects began moving from one spot to another, their thin whining growing then fading.

Jessi opened her eyes. The first thing she saw was the delicate shafts of sunlight filtering through the trees overhead. She was cold, but the fresh air and melodic noises of the forest brought a smile of contentment—in spite of their crazy circumstances. Even though it was June, the large leaves were still the bright green color of early spring when they first come out. Tyler was asleep to her left; his right arm cradled under his head.

As she leaned towards him her back cramped up, and she fell back onto the tarp, whacking her head on the ground.

"Ow!" She slowly sat up, rubbing her head.

Tyler woke up and looked at her. "You okay?" he mumbled. He then pulled his arm down to his waist with a groan. "Uuh! My shoulder hurts, and my legs! Man! I'm hungry."

"Aww, quit whining. I'm sore too."

Tyler lay still. With a sigh Jessi lay back down next to him. Silence ushered in like a dark cloud. They were cold and wet; their sleeping bags were damp and heavy, and the tarp all around them was wet with dew.

Eventually they both got up and walked slowly around their campsite. After a few minutes they started feeling better and then sat back down again on the cold wet tarp. They each ate an energy bar as they watched and listened to the forest creatures. Birds were twittering all around them, almost to the point of being obnoxious. Squirrels chattered to each other as they ran up and down the tree trunks; sometimes jumping from one tree to another.

"You know, I've climbed a lot of trees, but I've never gone down a tree headfirst like those squirrels," Tyler mused as he looked overhead.

"Yeah," Jessi nodded. "But don't try it, okay? We need to get home injury-free."

Once they were done eating there was no reason to hang around, so they each rolled up their sleeping bags; they then folded up the tarp, stuffed it into Jessi's backpack, and headed out.

They stood at the edge of the road, examining it skeptically. It wasn't too impressive. Rocks and tree roots stuck out of the ground, sometimes as much as four to six inches. It was so uneven with bumps and holes everywhere that only some kind of off-road truck would be able to navigate it in one piece.

Jessi looked to the north, holding her right hand up to the side of her face to shade her eyes from the climbing sun. "When we see someone, let's just stay on the road this time. What d'ya think? If we stay together on one side single file, we'll probably be okay."

"Let's agree on which way we'd run if we have to," Tyler added. "Oh, and let me walk ahead of you, and I'll do the talking."

"Well, I sure won't. I don't know the language. Besides, aren't England and France enemies?"

"Here and now? I don't know. It was off and on between them for hundreds of years."

"Well, I'm not taking any chances. *You* can do the talking for us."

"No problem," he added with a smile. "I'll just tell people you can't talk 'cause you got brain damage."

"Hey!" Jessi play punched Tyler on the arm.

They both snickered and started walking. Even though they were still in the cool of the morning, it wasn't long before once again they had to peel off their sweatshirts. After a couple of hours they saw in the distance a tall figure walking towards them.

"Here we go, Ty," Jessi whispered nervously.

"Just stay behind me," Tyler advised. "We got maybe five minutes before we pass each other."

They exchanged anxious looks, then shrugged as Tyler stepped in front. Up ahead the road sloped gently downwards, trees on the right, an open area on the left. It was a wet, marshy field that appeared to collect all the rainwater in the area. As they approached the flatland, the smell of rotting vegetation slowly filled the air, and the buzzing of flies, chirping crickets, and frogs droned loudly all around them.

The space between them and the approaching figure quickly diminished. They could see it was a man. Tyler thought he looked a little younger than his grandpa. His long narrow face matched his nose, and his stringy, oily hair hung in clumps almost down to his shoulders. His short scraggly beard was sprinkled with gray.

"Good morning, sir." Tyler spoke confidently.

"And the same to you, young master," replied the man. He then glanced up at the sun. "Looks to me like it's a little after noon, actually," he added.

Tyler instinctively followed his glance up towards the sun, noting its location as indicating noon. He hoped they could just keep walking, but the man had stopped, and it looked like he wanted to talk. He leaned forward as he curiously examined them slowly from head to toe, and back up again.

"You two are dressed strangely. Where does such attire come from?"

"Not around here, that's for sure!" Tyler ventured, hoping that was a good enough answer. He saw it wasn't when the man's smile disappeared.

"I already determined that. Well, that's your business, not mine, I suppose. So what brings you out here? We're a long way from anybody's home in this part of the king's country." The man's eyebrows rose with the inquiry.

"Well, we're going to Lille, to see my ... uncle. He's expecting us there in about a week, so we need to keep going. Have a good day!"

The whine of a mosquito flew by Tyler's ear. He took a step forward, but the man's arm shot out as he planted his hand squarely on Tyler's chest, stopping him cold. "What is your hurry?" he asked. Tyler shrank back as the man loomed over him. His overcoat opened up and gently closed back together, sending out a very unpleasant odor. Tyler guessed he hadn't bathed in at least a week. Without waiting for an answer, the man looked back at Jessi.

"What about her? Are you two related, or married?"

Jessi stepped back, dropping her head slightly. She looked at Tyler.

Shocked at the question, Tyler hesitated. "She's my cousin. Her dad's my uncle—he's the one expecting us."

He looked at Jessi. "Is that right? Lille is a long ways away." He waited for an answer, his eyes narrowing.

"She can't talk, mister. She can hear fine, but her tongue doesn't work right. Please, mister. We need to go."

"Mmm hmm," was all he answered, never taking his eyes off of Jessi. "How come her hair's so short?" he asked.

Tyler's mind started racing. "Well, umm, she had a bad case of lice and had to cut it. Hopefully she got it all, but I'm not so sure." He turned towards Jessi and slowly winked as he pointed at a yellow flower among the weeds. "We gotta get him to back off, so laugh as soon as I stop talking to you, then scratch the back of your head like it really itches." She followed his lead, and a moment later the man took a slight step back.

Tyler felt a pin prick on the back of his neck. He slapped it and pulled a bloody mosquito out from between his fingers. *Too late*, he grimaced. The man kept staring at Jessi, and Tyler sensed that they needed to get away. "Mister, how far is it to Lille?" he asked, putting on as pleasant a face as he could, despite his growing anger.

The man pulled his gaze away from Jessi, and his hand dropped down to his side. "Huh? Oh, it's a long ways, probably about twenty–three Lieue. You'd better keep moving, and get out of these lowlands before nightfall. Try your best to make it to the Doullens' farm at the fork in the road." Nodding towards the bog, he warned them, "There are some strange creatures around here."

"Oh, that reminds me," Tyler began. "We passed some people who were talking about a serpent. What exactly would that be?"

The man looked at him in alarm. "Where was the serpent?" he asked sharply.

"A little bit this side of Amiens. Why?"

"Obviously because I'm heading that way!" he said scornfully, before glancing nervously at the road ahead of him. "You two get to higher and drier countryside. Good day!" Without another word he quickly left them behind.

"Thank you, sir." Tyler called after him. He watched as the man went away, at a pace just short of jogging.

They put about a half-mile between them before Jessi said anything. "So what was *that* all about?"

"Well, first he talked about our clothes, and then asked where we're heading."

"Maybe just to be nice?"

"Maybe, but he didn't like it when I didn't give him a direct answer. He said Lille is a long ways away."

"Did he say how far?"

"He said it was twenty-three Lieue."

"What's a … Leeoo?"

"Lieue. L-i-e-u-e. It's French for 'league', but I don't know how long a league is. Jim said it was seventy miles from Amiens, and we've gone maybe fifteen so far."

"So that's uh … twenty-three divided by fifty-five?" Jessi asked.

"No," he corrected her. "It's fifty-five divided by twenty-three, which would be about ... two and a half miles per league."

"That sounds about right. I'm not the math whiz here," she conceded.

"Well, he said we should try hard to get to the Doullens' farm, and out of this area. 'Strange creatures,' he said."

"Humph! I think *he* was the strange creature. But what did you say to him at the end?" she asked. "He was scared of something."

"I asked him about the serpent those people were talking about."

"What'd he say?"

"Nothing! He just asked where the serpent *was* and said to get away from this swamp. Then he just took off."

"Fine with me. Let's get moving. Oh, hey! What'd you tell him about me?"

"That you have the smarts of a donkey—Ow!"

9
Water

The sun started its slow descent towards the west. Clouds were now scattered throughout the sky in all directions, but rarely did they have any real relief from the sun. They were thirsty, but their water bottles had been dry for at least an hour. To make things worse, the last couple miles had been steadily uphill. Thankfully, the rotten scent of the lowlands was gone, replaced with the sweet smell of the tall, green grass on either side of the road.

A half mile before the crest of the hill, the dirt road suddenly became paved with smoothed stones that had been shaped to allow them to pack tightly together. In addition, squared stones were neatly laid in such a fashion that they formed a small curb on each side. Tyler slowed down as he intently studied the road.

"What are you thinking?" Jessi asked.

"I've seen this before, but I can't remember why."

"Last time you were in France?"

"No, I'm serious, this looks—oh, I know! Awesome! This is a section of road built by the Romans back in … whenever they controlled Europe. A friend of my dad is an engineer, and he was showing me a whole bunch of pictures on the internet of ancient Roman roads that are still being used."

He looked behind them. "I wonder what happened to the stones back there?"

"Well, some of them went into a building a mile or so back on the left. No roof, just walls. Didn't you see it?"

"No, shoot!"

"You didn't miss much, Ty."

They reached the crest of the hill but were unable to see what lay beyond because of the trees encroaching on both sides of the road, although there was a nice view behind them to the south.

They continued down the road a short distance.

"Yes!" Tyler said with a shout as he suddenly broke into a run. From higher ground on their right, a bubbling stream of clear water came down, hitting an embankment of paved stones against the road, which made the water run alongside the road for a couple hundred feet before hitting another paved embankment that forced the stream to go *under* the road.

Jessi caught up with him just as he reached the edge of the water. "Right ... there!" Jessi pointed further ahead to where the stream narrowed to about four feet wide. She walked over to the place she had spotted and easily jumped to the opposite side.

A few large flat rocks gave her a place to put down her pack, and she knelt over the rushing water. She filled her bottle and straightened up as she emptied it – one delicious swallow after another. As she leaned over and refilled the bottle, the noise of the water rushing among the rocks was music to her ears; since all they had been hearing for hours in the quiet countryside had been squawking birds, the endless drone of crickets, and the faint whisper of the wind through the trees.

Cupping his hands together Tyler drank four handfuls of water before looking up. "Hey! How do we know it's safe to drink this?" he asked.

"Doesn't matter *now*, does it? Besides, I *just* ran out of iodine tablets," she said with a wink, snapping her fingers. Water ran off her chin and dripped onto the rock next to her hand as she looked back to where the water came rushing into the open between two huge maple trees at the top of the hill. She was getting in the habit of constantly looking behind her. *Don't be so paranoid*, she thought.

While Tyler refilled his water bottle, Jessi hopped back over the stream and stepped up onto the road. She headed on downhill. The road leveled off briefly where the stream went underneath her, before going downhill again a short distance to the flatlands beyond. She continued to that point before she

realized Tyler wasn't with her. She looked up the road behind her
– he wasn't there!

"Tyler!" she screamed.

"I'm here. What's the matter?" she heard him respond. Relief
at hearing his voice, and warmth at hearing the *concern* in his
answer swept through her.

"Where are you?" she asked.

"I'm under the road."

"What?"

"I was looking at the construction of the arch that holds up
the roadway where the water goes underneath. It's pretty
amazing, and it's what? Maybe a thousand years old?"

"You made *me* old, disappearing like that."

"Oh, sorry. But it *is* pretty cool," he added as he finally caught
up with where she was waiting.

* * * * * *

A couple minutes later they saw that the stream, which had
been hugging the side of the road, now turned off to the left.

"Oh, wow!" Jessi breathed.

Hardly 20 feet away, the stream emptied into a lake that must
have been a half-mile across. Jessi immediately headed for the
water, dropping her backpack on the ground under some trees.

She approached the edge and leaned over, peering down to
the bottom. It appeared to be only a couple feet deep, so she sat
down, took off her shoes, hiked up her pants, and waded into
the cool water. "Ooh, Ty! This feels sooo good. You gotta try it."

He glanced both ways along the road, saw they were alone,
and probably would be for a while. As he approached, he put his
backpack next to hers. "Sure, I think we can relax for a few
minutes. No one's coming."

"Relax for a few minutes? Are you sure you can let your guard
down that long?" she said teasingly. "I swear, Tyler, you're gonna
be an old man before you graduate from high school!" She
reached down and threw a double-handful of water at him.
"Come on, the water's fine!"

"Really?" he said with a smile. A moment later he launched himself directly towards her; landing a perfect belly flop that pushed a mountain of water on her. When he stood up out of the water he saw that she was almost as soaked through as he was.

"That's more like it!" she said with a grin. "It's on!"

Ten minutes later Tyler stepped out of the water and under the trees. "I've always wondered what it'd be like to go swimming with all my clothes on!"

Jessi, still in the water, looked up at him. "So ... what do you think?"

"Nice," he laughed, "but I think I prefer board shorts."

"That's a big surprise," she said mockingly. "I don't know about you, but I don't think I've had this much fun in two feet of water since I was four."

"Yeah, me neither." His eyes rested on her as she looked around. "I ... I'm thirsty. I'm getting another drink." He glanced briefly at the mud they had stirred up. "But I think I'll get it upstream," he added as he walked away.

A couple minutes later he returned and sat down next to Jessi, leaning his back against a tree. "Maybe we should spend the night here. What d'ya think?" He pulled out the rest of the food they had earned by moving the firewood. Using his legs as a table, he put the remaining portions of bread and cheese on his lap and started to prepare their lunch. He cut both the bread and cheese in half and started to put half of it into his pack, as Jessi reached for the portions that were still out.

"Hey! Not so fast!" Tyler snapped. "We're splitting that between us! We gotta save the rest for later."

"Well, who made you the food police?" Jessi retorted.

"Look, I'm just trying to plan ahead! I'm getting tired of energy bars *too*, okay?" Tyler aimed for the middle of the bread and angrily plunged the knife in – a bit too far; the knife poked through the bottom of the loaf and into his leg. "Oow!" he yelped, as he pulled the knife back up. A small spot of blood appeared through a little hole in his jeans.

Jessi twisted around in concern. "Hey, you okay?" she asked, her anger vanishing.

"Yeah, I'm fine. It just nicked me," he answered sullenly. "Just eat your food, okay? Here, have an apple."

They ate in silence, except for the occasional whine of a mosquito and the usual cricket that could always be heard but never seen. The air felt heavy and thick, and they were glad for the shade.

Jessi took a swig of water from her bottle. "You know, Ty, we're really doing pretty good here. Ya know what I mean? After all we ... what?"

Tyler had grabbed her arm as he pointed towards the water about a hundred feet away from where they had their water fight. Without taking his eyes off that spot, Tyler slowly lifted his index finger and placed it over his lips. "Shhhhh."

Jessi turned and looked. "I don't see anything, Ty," she whispered.

"Wait ... keep looking ..." There was tension in his voice.

Twenty long seconds passed by. Slap! Water splashed high up onto a bush that hung over the water's edge.

"That's one big fish!" Jessi gasped, wide-eyed.

"That's no fish," Tyler quietly answered. "Are there hippos in Europe?"

"I don't think so."

"There's something big down there, Jess."

The idea made her heart sink. *We were just in there*, she thought. She wanted to turn and run, anything just to get away from the water and back on the road. Her eyes darted down to her feet, and then slowly tracked along the path to the water. Their sneakers weren't the only prints to be seen! She silently pointed them out to Tyler.

Tyler began examining the soft earth, as he silently pointed out the six-inch-wide round prints with four stubby toes that were all around them. They were so obvious; how could she have missed seeing them before?

Tyler looked at Jessi. "Are you *sure* there are no hippos in Europe?" he quietly asked.

"I dunno, Ty. Let's get out of here," Jessi answered as she grabbed her backpack. "C'mon!"

"Hang on!" Tyler hissed. "There's no way a water creature can run faster than us on land! I want a closer look." Crouching low to the ground, he crept down to the edge of the water next to the bush from which a few random drops of water were still falling. Jessi followed close behind.

He stood on the soft turf at the water's edge, his toes less than an inch from the water. Jessi came alongside and peered down into the murkiness. She saw that here the depth of the water was at least three or four feet deep right at the edge, as if someone, or some *thing*, had burrowed it out. Then she noticed the turf they were standing on was actually over the water and was slowly sinking under their weight! In a panic she jumped back as the portion of earth that had been under her feet broke and dropped into the water. Startled, Tyler pulled back and fell to the ground as the turf under his feet collapsed as well. He quickly scrambled to his feet and grabbed her arm.

"Let's get out of here," he hollered. "There's something … big … in there, and I almost fell on top of it!" They each grabbed their backpacks on the run and didn't stop until they were back on the road. One quick look behind them told them they weren't being followed, yet they kept moving faster than usual until they were far away.

From the water's edge two large greenish-yellow eyes broke the surface and watched as the forms of the two visitors disappeared, its long tail roiling the water behind its stout body. It slapped more water up into the bush, knocking a small frog off a branch and into the water, and with lightning speed seized the frog in its mouth before it could swim away. After swallowing the frog whole, it slowly descended back below the water's surface.

* * * * *

The late afternoon flew by as they continued their journey. It took at least an hour before their clothes dried out, but Tyler's sneakers squeaked for another hour beyond that.

"Ty," Jessi growled. "Next time, take off your shoes before you go swimming, okay?"

They tried to keep track of how many miles they were covering but just couldn't be sure. What bothered them more was not knowing how close they were getting to the farm the man had told them to look for. In addition, all Jim had told them was to go north for about 20 miles, then east to Lille. But how would they know for sure when they had walked 20 miles?

With the sun now below the trees and the temperature starting to drop, they knew it was time to find a place to camp for the night. The Doullens' farm would have to wait until tomorrow.

After several unsuccessful attempts, they finally came across the perfect site: a large tree that had been blown over in a windstorm many years before. The roots that had been torn out of the ground formed a vertical wall about eight feet high, and coarse grass a foot tall grew where the tree had once stood upright.

"What d'ya say we put the tarp over us this time?" Tyler suggested. "We were wet this morning from the dew anyway."

"And if it rains, we're ready for that! Brilliant, Ty."

They stretched their rope about three feet off the ground between the root ball and another tree, threw the tarp over it, and pulled the four corners out with rope attached to any bush or rock they could find.

It had been a long day, and they were moving slowly, hardly saying anything to each other. They sat down and pulled some food out of their backpacks and ate the last of the bread, cheese, and apples. By that time it was almost too dark to see. "Let's make a fire, Jess. What do you think?" Tyler asked.

"Sounds nice, but I don't think we can. After all, we don't have any wood, and now it's too dark to go out and find any." She glanced nervously into the gathering gloom. "And I sure don't wanna go out there *now*. What about you?"

Tyler sighed. "I think from now on we need to start making camp sooner."

"Yeah, well *I* think it'd be nice if we had a flashlight. Of course then we'd probably run out of batteries," Jessi said despondently.

They were both discouraged. Though neither one had said anything about it, they had both secretly been looking forward to sleeping in a bed, not under the tarp on the hard ground. But more than that, the idea of spending another night unprotected in the forest was unsettling, but neither was willing to voice their fears to the other. Fortunately for them, the tall grass provided a little bit of a cushion, but nothing like their beds back home. They were tired, and since they weren't used to this much walking, they quickly fell asleep.

10
Turn and Turn Again

June 14, 1614

The early morning sun crept over the eastern horizon and struck them full in the face. Within five minutes they were awake enough to know their sleep was over.

Jessi fished around inside her backpack. "All right!" she exclaimed.

Tyler didn't move. "What?" he finally asked.

"Energy bars for breakfast! Woo hoo!"

"You're so weird," he answered. Without opening his eyes he slapped the back of his hand onto the ground, palm open. "I'll take one," he said flatly.

Despite their taking the smallest of bites and chewing slowly, they were done way too soon. Their stomachs were telling them breakfast was just getting started, but they didn't dare eat more of their already dwindling food supply.

The sun was up, but its warmth was slow to dispel the damp chill under the trees. They weren't in a hurry to get back on the road, but since there wasn't anything else to do, they decided to break camp anyway. Tyler grabbed two corners of the tarp.

"Get a hold of the other side there, and let's shake off the dew, Jess."

They shook the tarp, but out of rhythm. It flew out of Jessi's hands and the rope off one corner whipped around and lashed across her fingers.

"Oww!" she yelped, jumping up and down as she shook her hand. After a few seconds she looked over at Tyler, who was rubbing the back of his neck.

"Feels like the rope scraped half my neck off," he grumbled. Without another word they knelt and untied the ropes from the tarp. Tyler folded up the tarp and stuffed it into Jessi's backpack. He picked it up to help her put it on when he saw her approaching him with the four ropes all neatly coiled. With a sigh he set it back down and unzipped it, put the ropes in, and zipped it back up. He silently picked it up again and helped adjust it comfortably on her back, and a minute later they emerged from the trees that concealed their campsite.

They looked up and down the road in both directions, then at each other. Without saying a word they shrugged their shoulders and headed north. They knew a good fast pace would warm them up against the early-morning chill, but they just didn't have the heart for it, as the gloom each one had felt the night before still held them in its grip.

Within half an hour they had settled into a decent pace. The sun was rapidly warming things up despite the clouds that filled half the sky. They couldn't have asked for a more perfect day for a hike: sunny and bright but not too hot; but the gloom in their hearts tenaciously held on, and as a result they trudged forward with their eyes on the ground barely 20 feet in front of their bowed necks. Neither one spoke much, nor cared to try.

By midday they estimated they had covered six to eight miles and passing other travelers on the road had now become commonplace. Each time their odd clothes brought stares of curiosity and occasionally what may have been hostility, but they got in the habit of avoiding eye contact and picking up their pace when anyone passed by.

The sun was high overhead now, and they were uncomfortably warm—and thirsty. They'd come upon a stream only once all morning, and now with every step, the hollow thump of their empty water bottles reminded them of just how thirsty they really were.

Jessi stopped abruptly and held up her hand.

"What's up?" Tyler asked.

"Shhhhh," Jessi responded. "Hear that?" she asked, her lips curling into a faint smile.

Off to the right and out of sight they could hear the faint gurgling of a stream. Without another word they left the road, and two minutes later their bottles, and stomachs, were full of water. The fresh water revived their spirits as well as their bodies, and they set out once more.

Barely five minutes later they stopped. Until now, the road had always made many gentle twists and turns, yet consistently took them north. Now the road made a sharp turn to the left as another road was coming from the right. Tyler stopped and looked both ways. Which road to take? They had to make a decision, and the choice wasn't obvious. Go east, or stay on their road that now was turning to the west?

Jessi lowered her pack to the ground. She looked down the road coming from the right. It was very straight for half a mile before turning slightly to the left—towards the north. "Let's go, Ty." She picked up her backpack and started walking.

"I'm not so sure about this, Jessi."

"About what?" she answered curtly. "Jim said go north, then east to Lille. Do I need to show you the compass?" She turned on her heels and headed down the new road.

"It's not *that*, Jessi. I don't need a compass," he shouted indignantly.

The road *did* appear to go in the direction they wanted, so he swallowed his misgivings and caught up with her.

Immediately on their left they passed a farm, and in the distance a girl was leading a flock of at least 30 sheep. Between themselves and the sheep, a couple of men were working on a fence that secured about 20 large pigs. The scent of the pigs wafted through the air on a gentle breeze coming down from the north.

"Whew!" Jessi grunted. "That smells terrible!"

"Just keep moving, Jessi. I don't want to spend another night in the forest," Tyler said as he picked up his pace.

* * * * * *

Over the next two hours they passed by the occasional farm. With their thirst quenched, a little water in their bottles, and seeing they were getting closer to civilization, their sense of isolation subsided. As a result, they finally started enjoying the summer afternoon.

In front of them the road wound gently down into a little valley where cultivated fields, separated from each other by rows of trees, reached to the foothills in all directions. Trails of smoke rose from the chimneys of three houses set amongst the fields.

Suddenly a crow, startled by their advancing footsteps, leapt into the air. Jessi paused, her gaze following its path to their right as it disappeared into the distance where the sun was poised just above the treetops. She looked behind her, a sinking feeling filling her body. *Oh crap!* she thought. They were heading south, and had been for a long time!

After a few paces, Tyler realized she had stopped. "What's the matter?" he asked.

Jessi looked around. "We need to go back, Ty. We've been going the wrong way; look where the sun's going down!" She pulled out the compass and carefully held it flat in front of her. The needle was pointing directly at her. "Noooo!" She angrily kicked the dirt, and a few small pebbles flew into the stubby grass at the side of the road. "We're heading south, Ty. We gotta go back. And look down there. That stupid little cul-de-sac of houses is a dead end!"

"That's redundant," Tyler answered.

"WHAT! *What* are you talking about?" she hollered in frustration, fists clenched.

"You just said a dead end is a dead end."

"Huh?"

"'Cul-de-sac' is how you say 'dead end' in French."

She threw her head back and sighed in annoyance. "Ty, not *all of us* got the gift of French two days ago. Grammar is *not* the issue here!"

"Just saying ..." Tyler shrugged. He looked back where they had come from, then again towards the valley. "We've got a long ways to go back. What d'ya think, any chance that's the Doullens farm down there in the valley?" he ventured

"I really don't think so. After all, this is *clearly* not the road to Lille."

"Yeah, but we can be down there in fifteen minutes! It'll take at least a couple hours to get back to the main road, and then what? A night under a roof, any roof, would be better than under the trees."

Jessi turned around and started heading back. "Come on, Ty. Let's go back. That man yesterday mentioned the Doullens' farm for a reason. I couldn't understand his words, and he *was* kind of creepy, but I really do think he was trying to be helpful."

Tyler plopped down and started to take off his shoes. He started muttering to himself in frustration, just loud enough so Jessi could hear him and apparently hoping she would. "We shouldn't have taken this road in the first place. I knew it!"

Anger boiled up inside Jessi. "What are you doing?" she shouted angrily. "This is *not* the right way. We have to go back!"

"I have a blister and it *hurts*, so back off!"

Jessi knew this mess was her fault, but she was still so anxious to head back and make up for lost time she couldn't stand still. She paced around in circles a few times and found herself heading up the road, leaving Tyler behind. A couple minutes later she slowed to a stop, found another rock to kick, and sent it flying into the knee-high grass that was growing just in front of some bushes.

Tyler looked up and saw her pacing in circles, waiting for him. He folded his sock double-thick on his heel, put his sneaker back on, and stood up. With one final glance at the homes in the valley behind him, he moved double-quick to where she was waiting.

He caught up with her, and together they started heading back the way they had come. The sun was dropping rapidly now, but they still had plenty of daylight left. It was then that they saw what they should have noticed sooner: this road was narrower, and much less used—probably just by those three families in the valley.

They moved as quickly as they could, but they were tired. They still weren't used to this kind of exercise, and their legs and backs were hurting. Even so, they kept up a fast pace and returned to the main road in much less time than they had spent going the wrong way; but one glance at the setting sun told them their time was short to find a place to spend the night.

They discovered that the main road soon turned back northward again, which lifted their spirits, and saw that the farm where they had seen the sheep and the pigs extended to the north alongside them on their right. Then the delicious smell of smoke from someone's chimney filled the air.

"Tyler! Look!" Jessi shouted as she pointed ahead. "I knew it!"

They walked another hundred yards or so to where the road abruptly ended. *This* was obviously the real end of the northbound road. This new road running east and west was definitely what they were looking for. About 10 feet away in each direction there were signs about five feet off the ground nailed to small rough-cut posts. The one to the right said Arras – 8.

They looked at each other, and then Jessi looked back at the sign. "I don't read French, but I know that doesn't say 'Lille'."

Tyler dropped his backpack to the ground to pull out the map. "Maybe Arras is on the way to Lille."

Jessi exhaled slowly as she looked around them, then her face brightened. "Look there, Ty."

Farther along the road to the right they saw the source of the smoke. A house was there, with acres of open farmland behind it. Tyler stuffed the map in his pocket – it could wait. They ran forward, slowing to a stop in the road in front of the house. A driveway paved with smooth stones wide enough for a wagon stretched ahead of them until it disappeared around behind the house. They stood there, suddenly reluctant to step foot onto someone's property, but it was already getting hard to see anything distinctly in the shadows under the trees, and it would be dark soon.

"Shoot." Tyler said disgustedly.

"What?"

"I should have known. That creepy guy said the Doullens' farm was at the fork in the road. I forgot all about that."

"Yeah, well, we made it before dark. I won't hold it against ya."

Timidly walking towards the house they passed by a white goat tethered to a post by a long rope. They could see exactly how long the rope was, based on the short grass in a huge circle around the post. The goat could reach them as they walked by if it wanted, but it barely paid any attention to them.

Tyler knocked twice on the door before they heard the tread of footsteps made by shoes on a wood floor. The door opened.

"Madame Doullens?" Tyler asked.

"Yes. How do you know my name?"

"We are travelling to Lille, and on our journey met a man who told us that your farm would be a safe place to spend the night. Do you have room for us in your barn, perhaps? We'd be happy to do some chores in return."

"Hmm." She cast a quick glance beyond them. "I'm sure we can find a place for you. Come inside, children. It's getting dark out there. Come in, come in."

11
An Agreement

Mrs. Doullens gestured for them to sit down, so they quickly sat side by side at a large kitchen table that could easily seat eight. They were in a combination kitchen and dining room, with a woodstove against the back wall. A counter on the wall to the right comprised the kitchen. To the left of the stove in the middle of the room was a door, presumably to the back half of the house.

"We finished dinner half an hour ago, children, but you're in luck. We had some stew left over." She glanced at them; one had a look of appreciation, the other uncertainty. "I'm thinking you're hungry, am I right?"

"We really are. Thank you so much, Mrs. Doullens," Tyler answered. He nudged Jessi and quietly whispered something to her. Her face quickly brightened as she smiled at her.

Mrs. Doullens' eyebrows lowered a little as she looked intently at her. "You all right, child?" she asked.

"She's fine, ma'am," Tyler offered. "She can't talk, so I do her talking for her."

"Is that right? Hmmm." She went back to the stove, ladled some stew into two large bowls, and set them on the table. She then took two copper mugs off a shelf and reaching to the bottom of a water barrel, brought them up full of water. She set the mugs and a couple of spoons on the table and sat down across from Tyler and Jessi. As she slid the mugs towards them, some water splashed onto the table, but she took no notice of it.

Placing her hands flat on the table, she leaned forward on her elbows and looked directly at Tyler. "This will be your only meal here if you keep lying to me, young man."

Jessi looked at the woman and then gently elbowed Tyler, shooting him a questioning look.

"Ma'am?"

"Your friend here might or might not be able to speak, but what is certain is she can't understand me." She looked sternly at Jessi. "Right?"

Jessi looked at her blankly, then over at Tyler, confirming her statement.

Tyler looked down at his plate and stammered, "Yes, ma'am, she can talk just fine; she just doesn't know French. She ... she only speaks English. We thought it would be safer for us if people didn't know she was Amer ... uh ... English."

Mrs. Doullens leaned back and laughed. "Well, if that's all this is about, you'll have no worries with me. Besides, not too many people will be concerned about an English-speaking child around here. Now eat your stew." She leaned forward again. "After you're done, we'll talk about what we're going to do with you two."

"What was that about?" Jessi quietly asked. "I don't know what she said, but I knew that look meant trouble. It's the same look Mom gives me when she catches me trying to get away with something."

"It's okay," Tyler reassured her. "She could tell you didn't understand French and *not* that you aren't able to talk."

It didn't take long for them to realize their good fortune. Mrs. Doullens talked to Tyler as they ate, Tyler translating for Jessi. The Doullens ran a family farm, and apparently they were doing well. The three Doullens children were at a neighbor's home for the night and would return tomorrow. They had a lot of land and crops growing on most of it, with only one field left fallow.

"Fallow? What's that mean?" Tyler asked.

"Good Lord, boy! You don't know what fallow means? Where are you from?" She gave another curious look at their clothing. "Fallow means to leave the land alone for a season to let it rest. Most people just let the weeds grow, but we plant legumes—usually peas or beans—because somehow it's good for the soil just like the weeds. So we get food even during the fallow year. We do very well because of that."

She stood up from the table, and with one smooth motion double-folded the bottom of her apron and opened the door in the front of the stove. The apron acted as an oven mitt, but burn scars on her hands and wrists showed that she had lost a number of battles with the hot stove. With her other hand she added some wood to the fire inside, then closed the door.

She was in her midthirties, but she looked rather older, with one significant exception: her demeanor. In a moment she would go from serious attention to her work to a quick laugh or joyful expression, revealing that a young woman still resided inside. Scraping the bottom of the water barrel with another copper cup, she poured the water into a teapot, and placed it on the stove. "Tea for Mr. Doullens," she chimed.

After they finished their stew, she took their bowls and gave them each a dried apple. "Not too much longer and we'll have fresh apples," she said longingly as she unbraided her long hair. "We have several trees that—" She interrupted herself as she cocked her head to one side.

Outside they heard someone talking, but there was no voice in response. Then they heard someone stomping their boots on the pavement, as if to knock off some excess dirt. "Ready to go inside?" someone asked. A few moments later the door flew open, and a large dog came bounding through the doorway, followed by a slender, well-muscled man. His dark hair was cut short, yet it lay down close to his head; his brown eyes were friendly, but, like his wife, he appeared older than his 38 years. The dog immediately froze and faced the visitors. It appeared to be some sort of German Shepherd mixed breed. It let out a low growl, legs slightly bent, as if ready to defend—or attack. Jessi and Tyler watched the dog carefully, afraid to make even the slightest move.

"Pierre! Down!" Mrs. Doullens commanded.

The dog retreated slowly to a spot near the front door, never completely taking its eyes off of them. It made two complete circles before deciding to sit on its back legs, directly facing them.

Mr. Doullens smiled as he watched his dog begin guard duty, then said to his wife, "Horses and cattle are in for the night."

"That's good," she replied. "The boys secured the pigpen and Camille took care of the sheep before they left. We have company, as you can see, and we've been getting acquainted."

"Eh? All right. Tea ready?"

"Just about. Have a seat and greet our guests."

He sat down opposite them where his wife had just been sitting. Leaning forward, he pointed his thumb towards his wife and said in a low voice "She likes tea, and I'm getting used to it." He smiled and winked.

"I heard that!" she called over her shoulder.

"Well, it's true!"

"All right, all right. Just remember, the best part is you get to drink it with me!"

"No doubt about that!" he laughed with a twinkle in his eye. He turned back to his visitors.

"I'm Gilles Doullens," he said as he extended his hand.

Tyler gave as firm a handshake as he could. "My name is Tyler, and this is Jessi." The man's hand was hard and calloused, his grip strong.

"Hello, Jessi."

At the sound of her name Jessi looked at him, stood halfway up, and shook his hand, then slowly sat back down.

"Sir, she doesn't understand French."

"But you do, and with a slight, and rather curious, accent."

Mrs. Doullens came to the table. She set a mug of tea in front of her husband, and one for herself next to him. "Gilles, I was just about to ask these two how it is that they're here," she explained as she sat down. "So just how *is* it that you are here?" she pointedly asked.

Tyler looked straight at her, his mind racing. How much could he say? She certainly wouldn't believe they were from the future, but she would know if he were lying.

"Uh ... I don't really know how it is that we're here," he stammered. "We got ... left here, South of here, that is, about ... eight Lieue." He looked at Jessi. "She got hit real hard on her head." He gestured at the cut, which had scabbed over. "We're heading to Lille where our friend is meeting us in ten days next to a church, and he's going to take us home."

He looked back and forth between Mr. and Mrs. Doullens' faces. It was the truth, but it sounded pretty lame. He looked down at the empty bowl in front of him, figuring it would be his first, and last, under this roof.

Mrs. Doullens put her hand under his chin and lifted his face up until his eyes met hers. He watched her eyes shift back and forth as she looked intently at him.

"I believe you," she finally answered. "You say your friend expects you in ten days, yes?" She turned to her husband. "I have an idea."

* * * * * *

The barn door scraped and creaked on its hinges as Tyler pulled it shut. He turned around, lifted the lantern, and looked at their new home. Then he looked more closely at the lantern.

It was a tall skinny box, with the four sides made of glass. Open slots down low on each side allowed fresh air in to feed the candle that was placed into a hole in the bottom. The metal lid had holes around the edge to let out the heat from the flame without burning his hand as he held the handle attached on top. It looked a lot like the gas lantern his family used when they went camping.

The lantern cast a dim light about him, creating a circle of shadowy darkness not very far away—in fact far too close. He took a deep breath. The air was fresh and sweet; the rolls of grass stacked high were still a strong shade of green. Mr. Doullens had said it was their early crop, with another crop still in the field.

Jessi was already going up the ladder to the hayloft overhead. When she got to the top she put her lantern down on the floor of the loft, but the weight of her pack prevented her from easily stepping off the ladder. With one hand firmly gripping the top of the ladder, she swung her pack off her shoulders and tossed it on the hay, then lightly stepped into the loft. Setting her backpack to the side, she spread out a blanket on the hay. She dropped down and pulled a second blanket up to her chin. "I'm so tired I could sleep 'til noon," she murmured.

Tyler was right behind her. "They said we could sleep in 'cuz tomorrow's Sunday. But I think what they call 'sleeping in' won't be noon."

"Yeah, I suppose not."

Tyler carefully placed his lantern on a little shelf against the wall opposite Jessi. He hesitated, unsure how close to Jessi he should place his blankets. Too close would be awkward, too far away could be insulting. He decided to play it safe and settled in with his feet facing hers. Placed on opposite walls, it was surprising how much light their two candles made together.

Jessi tucked her hands behind her head. "So Ty, tell me exactly what kind of a deal you made with the Doullens."

"Well, the Doullens were gonna have a kid about our age spend the next week here working on their farm, but he broke his arm a couple days ago. So you and I are gonna fill in for him, and they'll feed us in exchange. Then next weekend Mr. Doullens will take us to Lille in their wagon, 'cause he's going there anyway."

"We don't know anything about working on a farm, Ty."

"I told them that, but they said it'd be okay."

Jessi sat up to blow out her candle, but started examining her backpack instead. Jim had sent her a nice one, much better than her own. On one side of the pack was a short zipper at the top of a long, narrow pocket that she hadn't noticed before. She pulled on the zipper.

Tyler blew out his candle and looked at Jessi. "How 'bout you turn off ... er ... blow out your light, Jess. What 'cha looking for?"

Jessi's face lit up as she looked at Tyler with a smile. "Thank you, Jim!" she called out towards the roof overhead. She was holding two toothbrushes. "And to think I *ever* gave my mom a hard time about brushing my teeth before bed!"

12
Sunday Morning

June 15, 1614

The sun had already burned the morning mist out from under the trees when Mr. Doullens reached the top of the ladder. He smiled and shook his head, then hollered, "I don't feed lazy children!"

They barely stirred. He climbed up the remaining rungs on the ladder, and dropped a double-armload of hay over their heads.

"Okay, okay, you could've just called us, or something," Jessi sputtered as she sat up, pulling hay out of her hair.

Mr. Doullens looked at Tyler, eyebrows raised.

"She said 'good morning,' sir. She wakes up grouchy sometimes."

Jessi eyed him suspiciously. "What did you just say?"

"I said you're a sound sleeper, and that it was hard to wake you up sometimes," he answered with a mischievous grin.

"Uh huh, right."

Mr. Doullens had left one cow for them to milk. He had already milked the other seven directly below them, but they never heard a sound. Starting that evening, they would milk all eight. He correctly assumed they had never done it before, so he led them to the milking stall, gave them a brief lesson, and told them to bring the pail of milk to the kitchen when they were done. It would be all they would have to do to earn their breakfast. "After all, it's Sunday," he said, as he turned away and headed to the house.

As Mr. Doullens walked away, they looked back and forth from him to the cow. It shuffled around a bit and looked back at the two strangers. A low rumble came out its throat, and they each took a step backward. "This isn't good," Tyler said apprehensively.

"Aw, we can do this." Jessi said hopefully. "You stand and stroke its back to keep it calm, and I'll milk it. We'll take turns, okay?"

The pail was full and the warm foam just reaching to the top, when the cow ran dry. It started to walk away and they both stepped back. The cow bumped the pail, sloshing some milk out onto the ground.

"No!" Tyler cried out as he tried to stop the cow.

Jessi reached down and quickly pulled the pail out from under the animal, making more milk spill out, this time onto her left shoe. "Aw, man!" she exclaimed as she stepped back, her toes getting wet as the warm milk seeped into her sneakers.

The cow lurched forward and quickly left the milking stall, anxious to start grazing in the pasture. Jessi wasn't ready for that and took another quick step back. Her elbow struck the wall behind her, and even more milk sloshed out of the pail, this time spilling down the front of her jeans. "Dang it!" she shouted. On her right leg her jeans were sticking to her skin from the middle of her shin to her shoe. As she trudged to the house her left shoe squeaked, and with each step the right leg of her jeans would stick, then unstick, stick, then unstick, to her leg. *This is SO gross*, she thought.

As they approached the house they saw that the kitchen was actually separated from the rest of the house. Paving stones lay between, and a roof overhead provided protection from the rain.

"Why are they separated?" Jessi asked.

"In case the kitchen catches fire, you don't lose the house as well."

"Oh," Jessi answered, as she opened the kitchen door.

Jessi handed the now half-full pail to Mrs. Doullens, who noticed Jessi's milk-covered jeans. "Hmm," she said, looking intently into the pail. "It looks like that last cow was a little dry this morning." She looked at her husband, winked, and then nodded slightly in the direction of Jessi's pants.

"So," she said. "Are you ready for breakfast?"

＊ ＊ ＊ ＊ ＊ ＊

They had just finished eating when the front door to the kitchen burst open. Two older boys and a younger girl came through the doorway, full of noise and laughter. All three had full baskets that were mysteriously covered with white linens.

They set their baskets down, and the constant stream of chatter and excitement continued. Jessi watched the commotion, not understanding a word being said, but certain they were telling their parents about their overnight stay.

The girl started twirling in a circle. Midway through her spin she noticed Tyler and Jessi. She stopped as quickly as she could, but not until she was facing away from them. She turned back towards them.

"Hello there. Who're you?" she asked, cheeks flushing. She reached up and untied her hair, letting it fall forward to hide the evidence of her embarrassment.

Jessi looked over at Tyler and waited for him to answer.

"Hi, I'm Tyler, and this is my friend, Jessi."

"My name is Camille. Nice to meet you," she said as she turned to her mother. "I'm going to put my things away, and then I'll be right back." She left by way of the back door towards the house.

"Always in motion, that girl." Mr. Doullens shook his head.

"Well, she IS fifteen," his wife replied.

"Hello there. I'm Jacques," the oldest of the Doullens children said as he hooked his thumbs into his belt. "This is my brother Luc." He nodded towards his younger brother. "Are you staying with us for a while?"

"Yes, sir. For about a week," Tyler replied.

"Sir! You don't need to call me that! 'Mr. Doullens' would be better."

His father laughed and growled good-naturedly at him, "There's only one Mr. Doullens in this house!"

He gave a long and overly dramatic bow to his father, turned towards Tyler, and smiled, "Just kidding. Call me Jacques."

Mrs. Doullens rolled her eyes and chuckled. "More tea, Mr. Doullens?"

He glanced at the clock on the wall. "That'd be fine. We won't be leaving for another forty-five minutes."

"Where are you going?" Tyler asked.

"*WE* are going to church, boy," he replied.

"But we do not go dressed like *that*," Mrs. Doullens exclaimed, looking pointedly at Jessi's pants. "No young woman in my care will be seen about the village in men's clothing! The very thought of it! I may not be able to do anything about your short hair, but I can find you a dress." Jessi's cheeks flushed in embarrassment. She didn't know what was said, but she knew she'd done *something* wrong.

The door opened and Camille reentered the room.

"Camille, we need to find our guest some appropriate clothes. I believe your Sunday frock from last year will suit her. Find it quickly so adjustments can be made if necessary. I'll join you ladies in a minute. Meanwhile, Luc will find something more appropriate for *you*, Tyler. Go on now."

Camille grabbed Jessi by the hand and headed back out the door. As the boys scuttled away, Mrs. Doullens muttered to herself, "I don't know where they're from, but their people certainly did *not* teach them how to dress properly."

* * * * * *

Their first-ever ride in a horse-drawn wagon was not what they expected. Holes, dips, and rocks created jolts and bumps that had everyone constantly bumping back and forth against each other. The road gave way to cobblestone as they neared the town, which then put the wagon into a constant rattle like a nonstop earthquake.

Tyler and Jessi sat in the back of the wagon, facing backwards, their legs dangling towards the ground. Stone and brick buildings appeared from behind them on their left and right, and they watched as everything slowly receded into the distance. Tired of looking at where they had been and wanting to see where they were going, Jessi twisted around and peered ahead. All she could see were the backs of Mr. and Mrs. Doullens and an occasional glimpse of the backside of the horses slowly pulling them forward.

Finally, with a "whoa" from Mr. Doullens, they came to a stop in a small field next to a number of other wagons. Next to the field was a church, a small one-story building with a bell tower above the front door. Maybe 50 people were milling around, engaging in quiet conversation. Reaching down on his left, Mr. Doullens pulled up on a bar attached to the outside of the wagon, and a square iron brake clamped tight against the left wheel, securely stopping the wagon's slight rocking back and forth caused by the horses stomping the ground underneath their hooves.

While Mr. Doullens calmed the horses and put a thin blanket over their backs, Mrs. Doullens secured their few belongings in the back of the wagon. Their three children had quickly jumped out and found their friends nearby.

Mrs. Doullens noticed Tyler and Jessi standing together, looking nervously around. She spotted the Leveau child not too far off. "Robert!" she called out. "Robert Leveau!" The boy looked at her. Beckoning with her hand she explained, "Come here; I'd like you to meet these two."

Jessi leaned over towards Tyler, "Row Bear?"

"It's the French way to say 'Robert'. It's even spelled the same," Tyler answered.

"Tyler, how do you know this stuff?"

"I dunno," he shrugged. "Just do."

"Robert," Mrs. Doullens began. "This is Tyler and Jessi. Be a dear and see they enjoy themselves today—yes? I'll talk to your parents about—"

The clanging of bells from the tower overhead stopped her in midsentence. Robert gave them a quick nod and ran off to join his family. Within the minute the entire Doullens family was together, and all seven of them entered the church.

After a couple minutes of steady clanging, the bell tower finally grew silent. Meanwhile the people had entered and were almost as silent as the now-still bells. All that could be heard was the rustling of clothes and an occasional creak, or pop, as someone would shift their weight in a useless attempt to get more comfortable on the solid oak pews.

From the front of the church, off to the side and out of sight, someone started singing. It reminded Tyler of music one would hear in a movie taking place in a middle-ages monastery, only this guy—whoever he was—didn't have that good of a voice.

"Is that French?" Jessi whispered.

"Umm ... Latin, I think," Tyler answered.

A quick rap on Tyler's knee by Mrs. Doullens quieted them both. As the song ended, a priest appeared—probably from where the guy was singing—and stood behind an ornately made pulpit, on top of which was an already-open book. He looked really old—maybe 70 or more. His thin gray hair was all the same length, cut just below his ears, which made it look too long on the sides and too short in the back. With barely an acknowledgment that anyone else was there, he began to read in a raspy, low, monotone voice.

Tyler strained to hear the words. He decided the priest must be speaking Latin, since between his English and French, he could understand some of it. Looking around, it appeared that a lot of the people looked bored and were just waiting for him to be done. He was wondering if the villagers knew Latin when he spotted Robert just as Robert was looking his way. He shrugged slightly at Tyler and looked back towards the priest. *Well, if he could do this every week,* he thought, *Jessi and I can do this once.*

The priest finished his reading and sat down on a huge throne-like chair facing the opposite wall. He wrinkled up his nose, scratched his ear that faced away from the people, put his hand back in his lap, and sat motionless. He seemed bored too.

Another man stepped forward to the edge of the platform. The congregation all stood and opened little booklets that were on the backs of the pews in front of them. The man called out, "Number twenty-seven," waited briefly while the people turned the pages of their booklets, and then began reading out loud. After reading for a few moments he stopped, and the people then read several lines from the booklet in response. This went on back and forth for about five minutes.

When they were done the priest stood up and prayed a brief blessing. As soon as he said "amen," he turned and walked back through the door where he had first come out, after which the people filed outside. As they stepped into the bright sunlight Jessi leaned over to Tyler. "Well, that was, um … different," she muttered. "Did you understand any of it?"

"The reading back and forth part was in French, so yeah, but pretty much none of the rest," he answered. "I don't think anyone knows Latin, 'cause it looked to me like no one understood what the priest was reading either."

"Maybe that's why they call this the Dark Ages," Jessi added.

"I think the Dark Ages was like … I don't know, a long time before this. It makes me wish I studied European history a little more."

The Doullens family proceeded together to their wagon, Jessi and Tyler dutifully following along. Mrs. Doullens pulled out various baskets from under the wagon's front bench and passed them to her children. Jessi and Tyler were each given large heavy blankets.

"Looks like picnic time, Ty!" Jessi ventured.

"Yup. Oh, by the way, nice dress!"

13
Sunday Afternoon

It was a picnic to remember, not only for the food, which was a welcome relief after eating energy bars, but also for where, *and when*, they were eating it.

Jessi took her last bite, licked her fingers, and lay down, looking up at the clouds overhead. "I'm so full … this is great!" She looked at Tyler. "Hey, how do they say 'full' in French?"

Tyler pictured a full cup of water in his mind and started to answer, but stopped himself. "Umm … that's weird!" he shrugged. "The French don't say 'full'; it's translated … 'eaten well'."

"How do you know—" Jessi interrupted herself, cupped her hands behind her head, and looked up at the clouds. "I've eaten well," she said with a smile.

Robert walked up. "Do you want to play Nine-Pins with us?" he asked. "Come on," he added without waiting for an answer.

They jumped up and started to follow him when Mrs. Doullens called out. "Not so fast, you two! Fold up those blankets and put them in the wagon; then you may go."

They quickly caught up with Robert and followed him through the streets to a wide-open area at the edge of a forest. Robert led them towards a flat space under a massive old oak tree. "Over here we have our own area," he explained. "The older kids leave us alone, especially on Sundays when there are lots of adults around."

"Some things never change," Tyler muttered to himself.

The space they had to themselves was about the size of a football field. Under the tree were two flat platforms with nine circles painted in a square pattern. On one platform, two boys were just finishing setting up what looked similar to bowling pins on each of the circles. They then walked back to a spot on the ground about 10 paces away. One of them took a soccer-sized ball and threw it at the pins, knocking six over. They ran forward, and the boy that threw the ball picked it back up and walked around the platform studying the remaining pins. He tossed the ball a second time from only a few feet away on the right side, and the last three pins toppled over. He raised his fist in triumph, while the other boy grimaced and shook his head. They reset the pins, and the same boy set up to make another throw.

"How does this game work?" Tyler asked.

"You've never played Nine-Pins before?" Robert asked in surprise.

"Uh-uh."

"Well, each player gets three throws per turn. The first from the far mark, the second and third from anywhere he wants. BUT if you knock all of them down, your next throw is back at the far mark, like Jean-Claude just did there. You get a point for every pin you knock down, and the first one to reach fifty is the winner."

Tyler started to explain the rules to Jessi, but she cut him off. "Primitive bowling? Yeah, I think I've got this; I was watching those other guys. They're writing their scores in the dirt. How high do they play to?"

"Fifty," Tyler answered irritably. Now Jessi assumed she knew all the rules too.

"We'll show these country boys how to play a game!" she said arrogantly.

After setting up the pins on the second platform, Robert went first, explaining strategies as he played. He cleared the board on his second throw and ended up scoring 14. They reset the pins, and Robert tossed the ball to Jessi.

"Whoa!" she said, "This ball is heavy. No air in *this* thing." She squeezed it as hard as she could, but could make only a small indent. Robert explained they made it by wrapping rags around a rock and sewing leather around that.

Jessi tossed the ball in the air a few times to get a feel for it, then took aim at the pins and let it fly. It went too far, taking down only two of the three pins on the backside of the platform.

Her next two throws cleared the remaining pins. With a scowl, she handed the ball to Tyler.

Not wanting to throw it too far like Jessi, Tyler ended up throwing it too short. It hit the ground in front of the platform and bounced slightly to the left, taking out only one pin. As he was lining up for his second throw, he realized the pins were spaced farther apart than the diameter of the ball. It would be possible for the ball to go right between all the pins without knocking any over! His first turn ended with a score of eight.

"What did you wanna show these country boys?" Tyler muttered.

"Just give me a few more turns," Jessi growled.

They did get better with practice, but they never came close to beating Robert even after spending several hours at the game.

Near the end of a game between Robert and Tyler, the bells in the church tower rang out the time. "It's three o'clock," he said. "I have five minutes to meet my parents to go home." On his next turn Robert pushed his score to 51. He said his good-byes to everyone, and left, as Jessi finished her game with the other two boys.

"If it wasn't for this stupid dress, I would've won that last game. Who bowls in a dress anyway?" Jessi grumbled.

"Yeah, I'm sure that was the only thing holding you back, Jess," Tyler sneered good-naturedly, dodging out of the way just in time to miss taking an elbow to the ribs. "Careful! What would Mrs. Doullens say about such unladylike behavior?" he laughed.

The other boys tossed all 18 pins and the two balls into a large bag, and started walking away. "Hey!" Tyler called out after them. "What do we do with the bag?"

Jean-Claude laughed. "Take it to the Twin-Goats," he shouted out over his shoulder. "Over there," he added, waving his hand towards a road lined with shops.

"Where are we headed?" asked Jessi as she heaved the heavy bag over her shoulder.

"Some place called Twin-Goats," Tyler replied. "Hopefully it's easy to spot." They took turns carrying the heavy bag as they trudged down the road. Near the end of town their attention was drawn by a roar of laughter coming from the last building on the other side of the street, beyond which was a large clearing next to the forested countryside. In front of the stone building, just inside the ditch that ran alongside the road was a large sign that read, "Twin-Goats Inn." Under the name were painted two goats standing side by side, both of them with raised heads as if in the middle of bleating … or maybe singing.

They hesitated in front of the door, suddenly uncertain whether they should go inside or not. Tyler was just reaching for the door when it burst open, and a man stepped outside, blinking in the bright sunlight. After a moment he spotted them. "Come on in," he said, as he swept his arms back and held the door open for them. "You can give your … toys … to the master of the house." He gave a loud belch, patted his belly, and stumbled down the road towards town.

They stepped inside as the door closed behind them. The large room was lit by two small windows on opposite walls and oil lamps hanging from the ceiling throughout the room. Compared to outside it seemed very dark, so they stood still and waited for their eyes to adjust, looking around them first with curiosity, then with growing alarm.

It was a loud and busy place. Almost every table had two or three men, young and old alike, all of them engaged in active conversation. Tall bottles of wine and loaves of bread were on every table, and many of the men were holding large mugs of beer. A thick layer of smoke pressed against the ceiling, trapped, with no place to go.

A man with a close-cut, jet-black beard looked carefully at them. "Looking for someone?" he asked. Leaning forward with a mischievous grin on his face, he added, "Or just looking for a drink?"

"We … we need to give this to the master of the house," Tyler stammered, pointing at the bag.

"Over there, in the red cap," the man replied, hooking his thumb towards the back of the room. Their attention was immediately taken to a large, burly man with a massive brown beard. He was wearing a bright red beret and leaned back at that moment in a loud outburst of laughter with a customer.

They started to wind their way between the tables, Jessi carrying the bag over her shoulder. As she turned, the bag swung out and hit a table, knocking over a bottle of wine. A red-haired man swore as he grabbed the bottle and set it back upright, but not quickly enough to prevent a large red puddle from splashing across the table. He lifted his arm to strike her for her clumsiness, but when he saw her shrink back, he composed himself and scolded her with a "Careful there, miss!" He took a cloth napkin from his knee and sopped up the wine dripping off the table, then dropping it on the floor, he pushed it around with his boot. Not bothering to pick up the napkin, he returned to the conversation at his table.

Tyler took the bag from Jessi and dragged it along the floor behind them until they got to the back. He nervously cleared his throat as he tapped the master of the house on the shoulder.

"What can I get you?" the man asked as he turned around; then his gaze dropped down to the bag on the floor. "Hang that on the hook in the corner," he said with sudden disinterest. He watched as they put the bag in its place, and as they filed past him to leave, he stopped them with an outstretched arm. "Aren't you thirsty? How about something to drink?" he asked hopefully. "I need to make a living, you know!"

Tyler glanced at Jessi in alarm.

"What does he want, Ty?"

"I think he wants a tip or something."

A man stepped up next to Tyler, resting a hand on his shoulder. Tyler looked up and relief washed over him like a cool breeze. "Now, Marcel," Mr. Doullens began, "these young guests of mine don't owe you any payment. After all, what I've spent here today is much more than you usually receive, yes?"

He leaned over and spoke quietly in Tyler's ear. "It would be best if you two went to the field behind us and watched Luc play Paille Maille." His speech was slow and a little slurred, the smell of wine strong on his breath. "Stay with him until it's time to go."

As he straightened up, he gave them both a gentle push behind their shoulders towards the front door.

They stepped through the door and paused to let their eyes adjust, squinting in the bright afternoon sun as a man and woman passed by in a wagon. The woman looked at them with a long and disapproving frown, turning her gaze away only after she was well past them. They walked around to the back of the building as they were told.

The large open space in front of them was a mixture of low-growing crabgrass and dirt that curved out of sight off to their left. Directly in front of them was a tall pole with a long arm attached. About 15 feet in the air an iron hoop three feet in diameter hung from a chain attached to the arm. A goat tethered to a stake behind Twin-Goats was quietly eating grass next to them.

Tyler paused to check out the goat. "Now *that* is a low maintenance lawn mower," he said with a wink.

They looked up as they heard a crack, and moments later what looked like a large softball came bouncing toward them. Soon two more balls landed near the first, and they saw Luc approach with two other young men.

"It looks like they're playing golf!" Jessi said in amazement.

"It must be the Paille Maille game Mr. Doullens mentioned," Tyler answered.

Luc nodded a greeting in Tyler and Jessi's direction as he set down the mallet they were sharing. Another player took up a mallet that had a spoon-shaped head and walked over to his ball. Using a one-armed swing, it took him three attempts before he finally put his ball through the hoop. It took Luc two tries, and the same for the third contestant.

They wrote down their scores, switched back to the other mallet, which had a different shape and was apparently made for distance, and started another round back towards where they had come from.

"Care to join?" Luc asked, waving them over.

Jessi and Tyler followed the players as they worked their way along the course, which they guessed to be over half a mile. At the other end was a hanging hoop identical to the first one. After playing back to the hoop behind Twin-Goats, they tabulated their score. A disappointed Luc shook his head and congratulated the winner, who smirked as he walked back towards the starting line. With a scowl and a sigh, Luc and the other player stayed behind, as two other young men stepped forward.

"Losers out, winner stays in," Jessi observed.

Luc sat down against a tree. "We play back and forth twice," he explained. "We add up our scores for the four trips, low score wins. I don't like to lose, of course, but Arnaud makes it really hard because he's so ..." Luc pursed his lips tightly together. "... so arrogant." He leaned forward and spat viciously at a clump of grass in front of him.

"No matter what game you're playing," Tyler answered, "it seems like there's always somebody like that. My dad plays a game that's a lot like Paille Maille."

"Oh? What's that?"

"It's called golf, but the ball is real small." Tyler held up his hand and formed an "o" with his thumb and forefinger to show the size. "And you hit the ball into a hole in the ground, not a hoop up in the air."

"How can that be?" Luc asked. "It would be next to impossible to make a ball that small roll straight on the ground. It would hit a rock or clump of grass and stop!"

Luc's comment surprised Tyler. "Well ... the grass in the greenway is cut very short."

"I see, but the grass would have to be a lot smoother than a goat could manage, wouldn't it?"

Pictures of men riding on lawn mowers flashed through Tyler's mind. He knew there was no way he could explain all that to Luc and make it sound believable. "Yes, that's true," he admitted. Awkward and embarrassed in front of the older teenager, he felt his cheeks getting red.

He looked overhead and jumped up. "Hey, Jessi! Let's climb this tree!"

"Tyler, I'm wearing a dress! I don't know much about the rules in 1614, but I'm pretty sure climbing trees in a dress is frowned upon."

"Hmm. Rules never stopped you before," Tyler said with a grin.

A few moments later they were working their way up through the branches. Without anyone to stop them, they felt free to climb as high as they wanted. It was only when the branches were getting thin and shaky that they stopped and looked down.

"Whoa!" Tyler remarked.

They each found a secure place to sit and watched the game going on below. Behind them they could see over the rooftops of the nearby houses, giving them a clear view of most of the town, except for the part behind the tall bell tower of the church a couple blocks away. After a while a few birds came back into the tree and joined them.

"This is so awesome!" Jessi quietly exclaimed.

"What do you mean?"

"Think about it. We're sitting in a tree in a French medieval village in the seventeenth century! It's just plain *awesome!*"

A few moments passed by. "And a bit scary," Tyler finished.

"Yeah." Their eyes locked on each other as they each took a long deep breath before looking again across the rooftops.

By the time the game finished below them, and Luc was once again playing Arnaud, they were uncomfortable enough sitting in the tree that they were glad to get back on the ground. They followed the three players in their game, and once again Arnaud was the winner, and he once again smugly walked away. Luc crossed his arms and looked up at the clouds while the other player silently took the goat and tethered it to the Paille Maille pole. Soon the church bells tolled five and the day's activities were over.

Luc scooped up the three balls and two mallets and headed towards Twin-Goats Inn, Tyler and Jessi following. They were happy to stay outside while he took the equipment into the inn. A few minutes later he reappeared still carrying the mallets and balls. Holding them close to his body he walked quickly to the family wagon and placed them in the back. Looking at Tyler and Jessi, he smiled grimly and said more to himself than them, "I'm practicing this week—a lot."

Soon all the family were back together at the church. Upon seeing her husband's flushed face and rather unsteady walk, Mrs. Doullens quietly turned her face away and looked at the ground, shaking her head. She took her place next to him in front, not speaking a word to him, or anyone else.

Tyler leaned over and whispered in Jessi's ear, "If Mama ain't happy … "

"Ain't nobody happy," she finished with a broad grin.

It was a very quiet trip home.

After unloading the wagon, unhitching, grooming, and feeding the horses, Camille gave Tyler and Jessi a brief lesson on how to milk a cow.

"I don't intend to offend, but after the mess you made this morning, it's obvious you don't have much experience milking cows," Camille declared. She hesitated before adding, "Besides, the better you do this, the more likely I won't have to—at least for the next week!"

Tyler watched as she quickly worked the cow's udder, filling the pail with warm milk. For the first time he noticed the muscles in her forearms and saw he wouldn't stand a chance in an arm-wrestling match with her.

Sunset found them walking in the fields around the Doullens' home. Their farm was a lot larger than they thought, and it was then they realized it was Camille they had seen yesterday afternoon with the flock of sheep. They were at the Doullens farm when they took their wrong turn and walked for an extra five hours!

Tyler looked around at the trees wrapping the different fields. Each field, no matter how small or large, had a row of low-growing trees or tall shrubs between them. "Why don't they take out the trees and make more room to grow stuff?" he wondered out loud.

Jessi glanced sideways at him. "Cause it stops the wind from blowing away all the dirt, didn't you know that?"

"How'd *you* know that?"

"Last semester in first period science class; the one you were always sleeping through."

"I did *not* sleep!"

"Take it easy, Ty. I was just kidding. My grandpa told me about it. He said that's what made the Dirt Bowl of the 1920s."

"When you say it that way it sounds like a college football game. Besides, it was called the Dust Bowl, and I think it was in the 1930s," Tyler responded, his wounded pride recovering a bit. "You know, " he continued, "we landed here about this time ... umm ... four days ago and ... I don't know, but it seems like it's been longer, doesn't it? Especially when ya think about how far away home is."

"Tyler, if you're trying to make me feel better about all this, it's not working."

He shot a quick look at her. "I'm sorry, Jess, I didn't mean to—"

"Nah, it's okay really," she interrupted. "I'm okay—mostly," she added with a chuckle.

Tyler looked around. Everything appeared so peaceful, so quiet. Yet he wished he could hear the sound of a car driving by, or a television playing too loud at a neighbor's house. Sounds of home—comfort. He took a deep breath and let it out slowly, sadness inside his chest.

Suddenly a flash of black shot up right in front of them. They cried out and jumped back, as a black bird angrily cawed at them as it circled overhead at a safe height, angry at having its meal interrupted. They looked down at the remains of an animal.

"What in the world is that?" Jessi asked.

"The long neck looks like a llama, but with a foot-long tail?" Tyler added.

"But the body's only two feet long!" Jessi observed.

They kept walking, and when they were deemed a safe distance away, the bird returned to its dinner and quietly resumed picking the bones of the animal.

"Maybe it's not as peaceful as I thought," Tyler muttered.

"What's that?" Jessi asked.

Tyler sighed. "Oh, nothing."

14
A Very Long Day

June 16, 1614

At dawn the next morning Luc opened the man-door into the barn; the cows stirred, expecting him to begin the morning milking. They began lowing in complaint when he walked past them and up the ladder to the loft.

"Hey, you two!" he hollered. "Get up! Milking's gotta be done before breakfast, and if you wait too long there won't be any left for you, 'cause I'm hungry this morning!"

Tyler and Jessi sat up and stretched; going to bed at sundown had given them enough rest.

"What time is it?" Tyler asked.

"It's time to get up and get going!"

They set to work. Tyler collared the first cow and led it into the milking stall. He secured the animal, and Jessi started milking her. By the time she was done, her arms ached and she had no strength left in her hands.

"I can't do this for eight cows, or even four," she complained as she rubbed her wrists and forearms, and then stopped. "I'd rub them harder, but I don't have the strength for it," she smiled weakly. "Tyler, you gotta do the next one."

They took turns to give each other a break, but by the time they got to the last two cows they were swapping back and forth every few minutes. They put out the last cow, which ran out through the wide-open animal doorway as if happy to get away from them. Their arms and backs ached, and sweat was dripping off their chins.

Tyler dropped to the ground and leaned against the wall of the milking stall, "I'm so tired."

"Yeah, me too, but I'm *more* hungry. Let's go eat!"

Mrs. Doullens looked at them as they came through the back door into the kitchen. She scowled and shouted at them, "Out!" Her long braid danced between her shoulders. "Don't come in here like that; go back outside and wash up. Wash your hands and faces in the outside water barrel; in fact, dunk your heads and use the towel to dry off."

They backpedaled out the door, where to their right they saw the barrel she referred to. It was small, about two feet high and a foot and a half wide. Jessi plunged her hands into the water and vigorously rubbed them together. She then kneeled in front of the barrel, lowered her face and stopped, her nose barely two inches above the cold water. The idea of dunking her head clear in was almost too much. It reminded her of the time Tyler had dared her to dive off the 3-meter diving board at the pool last summer—four hundred years from now! She shivered. It didn't look so high when they were standing next to the pool, but she fixated on that water a long time from the edge of that diving board until she could think of nothing else. That's when Tyler had sneaked up behind her and … water flew in all directions as Jessi pulled her head out of the barrel and flew to her feet, her fist ready to swing. Tyler stood there laughing, backing up just beyond the reach of her fist.

"You did it again! Just like at the pool!" Jessi shouted.

"You looked like you needed a little help." Tyler was laughing so hard he almost lost his balance.

"Yeah, well, your turn's next." The shock of the cold water had already subsided, and she grabbed the towel off the hook above the barrel. She swept her hand backwards as she bowed. "Now! Or I'll eat *your* breakfast too!"

She turned and went quickly inside. She'd get even someday. *Make him wait and wonder when I'll strike*, she thought smugly to herself.

Tyler wasted no time cleaning up and was sitting next to Jessi within a minute. Mrs. Doullens looked them over, smiled, and brought them two bowls full of some kind of mush. Steam rose from the bowls.

Tyler lifted up a spoonful. "Thank you, but what is it?" he asked, as he turned his spoon sideways and watched the contents slip off and drop back into the bowl.

"Oatmeal, silly boy." She looked at him quizzically. "Haven't you ever had oatmeal before?"

"Not like this, ma'am," he replied.

"Well, add some butter from the bell. Milk's in the jug, add some honey, and put in some berries too, if you like."

"Bell?" He asked in confusion. "What's butter doing in a bell?"

"The butter bell, boy! Don't you even know what *that* is? Look right in front of you!"

The only thing in front of him was a stoneware pot, upside down, resting in a big saucer. A knob was on the top—or bottom? His nose wrinkled up as he tried to make sense of it.

"What's goin' on, Ty?" Jessi whispered out of the corner of her mouth.

"Wait a sec, Jess."

Mrs. Doullens strode quickly over to the table. "The butter is in here, boy," she said as she tapped the pot with her finger. She shook her head as she went back to her work, cutting up some greens with a large knife.

Tyler lifted up the pot, but there was no butter on the saucer. "Ma'am, there's no more butter."

Mrs. Doullens looked at him, leaned forward, and shook her head again. "Boy, look inside the bell! You're holding the butter in your hand!"

Tyler looked inside the lid. Pressed up into the pot was the butter. He heard Mrs. Doullens chuckling to herself, muttering something about "strange children."

They helped themselves to the butter and watched it quickly melt into a puddle on top of their oatmeal. Mrs. Doullens came back to the table and sat down opposite them. Placing both of her elbows on the table, she rested her chin on her hands.

"You really *have* never seen one of these before, have you?" Her tone softened. "Listen. We put the fresh butter in the bell here with a big knife or spoon and set it down on the saucer to keep the flies off it. The butter sticks to the lid and doesn't drop down. Also, on hot summer days we put water in this trough here around the edge of the saucer, and the evaporation keeps the pot cool so the butter won't melt! Understand?"

Tyler nodded. "I'm sorry, but where we live things are very ... different."

"Well, finish up quickly, then go find Mr. Doullens in the wheat field straight back behind that first row of trees. He'll set you up for your work today."

They found Mr. Doullens examining a fence. "Something rather large broke through last night," he explained. "We didn't lose any stock, so it didn't find any food to its taste, I presume," he said. "It's fortunate we had the chickens closed up." He frowned as he knelt and studied the ground. "I haven't seen tracks like these since—" He abruptly stood up and carefully surveyed all his land. "Hmm," he muttered to himself. He smiled when he saw the look on Jessi's face, but wasn't able to hide his concern. "Follow me."

He then led them to a field immediately to the north. It had been planted a month earlier with beans and peas: the legumes Mrs. Doullens had mentioned before. The field was tilled into straight rows, and small green plants had sprouted about five inches above the soil.

"We've not had rain in three days, and the plants are too tender to go another day without water. Trouble with the pigs breaking down their fencing kept us from getting the irrigation set up for this field, so in the meantime we'll have to water the plants by hand. Each plant needs to be watered every day until we get rain. Outside the shed over there are the buckets and shoulder poles. Inside each bucket is a scoop. Each plant gets one scoop of water." He motioned further to the north. "Get the water from the river over there." Darkness clouded his face as he turned to go back to his broken fence.

Jessi and Tyler stood and watched him leave. "What's going on, Ty?" Jessi asked.

"Well, we gotta water all the plants in this—"

"No. I mean what's going on with Mr. Doullens? He's worried, or scared even, with what he saw at that fence."

"Oh yeah, when he got a look at the tracks the animal left, it reminded him of something he'd seen before. We'd better keep our eyes open around here."

"Awesome," she said sarcastically. They surveyed the field. "Wow, there's a lot of legomes here, Ty."

"Legumes, and yeah, there are. This is almost the size of our soccer field at school! We'll never get it done."

Tyler sighed and headed for the shed, as Jessi silently followed.

Inside each bucket was a large drinking-style mug made out of some dark metal. They left the mugs in the buckets and walked to the river. Finding a large flat rock just at the water's edge, Tyler squatted down and scooped the bucket into the stream, and it quickly became heavy with water. His arms, still tired from the morning milking, complained as he slowly pulled on the handle of the bucket, his grip barely strong enough to hold on. As he stood to go towards the field, Jessi shouted out.

"Ty, the scoop!"

Tyler looked back and saw the scoop floating away; it was already too far to reach, collecting water, and starting to sink. He put the bucket down, and not seeing any other choice, jumped in. He grabbed at the scoop, and missed, as it kept drifting further away and down. He made another grab for it and felt his fingers close around the brim.

"I got it, Jess! I ..." Tyler slipped and fell.

Jessi watched him slosh out of the stream and smiled. "You know, I think that makes us even for you dunking me this morning, and all I had to do was watch!" She then spoke in as deep a voice as possible. "So, what have we learned just now, young man?"

Tyler stared hard at her. "Your turn's coming, that's what!"

The job was simple but hard work. The weight of the buckets made their already sore arms even worse. They kept at it, filling their buckets only half full because of the weight, and making more trips. They were making decent progress when Luc came by.

"Time for lunch, you two. Now!"

They gratefully tossed their scoops into the buckets and slowly walked to the house. As they approached the door, Luc was hanging the towel back up on the hook.

"You're next," he said as he looked back at them. "I suggest taking your shoes off before going in. Mother won't like the mess."

Mrs. Doullens had a regular feast prepared. Roasted chicken, some greens they didn't recognize, and thick-sliced potatoes fried in bacon fat.

"Hey, Ty, look! Jo-Jo's!" Jessi exclaimed.

"What's that she said?" Mrs. Doullens asked.

"We sometimes eat potatoes like that, and we call them Jo-Jo's," Tyler answered.

"Well, there's one familiar thing at least," she said with a smile. Looking more closely at them, the smile disappeared as she turned to her husband. "They need work clothes, Gilles. Their strange clothes won't last the week."

* * * * * *

After lunch, Mr. Doullens took them out to a small shed behind the house. Following him inside, they found the room shadowy and gray; it smelled of cool, moist earth and metal. The only light was what came through the open doorway and a small window to one side. Clothes hung from a row of hooks on the left wall. Boots were lined up on the floor under a bench.

Mr. Doullens took various items off the hooks, placing them on the bench. "Here, see what fits. Men's things on the left, women's on the right. Ought to be a dress there that fits well enough for fieldwork. We keep all these for just this kind of thing. You made good progress on the watering. Make sure you don't miss any. You get them all, yes?" He pulled down a few more shirts and left.

While Jessi waited outside, Tyler tried on several different shirts and pants until he finally found some that fit reasonably well. "Your turn, Jess," he called out.

He stepped outside and waited, and before long heard her wail, "Really? I have to work in a dress?" A few minutes passed before Jessi hollered, "It's okay to come in now."

"I forgot to get some boots anyways," Tyler said as he came in. One look at her made him stop and do a double take. Wearing the worn work dress made her look like she actually belonged here. While it would be wise for them not to stick out like a couple of sore thumbs, this change made him feel uneasy. It was like they were leaving their real lives behind.

Jessi picked up a pair of boots. She turned them over and looked carefully at them, clearly puzzled. "Hey Ty, look at this. These are definitely a matched set, but there's no difference between left and right! So which is which? I can't tell."

Tyler looked closely at the boots in Jessi's hands. They *were* identical! "Lemme see." He looked at the wear patterns on the soles, and then put his hand down into the boot to feel the bottom. He felt something soft that moved slightly as he touched it. He yelled and dropped the boot. "Mouse!" he shouted.

Jessi jumped up on the bench, as if she expected it to run out the boot and up her leg. They both watched and waited. Nothing happened.

"Kick the boot; see if it comes out," she suggested.

"You kick it! I'm not touching it!"

"Come on, you're closer!"

"It's more your size."

"And that matters because . . . . ?"

Neither of them moved, uncertain what to do next. Someone opened and closed the back door of the house, the noise stirring them to action.

Tyler took a deep breath. "Okay, I'll pick it up. Maybe I can shake it out," he said, as his fingers gently closed around the heel. He lifted the boot upside down and shook it—it didn't fall out.

"Maybe it's up around the toe," Jessi ventured as she slowly got down off the bench. "Point the toe up so it will fall to the heel and then out."

Tyler followed the suggestion, shaking the boot hard. A furry lump fell to the ground at their feet. They both jumped back and waited to see which way the mouse would run. It didn't move.

Jessi leaned forward and looked more closely. By now their eyes had adjusted to the grayness in the room, but the lump was in the shadows.

"Tyler!" she laughed. "It's a rolled-up sock!"

Tyler couldn't believe it—he felt it move! "Are you sure?" he asked.

Jessi reached down and quickly flipped it up towards Tyler. Instinctively he jumped back, as it bounced off his knee and landed at his feet.

"Afraid of the big bad sock, huh?" Jessi mocked.

"All right, all right. It sure felt like a mouse."

The boots *were* made identically, but usage had worn the heels, and someone's feet had molded the insides, so that it was obvious which was which. They both found a pair that worked, although Jessi needed two pairs of socks to make hers fit.

They stepped out of the shed into the bright sunlight. After the cool darkness of the shed, the bright sun hurt their eyes, and it was already pretty warm; the few scattered clouds were too thin to give them a break from the heat of the sun. They headed back to the river, stumbling a couple times on the uneven ground as they got used to their new boots.

Pain shot through their aching arms as they once again started filling the water buckets, but it got better as they kept moving and got warmed up. Even so, the work was exhausting. By the time they were done with the watering, they were drinking from the stream every trip. They were putting their buckets away outside the shed when Jacques and Luc came by from one of the back fields.

"Good work," Jacques acknowledged. "That's a big field to water by hand. Now all you have to finish before dinner is the milking."

"Oh no!" Tyler moaned.

"What?" Jessi asked.

"We still have the milking to do!"

Luc wrinkled his brow. He walked up to Jessi, arm outstretched. "Squeeze my arm as hard as you can," he said.

Jessi looked at Tyler. "What does he want me to do?" she asked skeptically.

"He said to squeeze his arm as hard as you can."

Jessi had no strength left but did the best she could.

Luc shook his head and said to his brother, "We need to help them. They don't have the strength to do the milking alone."

"I suppose so," Jacques sighed. "After all, we'd be doing it anyway if they weren't here."

The two brothers made an extra milking stall out of bales of hay, then Jacques and Tyler worked at one stall, Luc and Jessi at the other. With the brothers giving helpful hints and working with them, the milking went quickly.

As Jacques and Luc were restacking the bales of hay, a gray cat came walking by. Tyler pulled a crust of bread left over from lunch out of his pocket and tossed it to the cat, who quickly gobbled it up.

"You better not let father catch you doing that," Jacques warned.

"Why?" Tyler asked, puzzled.

"That cat is a mouser, not a pet. It needs to find its own food—understand?"

Tyler shook his head.

"Look, it eats mice ... and rats. If we fed it, it wouldn't get hungry, and then you wouldn't be alone with just the cows while you sleep. Now do you understand?"

With a shudder, Tyler nodded in agreement.

After dinner they learned of another daily task assigned to them. The washing barrel, and the other like it in the kitchen that was used for cooking and drinking, were to be filled with fresh water every evening. After three more trips to the stream, their day's assignments were finally completed.

Back home they would've stayed up late on these long summer days, but not here. There were no more chores to be done, but they didn't have the energy to stay up for *any* reason. They received permission to go to bed, and after climbing up into the hay loft they fell asleep the moment their heads hit their blankets. An hour later the Doullens children brought in the cattle and shut up the barn. In the loft above, Tyler and Jessi were so exhausted they didn't stir, never hearing a sound.

15
Farm Life

June 17, 1614

When Luc woke them up the next morning, the last traces of night were gone, even though the sun was still below the horizon. He didn't mind waking them up as his new morning chore; it was a lot easier than milking the cows himself.

He stood near the top of the ladder, looking straight at them. "Up and at it, you two! Another day of work to earn your food and shelter. Let's go!"

They slowly made their way down the ladder, their arms aching as they held onto the railing to keep from falling. Once on the ground they stood shivering in the semidarkness of the barn, rubbing their arms.

Luc brought the first cow into the milking stall. "By the way," he began. "It's probably best you leave Marc and Bernard alone; they don't like strangers."

"Who are they?" Tyler asked.

"Our two bulls. To get milk the cows need to birth a calf, and to birth a calf we need a bull—right? Anyway, get too close to them and they'll run you down. Can you run fast?" he asked with a smirk as he left.

They got right to their task, now that they knew the routine. They also knew that if they didn't work, they wouldn't get to stay or get any breakfast. Besides that, riding to Lille in the wagon at the end of the week would be much better—and safer—than walking.

One by one they milked the cows; when they filled the pail, they'd pour the warm milk into the large cans just inside the barn door, quickly replacing the lid to keep the flies out. There were

111

fewer flies than usual buzzing around their heads in the chilly morning air, but they didn't want to take any chances.

Tyler sat on the short stool next to a cow, getting up only as Jessi returned with an empty pail. As she sat down and started working the udder, she asked "So do you know what happens to all this milk?"

"I dunno exactly. The last pail goes to the house for drinking, and they need some for butter. I guess they sell the rest. I'll have to ask."

Tyler didn't have to. During breakfast, once again consisting of a bowl of oatmeal, Mrs. Doullens was making plans to go to town with her husband.

"I need to pick up a few things too, Gilles," she began. "Some flour and sugar for starters."

"Well, I can get that for you; you needn't go."

"Except I also need to find some fabric for a new smock for Camille and myself, and you're not going to pick *that* out for me!"

Mr. Doullens knew that even if he were to pick the same fabric she would have, she wouldn't be content unless she looked at all the choices first. "Fine," he mumbled. "You can shop while I deliver the milk."

"Mrs. Doullens," Tyler asked. "What town are you talking about, and is it far?"

"What?" she glanced at him in surprise, as a suppressed laugh flickered across her face. "We live in Doullens, dear boy! That's where we were on Sunday."

"Oh. Wait! Your town is named after you?" Tyler exclaimed. "That's excellent!"

She chuckled at the thought. "No, it's not exactly like that," she said, a smile pulling at her lips. "It's more the other way around. My husband's family has lived here for many generations. We are one of several Doullens families in the area. Now off with you to your watering; today is going to be warm once again. Go, Go!"

Side by side they walked to the shed, Luc following behind. Jessi picked up their buckets, handed one to Tyler, and together they headed for the stream.

"Hey you two, you forgot your shoulder poles!" Luc called after them.

"What's a shoulder pole?" Tyler asked.

"You don't know ... wait!" Luc looked at them incredulously, then started snickering. "You mean to say you carried all that water yesterday by *hand*?" Soon the laughter spilled out. "No wonder ... you were so ... weak in the ... arms ... oh!" He paused and took a deep breath in an attempt to regain his composure.

He pointed to two long curved poles leaning against the shed. Attached to each end was a chain about two feet long, with a hook on the end of the chain.

"You each take two buckets, fill them with water, and hang them on the hooks. Then you kneel under the center of the pole and stand up with the pole across your shoulders behind your neck, like this," he demonstrated. "You really haven't seen anybody use a shoulder pole before?" He shook his head as he turned and walked away, laughing to himself, "Carried the buckets by hand! That's hilarious."

Five minutes later they were at the river. They filled up four buckets and placed them on the ground. Jessi put the hook under one pail's handle—but the other pail was too far away. She moved it closer and slipped that hook under the handle of the second pail, then started to lift the pole and saw that the first hook had slipped off. She then re-hooked the first pail and went back the center of the pole. She lifted the buckets off the ground, but knew she didn't have the strength to lift it up and over her head onto her shoulders. She put the buckets down, and the hook slipped off the first pail again. Tyler started snickering, "Nice!"

"Okay, wise guy! Let's see you do it!" she snapped.

"Watch this!" he said confidently. Tyler positioned the buckets at what he figured was the correct distance from each other, their handles up. Placing the pole across his shoulders, he leaned down on his right and snagged the handle with the hook. He started to bring the other hook to the second pail, but saw that he had to lift the first bucket really high to get the second hook down low enough. He then kneeled on the ground and hooked the second bucket. "See, like that!"

He started to stand up, and the buckets lifted off the ground, but he was too far forward, and the weight of the buckets pulled him backwards and he fell to the ground, landing hard on his backside.

Jessi stood watching, her arms folded across her chest. "I see all right. I just wish I had a video of that!" she said with a snort.

Tyler stood up, rubbing his rear. "Yeah, yeah, go ahead and laugh. I can do this."

On his second attempt, Tyler found the right balance point and stood up under his load of water, tottering slightly. "See! Now you, Jess."

They finished their watering task two hours sooner than the prior day, so Mrs. Doullens let them wander around the farm till supper was ready. They found themselves playing with the goat in front of the house for most of that time, to the amusement of those passing by on the road as well as themselves.

* * * * * *

The next day went slowly; everything just like the day before: The first milking at sunrise, and then without the slightest hint of a cloud, another full day of watering plants under a hot sun. Milking the cows at the end of the day was exhausting, but at least they were out of direct sunlight. The last cow was released into the corral next to the barn while the sun was still well above the trees to the west. Without their noticing, their arms were gaining strength and tone, their legs as well.

"Well, we sure are getting faster at this," Jessi said contentedly. "We're gonna have a little free time before dinner, but more than that I'd really love to see some rain." All through the day Mr. Doullens had watched the sky, and they were all praying for rain, but none came—nor any hint of it.

They walked around the back of the barn towards the chicken house. They had discovered that watching the chickens was guaranteed fun. Always on the move, pecking and pushing each other around for no apparent reason, they would fight over a food scrap when a larger scrap was three feet away.

Camille sounded the dinner bell and they jumped down from the fence they'd been sitting on. After cleaning up at the barrel between the house and kitchen, they went inside for dinner. The table was set, and everyone took their place. Mr. Doullens said grace and dinner was served.

"Pork pottage tonight," Mrs. Doullens announced brightly. She then proceeded to fill bowls as the family passed them around until everyone was served. The pottage was a thin broth with chopped cabbage, leeks, carrots, and onions. Bite-sized chunks of pork had been added, and she made sure everyone had at least four pieces each.

"There are two special ingredients tonight," she said mysteriously. "See if you can guess what they are." Her eyes danced with delight at the game she had started.

"Meanwhile, I'll pour the ale," Mr. Doullens said. Seeing the surprised look on Tyler's face he added, "The ale will help make the dinner last, or else you'll be hungry later tonight."

Tyler translated for Jessi. "The beer is needed to help us not get hungry later. I'm guessing because of the calories."

"Okeydokey," Jessi answered apprehensively.

"Pepper!" Luc exclaimed.

"That's one!" Mrs. Doullens laughed. "And the other?"

There was silence as everyone took a slurp of broth.

"Nuts?" Jacques said uncertainly.

"Very good!" Mrs. Doullens applauded.

"Where ever did you get the pepper?" Luc asked.

"I had a little set aside for a special occasion and thought it was fitting to share it with our guests," she explained.

Tyler translated the conversation to Jessi to keep her up to speed. "Sounds like pepper is very rare here, so make a big deal about it, okay?" he said with a quick lift of his eyebrows.

"Ah, yes," Mrs. Doullens continued. "I still remember as a young girl the first time I had pepper. That was about ... 1585, I believe. My mother had snatched the miller's young son out of harm's way from a runaway horse, and the miller thanked her with half a litron of pepper! It was better than a bag of gold!" she sighed contentedly. "My mother stretched that supply out for over four years!"

Tyler told Jessi about the miller's son, and the reward given in pepper. Jessi hopped to her feet and gave Mrs. Doullens a hug from behind. "Thank you for sharing something so special with us." Tyler saw a translation was unnecessary. -

When dinner was done and the water barrels were full, everyone was free for the rest of the evening. They spent their remaining daylight wandering around the farm, returning to the barn at twilight.

They secured the cows in their places as darkness fell, and by the time they were walking back to the house the night creatures in the woods had begun their chorus. The Doullens' kitchen was dimly lit, as usual, by just a couple oil lamps, so they stayed there just long enough to light their candle lanterns and head back to the barn. They were enveloped in the darkness as they stepped outside; night had fallen quickly. The comfort and security of being in a house and on a farm had easily trumped the sense of adventure that came with camping in the woods at night, and they walked straight to the barn and headed up the ladder to their welcoming blankets on the hay.

* * * * * *

Thursday morning found them once again moving buckets of water from stream to field. By midmorning Mr. Doullens and his sons joined them at the upper end of the field, right next to the river. They set to work digging trenches and preparing to install a water gate that would eventually allow them to irrigate the field by the simple lifting of a trapdoor. They expected to have it done by the weekend.

During lunch Luc abruptly asked, "Has anyone seen Bernard today?"

Blank looks on everyone's faces gave him the answer.

"Luc," Mr. Doullens began. "When we're done here I want you and Jacques to get the long spears out of the barn. I'll get the flintlock. The water gate will have to wait until we secure that break in the fence."

"Gilles!" Mrs. Doullens exclaimed.

"Not now, Christine," he tersely replied.

* * * * * *

After lunch Mrs. Doullens gave two candles to Jessi, their original candles having been reduced to stubs. After placing the new candles in the lanterns, she put them just inside the man-door of the barn and started to leave. The cat was at the door of the barn watching her every move. Laying down squat on all fours with its head up and following her with its eyes, it reminded her of the sphinx in Egypt.

The cat lifted its right paw and something shot out—it had caught a field mouse. With its left front paw the cat quickly swatted the mouse until it rolled back underneath her, as she now stood over it, her tail straight up in the air and moving slowly side to side. The mouse lay motionless under the whiskers of the cat. Jessi stood still, scarcely breathing, watching in fascination.

The mouse started to move again, and this time the cat swatted it three feet away and in one jump landed on top of it again. After playing with it a couple more minutes, it snapped up the mouse in its mouth and started to walk away. Jessi turned to join Tyler, and at the sound of her footsteps the cat stopped and looked back at her. The tail of the mouse hung out the side of the cat's mouth, twitching every few seconds. Jessi gave an involuntary shudder and headed towards the house, as the cat sauntered off, its prize still squirming.

* * * * * *

As they continued their watering during the afternoon, the sharp lines of their shadows grew less distinct until gradually there were no shadows at all. By late afternoon clouds had consumed the blue sky and there was a smell of rain in the air.

A steady wind was coming from the north, bringing with it a large bank of dark clouds filling half of the sky.

Mr. Doullens commended them for their efforts. "Well, I must say, you've done well this week. The plants are growing strong thanks to your watering. We've had no rain yet, but it looks like it's on its way. You can stop now, and the milking is all you need to do; the beans and peas will be fine."

Relief washed over their faces. They had hoped they would get to stop but were too timid to ask unless it was already raining. They put their watering tools away and returned to the barn, where Jacques was filling the cows' food troughs with grain.

"What did you find out about Bernard?" Tyler asked.

Jacques looked around for a moment before answering. "Follow me."

He took them to the field where the fence had been broken down. "Look here," he said pointing at some flattened grass.

The grass, and the ground around it, was heavily stained with blood. Cattle hoof-prints were everywhere, punctuated with those of another type: nine inches wide with long claws.

"It killed Bernard, and dragged him this way," he said as he led them towards the fence, following the claw prints partially covered by the dragging of the bull behind. Then there were only claw prints to be seen heading towards and out past the fence. "Here's where the creature threw Bernard on its back and walked off with him," he said bitterly.

"*Carried* the bull off?" Tyler exclaimed.

"I've heard old people in town talking about such things happening years ago, but I never believed them. I used to make fun of their 'stories,' thinking they were making them up. Poor Bernard."

"Maybe you can get another bull, only one that isn't so mean," Tyler offered.

"Mean? What are you talking about?"

"Luc told us to stay clear of the bulls, that they'd run us down if we got too close to them."

"Bernard and Marc are known for being kind and gentle, and other farmers pay us to let them breed with their cows!"

* * * * * *

They had a couple of hours to kill before dinner; Camille took them on a hike around their property, explaining to them how they grew the various crops, from tilling the soil to planting and harvesting.

"It's been nice having you here this week," Camille said gently. "I'll miss you when you're gone. Maybe you can come back sometime and visit?" she asked.

Tyler looked ahead at their pathway, snaking its way amongst the fields. "That'd be nice. But I don't think we will be coming back this way again."

"Are you sure?"

He looked at her out of the corner of his eye. It occurred to him that if things were different—like if she lived back home in their neighborhood or if they lived here all the time—she would be a good friend, even though she was probably a year older than him. His eyes returned to the path in front of him just in time for him to avoid tripping on a rock. "Yeah, I'm sure," he said quietly, with a trace of sadness.

All three of them walked in silence for a few moments. "Well," she said hopefully. "You never know, maybe someday."

* * * * * *

That night Tyler dreamt he was cruising with his dad on the freeway. It was warm outside, so he rolled the window down, closed his eyes, and leaned against the door, listening to the hum of the tires spinning over the concrete. They pulled off the freeway at a rest stop overlooking the Willamette River for a few minutes to look at the view. South of them, the trees grew close down to the water on both sides of the river, and it took little imagination to think it looked the same to Lewis & Clark when they first came through a couple hundred years earlier.

He walked over to the edge of the parking lot where there was a stream and a small waterfall. The image of the waterfall faded away as he opened his eyes. It was dark, and Jessi was sound asleep next to him. The roof of the barn was just a few feet above them—he could touch it if he stood up—and he realized the sound of the rain hitting the roof was similar to the waterfall in his dream. A very large emptiness filled his chest as he thought of home, worlds away. *Wait!* he thought. *Rain! No watering tomorrow!* He turned over and snuggled deeper into the hay and went back to sleep with a contented sigh.

* * * * * *

The rain continued steadily all day Friday, mud puddles accumulating everywhere. Tiny watercourses made their way from puddle to puddle, back and forth across the land, seeking the next available lower location. Mud was everywhere; every step becoming heavier with the mud that stuck to their boots.

There was no work to be done outside, so the Doullens busied themselves in the barn, tending the animals, and repairing the various tools that needed attention. Mr. Doullens prepared the wagon for their trip to Lille the next day.

That evening the rain slowly eased off to just a drizzle, and then the sky began to clear. The almost-full moon drifted in and out among the clouds, lighting up the thin ones, disappearing behind the thick. Eventually even starlight shone through the thinning clouds. Gilles Doullens stood in the open doorway, surveying the night sky.

"This will not be an easy trip this time, Christine. The road will be slippery and slow, and I'm certain we won't make it to Lille in just one day."

Mrs. Doullens tugged on the needle in her hand, raising it up over her head, the thread pulling taut on the fabric in her lap. She looked up. "I know you can't put off the trip, so I won't say more about that, but what about the children? What will you do with them tomorrow night? It's only been a week, but I've grown rather fond of them and their odd ways," she said with a sigh.

"We should easily make it to Jean Moreau's place on the far side of Arras by evening. He'll put us up in his barn, I'm sure.

Besides, it's been over two months since we last saw them, and it will let us catch up on any news."

"I'll make sure you have some food to add to their table, since you'll be dropping in on them without warning. Be sure to give my regards to Charlotte," she added, taking another sip of tea while Mr. Doullens cozied up beside her. They sat together in silence, listening as the crickets sang their night song.

Mr. Doullens frowned. The trip could well become dangerous.

16
Arras

June 21, 1614

Saturday morning the cows dutifully lined up for milking, but this time Luc and Camille joined them and the task was finished in record time. Best of all, it gave the four of them one last time together. When they were done, Tyler and Jessi climbed back up to the loft, grabbed their backpacks, and tossed them into the back of the wagon.

"Go up to the house and say your good-byes," Mr. Doullens told them. "I'll bring the wagon up in a few minutes."

They slowly walked up to the house, suddenly reluctant to leave, knowing there would never be an opportunity to see them again. In barely a week they had been welcomed in as if they were family, and they took pride in the fact they had made a difference in this year's crop. The Doullens family would have more food on their table this fall because of them.

They said their good-byes to each family member in turn and climbed into the back of the wagon. Just as Mr. Doullens was releasing the brake, Mrs. Doullens stepped forward. "Wait a moment, Gilles," she said.

From her apron pocket she pulled a small cloth with its four corners tied into a knot. "Here's something to make your meals a bit tastier," she beamed as she handed it to Jessi.

After untying the knot and peeking inside, she leaned over and gave Mrs. Doullens a hug. "Merci," she said warmly, clutching the pepper close to her heart.

Like just about everything in their adventure, their second wagon trip was not what they expected either. They were thinking they'd spend the day sitting on the back gate of the wagon, much like the prior Sunday, but instead found themselves huddled under damp blankets trying to escape the light rain that played hide and seek with the sun. They often had to get out and help push the wagon forward through the slippery mud whenever the iron-wrapped wheels sank too deeply into the muck for the horses to manage alone. Many times they'd slip and fall, then pull themselves up, only to fall right down again. It was miserable work.

Eventually the road improved, and they were no longer called on to help, and soon the rocking of the wagon lulled them to sleep. Cobblestone replaced mud as they approached the outskirts of Arras, but they saw nothing of the town, waking only when the wagon lurched to a stop.

"Gilles, you dirty dog!" a friendly-sounding voice boomed. "What brings you here? Welcome, my friend."

"I need the use of your barn tonight, Jean." He then nodded behind him. "For me and my two young friends."

They sat up and looked around, rubbing their eyes. Tyler stretched and yawned loudly as a large, burly man walked around to the side of the wagon. With his large black mustache and dark brown eyes, he looked like he belonged in a wrestling ring on Saturday Night Fights.

"Welcome, boys!" he said as he extended his hands towards them. "Let me help you out." He grabbed Tyler by the waist and effortlessly lifted him over the railing onto the ground. As he turned to hoist Jessi out he stopped in surprise, "Ah, a young *girl*? Pardon me!" His large smile revealed a gaping hole where a front tooth had once been. "If Gilles calls you his friends, then you are mine as well."

Mr. Doullens dropped to the ground, stepped in front of the horses, and grabbed the reins. "Open the barn, Jean, and I'll lead my animals inside, if you please."

It took 20 minutes to maneuver the wagon into the barn, unhitch the horses, and get them situated in their stalls for the night. Tyler and Jessi helped as much as they could but ended up mostly watching the process.

They left the barn and trudged over to the main house, where Mrs. Moreau welcomed them inside. As they took off their boots and set them next to the door, she placed three more bowls on the table and ladled some barley soup out of a large pot. "There's plenty here. Just let me grab an extra loaf of bread, and we'll be set."

"Actually, Charlotte," Mr. Doullens said quickly. "I brought a few loaves with me. Christine sends her regards and thanks for taking us in unannounced. Tyler, go get the basket under the front seat of the wagon, yes?"

After dinner, Mr. Moreau lit a fire in the fireplace in an effort to drive out the cold and damp, and was soon rewarded with a roaring blaze, which drew them all in as close to the flames as they could bear. Tyler listened to the adults' conversation, mostly about local events, but his attention soon drifted away to his own thoughts. Jessi, understanding nothing being said, had already fallen asleep.

* * * * * *

June 22, 1614

The next morning dawned cold and grey; the clouds dark and full of rain. Mrs. Moreau bent onto her knees in front of her stove, gently blowing on the kindling that would soon be the fire she needed to cook breakfast. Her stove was similar to that of the Doullens': a small fire box at about knee-height that would heat up the thick iron stovetop above. Smoke from the fire went up a pipe in the back.

A few minutes later she heard Tyler and Jessi begin to stir. After they had fallen asleep next to the fire, she had laid blankets over them and tucked pillows under their heads. Now they awoke to a fireplace that was dark and cold; even the bright coals of the evening's fire had turned to ash. They looked out the small window at the dark sky, uncertainty on their faces.

"A pleasant Sunday morning to you both," she greeted them. "Last night Mr. Doullens wanted to take you out to the barn to sleep, but I thought it better to keep you here with us," she added with a smile.

"Thank you, ma'am," Tyler answered. "It's been a long time since we slept inside a house."

Mrs. Moreau watched them slowly survey the room. *They need a job,* she thought to herself. She picked up the bowl of eggs that was in front of her and placed them on an upper shelf. Grabbing an empty basket off another shelf, she turned back towards them. "Oh dear, we're out of eggs," she said. "Go behind the barn and you'll find a chicken coop. Take this basket and gather up a couple dozen eggs for our breakfast. Now off with you!"

She tossed them the basket and turned away from them, a smug smile on her face. Tyler scooped the basket off the floor, and she heard him say something in English to Jessi. As the door closed behind them, she pulled the bowl of eggs down off the shelf and pursed her lips as she tried to decide what to do with them. She then pulled a pot off a hook on the wall, filled it with water and a little vinegar, added the eggs, and put it on the stovetop to boil. *That'll be a nice something for them to take on their trip today.*

* * * * * *

Jessi and Tyler walked around to the back of the barn. A short distance beyond they could see a small building about the size of a large bedroom. The sounds, and smells, confirmed they were heading in the right direction. A tall fence enclosed both the chicken coop and maybe half an acre of land. On the right side of the fence surrounding the coop, they found a gate that was secured by a block of wood that lay horizontally on hooks fastened to both the door and the fence. Tyler lifted the board and pulled the hook to open the gate—it didn't budge. He stood there a moment, looking at it.

"Push on the gate, genius," Jessi said teasingly.

"Oh, right."

As they stepped through the open gate, a chicken started making a fast loop around their legs to make its escape before the gate closed. Jessi threw her leg out and pinned it against the fence. It uttered a complaining squawk, flapping its wings furiously as feathers scattered. It finally gave up and walked away, clucking angrily.

She laughed. "Ya know, I think it's swearing at me!"

Tyler walked up to the building. On each side of the coop a small ramp angled gently up from the ground to a little doorway about three feet off the ground. He leaned over one of the doorways and peered into the darkness inside.

"How do we get in there?"

"The door for us is over here. You need a cup of coffee or something?"

They cautiously opened the man-door and peered inside. The coop was quietly active with rows of chickens cooing and clucking amongst themselves. As they entered, the sound grew suddenly louder as the chickens acknowledged the intruders.

The door swung shut behind them with a bang, causing all the chickens to respond with a swell of squawking that quickly subsided. Along the two side walls were nesting boxes, about a foot square each, for the chickens to lay their eggs in. Under the nesting boxes, they could see the small doorways leading to the outdoor ramps. Against the back wall were a series of horizontal tree branches that had been planed smooth for the chickens to roost on. Jessi hesitated as she saw dozens of beady eyes watching her every move. She thought of them attacking her at any moment and pictured herself returning to the Moreau's house bleeding in tattered clothes.

"Do they fight back?" she whispered.

"Jess, I don't think you need to whisper," Tyler replied. "Just show them who's boss." He took a less than confident step towards the first nesting box in front of him. The chicken tensed and lifted up a little. It let out a continuous low clucking that was a definite warning to be left alone. "Aren't they supposed to run away from us?"

"He looks like he's ready to defend his eggs."

Tyler looked at Jessi, grinning widely. "*His* eggs? These aren't roosters, Jess; they're hens."

"Oh … right." *I got him about the gate,* she thought, *I guess we're even now.*

Tyler nervously reached his hand forward. "Okay, little lady, do you have something for me?" he asked. The chicken's head quickly bobbed back and forth, watching his every move. His hand started shaking a little as it came under the chicken's outstretched neck. Before Tyler could react, the hen gave him a hard peck on the back of his hand.

"Ow!" he yelped. "He bit me!" He put his hand to his mouth and quickly spat out a little pink–colored spit. "Eew, from his mouth to mine," he said in disgust.

"*Her* mouth," Jessi corrected with a smile.

"I'm definitely getting her eggs now! It's on," Tyler snapped. He angrily reached forward, and the chicken quickly moved aside, revealing an egg for the taking. This was a foe she didn't want to take on after all.

"Yeah! See, it's like I said. Show it who's boss!" Tyler stepped sideways to the next box. He gave a quick back-handed wave, and the chicken made way for him. "Who's the boss, who's the boss," he chortled.

A few minutes later they were closing the gate behind them. Looking to the east they could tell that the sun was now above the horizon, but because of the heavy gray clouds they could only guess at the time; a new day had begun. They saw ahead of them the footsteps they had made in the mud on their way to the chicken coop. *It's a good thing we had our boots on instead of our sneakers,* Jessi thought. *Our sneakers!*

"Ty!" Jessi grimaced. "We forgot our shoes at the Doullens! … *and* our clothes! Our *real* clothes. Oh man! We can't go back and get them now—they're probably still hanging in the shed! Aww, and you know what this *means?* I've actually gotten *used* to wearing a dress. I don't believe this!"

Tyler thought for a moment. "Probably just as well. They only draw attention to us anyway, and the more we blend in the better."

"Yeah, but my jeans were almost brand new! Mom's gonna kill me when she finds out I lost them." Mentioning her mom was a bit of a jolt, and she suddenly grew quiet. "We *are* gonna get home, right, Ty?"

They slopped through the mud to the front of the Moreau's door, then slipped off their boots and shook off some of the mud that had made each leg feel five pounds heavier.

Just before going inside Tyler caught Jessi's eye. "I want to go home too, Jess. And we're going home *today*, remember?"

"Yeah," Jessi said with a contented sigh. "Home."

17
𝔄 𝔙𝔢𝔯𝔶 ℜ𝔞𝔦𝔫𝔶 𝔇𝔞𝔶

After breakfast the two men strode out to the barn to hitch the horses up to the wagon. They had further to travel today than yesterday, "Over eleven lieue," Mr. Moreau had said, and the roads would be in about the same condition—muddy and slow. Tyler and Jessi shuddered at the prospect of repeating the prior day's travel.

Mr. Doullens pulled the wagon to a stop in front of the small house; Mrs. Moreau stood on the porch to see them off. They climbed into the back of the wagon and made their places as comfortable as possible. Mr. Doullens then gave two loud clacking sounds out the side of his mouth as he threw a quick snap into the reins. His motion with the reins traveled forward from his hand like an ocean wave and the horses started to move.

"Gilles! Hold on a moment; I almost forgot!" Mrs. Moreau called out. Mr. Doullens quickly stopped the horses as she did an about-face and ran inside. Moments later she reappeared with a small basket in her hand and stopped at the edge of the porch. "Jean, be a dear and give this to the children." The two men were talking again about the conditions of the road, and he stopped in midsentence with a shrug and a quick lift and drop of his bushy eyebrows.

He took the basket from her and brought it to the side of the wagon. "Here you are, young ones. Stay under the cover. You have a long wet day ahead of you."

They thanked the Moreaus for the gift, then their heads bobbed forward as the wagon lurched ahead. Their legs dangling off the back of the wagon, they watched as the Moreau's home slowly grew smaller. They waved one last time to Mr. and Mrs. Moreau as they rounded a turn in the road.

The first hour passed by pleasantly—not once did they have to get out and help push the wagon. Soon the mostly gentle rocking of the wagon lulled them to sleep under a heavy blanket that kept them warm against the cool morning breeze; even the occasional jolt of a wheel dropping into a hole in the road didn't wake them.

* * * * * *

The wagon rolled to a stop, and Jessi opened her eyes. She was looking straight up into the branches of a monstrous tree, its large flat leaves almost completely blocking out the gray sky above. She started to sit up and discovered that her foot had fallen asleep, thanks to her leg hanging off the back of the wagon cutting off the circulation behind her knee. She lifted her leg up and started rubbing her foot, the tingling growing painful as the nerve endings came back to life.

She looked over her shoulder towards Mr. Doullens, who was silently looking straight ahead. "Is something wrong?" she asked.

Mr. Doullens twisted around and looked at her uncertainly. "Qu'est-ce que tu me demandes?"

She frowned and jabbed Tyler in the shoulder. "Wake up, Ty. I think something's wrong."

Tyler grimaced and stirred. "Huh? What?"

"We've stopped for some reason. Mr. Doullens is just sitting there, and I don't know why."

Grabbing the side rail, Tyler slowly stood up, stretched, and yawned. "Mr. Doullens, why are we stopped?" he asked.

Looking towards the sky ahead he nodded with upraised eyebrows. "Rain, and lots of it, is blowing our way. I figure we've got a few minutes before it gets here. That'll give us time to cover up, and this tree will block the worst of it as well."

They hopped off the wagon and helped him open up a canvas tarp with which they covered the entire back of the wagon. They had barely finished tying down the corners when the first drops began to fall. They stood next to the wagon to watch the storm blow through. The rain found its way through the leaves overhead, as large drops of water randomly hit the ground around them. Once in a while drops would hit them on the head, sending tiny lines of water running down their faces.

Tyler slapped his palm against his forehead. "Jess, we forgot about the ponchos Jim sent us!"

A few minutes later they were keeping dry as they watched the storm slowly ease off. Water had accumulated on each side of the road, creating puddles as far as they could see in both directions.

Mr. Doullens took a particular interest in their ponchos. He found it very curious that water would float and run across the surface without *any* of it soaking into the fabric. "Tell me where you got this," he said. "I would very much like one of these. It would be very helpful to keep me dry on these trips during the winter."

Tyler interpreted his request for Jessi, after which they exchanged uncertain glances. Mr. Doullens had been very nice to them, and they didn't want to say no, but ... "Well," Tyler offered, "perhaps when we see our friend in Lille he can get you one."

"What do you think, Jessi?" Tyler asked. "Think Jim could send us one for him?"

Without waiting for an answer he looked back at Mr. Doullens. "If not, I can give you mine."

"That is kind of you, but I suspect it's a bit too small for me. Thank you anyway." He looked up at the road ahead and patiently waited. Time slowly dragged on. Finally, in the direction of the wind the clouds appeared lighter and thinner. "It's time we got rolling again," he finally said.

They covered the next few miles fairly quickly, considering how wet and sloppy the road had become. They saw no one else, as most people avoided traveling if they could in such weather.

Once again Mr. Doullens pulled the wagon to a stop, this time staying in the road, as he surveyed the scene ahead. The road gently descended before rising again about 30 yards further on. From the hill on the right a torrent of rainwater was rushing down and overflowing the road at the low point just before them. The muddy water concealed all evidence as to the condition of the road underneath, and there was no way to be certain how deep the water was. After crossing the road the water disappeared over a sharp drop-off on the left.

"Hmm, we'll see," Mr. Doullens muttered to himself as he gave his clacking sound and a shake of the reins to the horses. As they slowly pulled forward, Tyler and Jessi leaned over opposite side rails, intently watching their progress through the water. It looked to be about two feet deep at the lowest point, and the thin legs of the horses sliced through it easily. The horse on the right briefly stumbled, but quickly recovered.

Moments later the wagon suddenly dropped down on the right side and stopped. The water that had been flowing well under the wagon was suddenly at the floorboards, lifting and slowly pushing the wagon to the left.

Mr. Doullens looked down at the ravine. "Out!" he shouted, "Jump out NOW! Lift and push the wagon! GO!"

Tyler jumped down behind the wagon on the left side; the water sending a cold shock wave up his legs, as it started pushing him over. He grabbed the back of the wagon for support, got his footing under him, and started pushing. A quick glance to his left, down the hillside, scared him, and he pushed again with renewed energy. Jessi was alongside him on the right. They pushed forward, but the wagon didn't move.

"Ty, help me. I think the wheel over here is in a hole! Help me lift! Come on!"

Tyler moved over next to Jessi; the wagon lifted a little but not enough.

"Okay." Jessi shouted. "On three! One, two, three!" They lifted with all their strength, a strength they didn't have just a couple weeks earlier, as the horses pulled hard against their harnesses. The right wheel found higher ground under the water and slowly moved forward. Holding his left hand on the wagon for support against the rushing water, Tyler followed along. Jessi stepped forward into the hole and fell, causing her to strike her head against the wagon. She lost her grip and disappeared under the water.

"NO!" Tyler shouted when she didn't come right back up. He felt her limp body bump against his lower leg. She wasn't trying to get up, and she was floating ever closer to the precipice! Plunging his right arm into the water, he grabbed her just as he felt her spinning around and behind him. He lifted her with all his might, but couldn't get her head out of the water.

Suddenly he felt her body twist and pull on him. A moment later she broke above the surface of the water with a gasp. She threw her free arm around his neck and clung to him. He gripped her around her waist, and still holding on to the wagon, pulled her along until they were out of danger.

Once out of the water, Tyler half-carried her to some grass on the side of the road, where they both collapsed to the ground. After a few minutes she regained enough strength to sit up.

"You saved my life!" she exclaimed fervently.

The vulnerability in her eyes left him speechless, as he grappled with the realization that she was an awesome *girl*, not just his next-door neighbor.

"Aw, come on, Jessi. I didn't—"

"When I hit my head, I literally saw stars, and everything went dark for … for a moment." She shivered uncontrollably. "I could tell I was … was under water, but I didn't know whi … which way was up. Then you grabbed me and … and … I would've go …gone into that ravine if … if it wasn't for you! I … I'm so cold."

Mr. Doullens approached, and without saying a word, easily scooped Jessi up and placed her in the back of the wagon. He smiled at Tyler. "Good work," he said. He then went up front and quietly spoke with the horses, gently stroking them as he looked for any possible injures. Then, with a double "clack" and a flick of the reins, they were on the move once again.

They crawled under the tarp away from the rain, but it was wet there too.

Jessi couldn't stop shivering. "Ty … I'm … so … so c-cold."

Tyler looked at her, alarmed. He was wet, but she was in trouble. He started opening her backpack. "Ya gotta get out of those wet clothes. I'll find something else for you to wear."

"Ty, there's ... there's ... nothing else t-to wear. What we have ... have on is all ... all ...we got."

"Oh, yeah. I'm sorry."

Tyler helped her take off her poncho, but it was hard work in the tight confines of the swaying wagon, with the tarp pressing down on them. As he wrapped the damp blanket around her, they hit a rock, tossing her against him, and the warmth of his body drew her like a magnet. "Help me get ... get ... warm, Ty," she chattered as she put her arms around him. Tyler wrapped the blanket around them both as delight, and confusion, flickered across his face.

Tyler watched as their water crossing disappeared around a corner, and Jessi's shivering started to subside as she fell asleep with his arms holding her close.

* * * * * *

The wagon again pulled to a stop. Tyler looked up at the tarp overhead. How long had it been? Jessi was still pressed close to him, deeply asleep. He slowly pulled back and tucked the blanket around her, feeling awkward and grateful she didn't wake up. He looked out from under the tarp. The sun was shining, but everything around was wet from the rains. Mr. Doullens set the brake, jumped down, came around to the back, and lifted the tarp.

"Come on out, you two," he said. Jessi still didn't move. He smiled tenderly as he reached out and picked her up, blanket and all. He peeled the blanket off of her and stood her on her feet. He looked at Tyler. "Tell her to move around and warm up. We have a little bit of sunshine right now."

Tyler looked at the sky. "Little bit" was right. Most of the sky was thick with clouds, but a small section of blue was allowing a brief spot of brightness—and warmth—but it wouldn't last long.

Mr. Doullens grabbed the basket Mrs. Moreau had given them as they left. The basket had a woven top that hinged in the center under the handle. He lifted one side to examine its contents.

Ten minutes later the gap in the clouds closed, and the sun disappeared once again; but not before Jessi had dried out and warmed up. They had all feasted on hard-boiled eggs and bread, washing them down with water from the jug Mr. Doullens kept up front with him.

They climbed back into the wagon; there was the now-familiar "clack-clack" accompanied by a flick of the reins, and with a lurch their journey continued once again. Tyler hoped there would be no more incidents along the way.

18
Lille

They watched as this increasingly familiar world continued to recede behind them. Farmland could be seen everywhere, often bordering right up to the road. Cleared and cultivated land could be seen in the distance in one direction or another, but always trees, trees, and more trees, bright green with the fresh June leaves of an early summer day—a very wet summer day.

By early afternoon the countryside began to change, as the larger farmlands were replaced with smaller tracts of property. Groups of houses began to appear, each group surrounded by a wide section of tilled land, growing various crops they didn't recognize. They sensed they were approaching the city of Lille.

The thudding clip-clop of the horses' hooves suddenly brightened to a higher, harder sound. Moments later the smooth flow of the wagon was replaced with the drone of rough vibrations pushed up through the wagon by the hard cobblestones under the iron-clad wheels. They spun around to get a look at the city. Their destination at last—and then home! The bright hope on their faces quickly disappeared as they surveyed the scene around them.

"This is Lille?" Jessi asked.

As far as the eye could see there was nothing but a scattered collection of old homes, weathered rock porches in front of brick or rock-walled houses that had been occupied for countless generations. Some of the houses had the living quarters on the second floor, with horse stables at the ground level. As they watched, the distance between the homes steadily diminished until it was finally clear they truly *were* in a city. This had to be Lille!

Their eyes eagerly scanned the streets around them for the large tree located near a church. How did Jim describe it?

South—or was it east—of a church in a park about 50 yards away near a stream.

But where was the church, and with so many trees everywhere, how would they know which was the right one? Doubt slowly crept over them, crowding out the hope they'd been holding onto all day. It didn't take long before all the streets started looking the same, and though every house was different from the next, there was a dreary similarity to the look of most every dwelling. Soon another unpleasant aspect of city life became apparent: the smell. Everywhere they looked there were piles of horse manure, and no matter what street they traveled on, the smell filled the air.

With a "clack" sound to the horses, and a slight tug on the reins, the horses turned right onto a slightly less traveled street. They continued a few more minutes, making a few more turns. Soon they were completely turned around and had no idea from which direction they had entered the city. They kept looking for a church, with a large tree nearby, and a stream …

With a "Whoa!" Mr. Doullens pulled back on the reins. The horses obediently came to a stop. Without a word to Tyler and Jessi, he set the brake on the wagon, jumped down to the ground, and walked into the building to their right.

A few minutes later he returned. "Come on, you two. Help me unload the wagon," he commanded.

They dutifully put themselves to the task, and soon the wagon was empty except for their personal belongings. They waited in the street, where through the window in the front of the store, they could see the shopkeeper give Mr. Doullens some money. The men continued their conversation, looking several times in their direction.

"Why do they keep looking at us?" Jessi asked. "It's making me nervous."

"I don't know and I don't care. We need to find that church," Tyler said, scanning the area.

Mr. Doullens came out to the wagon then, and as he maneuvered the wagon away from the store, Tyler asked, "Mr. Doullens, what did we just deliver to that man?"

"What? Oh, this trip it was special spices made at a shop in Doullens. Now I'm picking up some colored glass to take back home with me—for an artisan in Doullens working on a large home. Every two weeks it's something different, back and forth, back and forth. It's a good way to make some extra money—necessary when our crops are short; and when our crops are bountiful, we expand our farm."

Tyler translated for Jessi. "Sounds like a 1614 version of a trucker," Jessi responded.

"Yeah, it does," Tyler laughed.

"What's that she said?" Mr. Doullens asked.

"She said we know of people where we come from that do this same kind of thing."

As they wound through the city, Tyler and Jessi were fascinated by the sights and sounds. They hadn't seen so many people at the same time since they had arrived, and in that respect the city reminded them of back home.

"Hey!" Jessi shouted, pointing to the left. "I see a church!"

Mr. Doullens twisted around, glanced at Jessi, then asked Tyler. "What's she so excited about?"

"We're supposed to meet our friend near a church. Maybe that one over there?"

"St. Maurice's? Well, let's go see."

He coaxed the horses into an about-face and headed towards the church. "St. Maurice's was built a few hundred years ago, I believe. Oh, and tell her to keep her English to herself. In the city it may get the wrong kind of attention."

He directed the wagon to the front of the church. Two huge black doors were set back inside an overhanging porch that stretched about 30 feet overhead. Above that were several stained-glass windows, and above the windows there were three stone figures of men. Then above them another set of windows seemed to stretch maybe a hundred feet to the top. They had never seen anything like it in their lives.

Mr. Doullens drove the wagon in a complete circuit around the church, pausing briefly once as a family crossed the street in front of them. In disappointment Jessi and Tyler looked at each other; there was no park, no big tree, and certainly no stream.

"He's not here," Tyler finally said. "Is there another church where we can look?"

"Hmm, well, there is St. Catherine's, to the west of here near a small park. It's not far beyond where I'm picking up the glass. So after we get the glass, I'll take you there."

It didn't take long to reach the glass shop. Mr. Doullens went inside, and they again waited in the wagon. They studied the buildings and the different businesses along the street. It seemed to them each business here had to do with making something.

"Let's go check out these places. They look pretty cool," Jessi said hopefully.

"But what if Mr. Doullens needs our help?"

"Don't worry. We'll be right here along the street. We can keep an eye—and ear—out for him. Come on, where's your sense of adventure?"

"You're kidding me, right?" Tyler asked, shaking his head.

They walked down to the end of the street and turned around. They would work their way towards the glass shop, and it would be easier to see Mr. Doullens when he came out.

The first business made blankets and sheets. An awning hung out from the building, and under its protection from the rain thick blankets were neatly stacked on two tables on opposite sides of the doorway. The thick blankets looked particularly good to Jessi, who still felt chilled after her dunking in the road.

She slid her hand between a couple of blankets. The material was rougher than what she was used to back home—a lot like the blankets the Doullens had given them to use in the hay loft. It needed to be thick to stop the hay from poking through; her blanket back home wouldn't have worked here. She could feel the warmth growing around her fingers.

The shopkeeper stepped out of the door. "Feels good, yes? Especially on a cold wet day like this!" He took a deep breath and exhaled with a smile of contentment. "I love how the rain cleans the streets and freshens the air." He leaned forward with a slightly hopeful look. "Would you like to buy a blanket?"

Jessi withdrew her hand as Tyler stepped forward. "Thank you, but no. We were just admiring your work."

They went to the next shop and looked through the window. Necklaces, bracelets, and all kinds of jewelry were displayed on top of, and behind, glass cases. A rather large woman, already wearing a lot of jewelry, had the full attention of the man behind the counter. It looked like she would soon be wearing even more, judging by the man's happy face. They weren't interested at all in going in there, so they moved on to the next store.

This store also had a large awning jutting out from the building. Rain started to fall again, and they were grateful for its protection from the light drizzle. Under the awning were ceramic and clay pots of all sizes, shapes, and colors. Some of them were made the same, but in different sizes, so they could be sold as a set. Inside the store they found stacks of dishes on shelves, with matching mugs and bowls. Each set had its own color and painted patterns, usually of flowers and leaves. They didn't stay long and wandered to the next store, which was right next to the glass shop where Mr. Doullens was still talking with the owner.

Bronze statues were arranged outside in front of the store, the smallest about two feet tall, the largest almost as tall as themselves. One statue in particular caught their attention. It was a small child about three feet tall, leaning forward and laughing with its hands on its knees. Rainwater ran down the folds and creases of the metal, like shiny miniature rivers; just looking at it made them smile as they walked past it and went through the door. Inside were hundreds of bronze statuettes, smaller pieces, all with unbelievable detail. The sculptor sat on a stool midway into the store.

"Come on in and take a look around. Then buy something expensive!" he guffawed.

"I didn't think they would be this good," whispered Tyler. "You know, without having machinery to use."

"Come on, Ty. These guys are artists."

"Tyler! Where are you?" they heard Mr. Doullens call out.

Jessi and Tyler spun on their heels and bolted out the door. The store owner jumped off of his stool in the corner and charged after them, as if certain they had stolen something. As soon as they were outside the door, they stopped and got Mr. Doullens' attention.

"Well, come on over here," he called. "I could use your help."

The sculptor went back into his shop and watched them briefly through his front window. When he saw them helping Mr. Doullens, he went back to his work.

Loading the wagon was heavier work this time. The glass weighed considerably more than the spices they had brought with them. Because of the weight, the wagon quickly reached the most it could carry, even though it didn't look very full.

Mr. Doullens took a careful look at the load. It was important it was balanced properly from both side-to-side and front-to-back, especially since he had a long and slippery ride back home, alone.

"Hmm," he said, "I'll be inside a couple more minutes. Stay in the wagon this time, understand? No wandering," he said sternly.

They climbed into the wagon, pulled the tarp up over their heads to keep out the rain, and waited. A minute later they watched as an older boy slowly walked towards them. He was wearing a long black cloak that hung down almost to his feet and buttoned about half way down. Tyler guessed he was about 18. The boy didn't see them under the tarp; he seemed pretty focused on the goods along the storefronts. He paused in front of the bronze figures and looked at all the pieces. He casually looked inside the store, leaning forward a bit, his cloak opening up in front. As he straightened up, his cloak folded together again. He turned around and nonchalantly headed back the way he had come.

Tyler blinked. He couldn't believe it! The statue of the laughing boy was gone! "Jessi!" he gasped. "He took the statue!" He jumped to his feet, shoving the tarp out of his way. "Robber!" he shouted. "I saw you take that!"

The young man looked at him in confusion. Tyler realized he had shouted at him in English.

"Help!" He shouted as loud as he could. "That guy there stole a statue!"

Anger flashed across the young man's face when he realized his theft was discovered. The sculptor came charging out his door and immediately saw that his Laughing Boy was gone. "Thief!" he shouted at him.

Glancing back and forth between the sculptor and Tyler, the thief started to cross the street, but stepping into a pile of horse manure, he slipped and fell, spreading the manure all over his long coat and pants. The statue fell to the ground with a clang as he released his grip. Jumping up, he pointed his finger and glared at Tyler. "I'll get you for this, rat-face! I'll make you pay!" He ran off down the street. "You'll be sorry, rat-face!" he shouted one last time as he disappeared around the corner.

Tyler's heart was pounding hard as he sat back down. He couldn't believe what had just happened. He took a few shaky breaths.

"Way to go, Ty!" Jessi nodded approvingly. "Way to go! He'd have gotten away with it if it wasn't for you!"

The sculptor picked up his statue that had fallen onto its back. "Are you hurt, little one?" he asked tenderly as he carefully turned it over and examined his handiwork. "Oh, a little scratch only. I will fix you as good as ever!" He stood up with a grunt, the Laughing Boy cradled in his arms.

"You, boy!" he called to Tyler. "Come here."

Tyler and Jessi both hopped down off the wagon, the sculptor motioning them to follow him. He went inside and set the Laughing Boy on his workbench. Then he walked over to one of the shelves that were full of tiny statuettes. His eyes scanned across all the pieces, then stopped as he smiled and picked one up.

"Here," he said gratefully, "is a small token of my appreciation. When you look at it, you think of me, and remember how thankful I am you were brave enough to face up to that horrible boy."

He placed a small figure in Tyler's hand. It was a miniature of the Laughing Boy, about two inches tall. Tyler was surprised at the amount of detail in such a small piece. This man was *really* good!

"Thank you, sir." Tyler put his hand out to shake the man's hand. The man laughed a loud "Ha" and took Tyler by the shoulders kissing him on each cheek. "No, thank *you*, young man."

* * * * * *

Twenty minutes later they pulled up to St. Catherine's. The church was constructed of large blocks of chiseled white stone. Stained-glass windows stretched the length of the building; the bottoms of the windows were over 10 feet above the ground, and the windows themselves were at least that tall.

Mr. Doullens pointed to the far side of the church. "The tower over there is used as a lookout for fires around the city," he said.

They looked up at the square tower. On each of the four sides they could see a large clock. Suddenly the air was pierced by a loud gonging as the bell in the tower struck five times. As the ringing died away, the sounds of the city seemed to recover after the momentary pause. When they made their way to the front of the church, they saw a park across the street containing several large fir trees and a massive maple on one side.

Tyler looked around at the sky but couldn't locate the sun. He pointed towards the park. "Is that way south?" he asked.

"No, that is north."

"Oh." Tyler frowned.

"What's the matter, Ty?" Jessi asked.

"Jim said the funnel was south of the church next to a large tree, but that way is north, and behind us are only streets. No trees, not even small ones."

"Are you sure?" she asked. "Maybe the church was south of the funnel, not the other way around?"

Neither could remember Jim's words for sure.

Mr. Doullens looked at them and gently asked, "Are you two all right?"

Tyler wasn't sure how to answer him.

19
𝔖𝔢𝔞𝔯𝔠𝔥𝔦𝔫𝔤

June 15, Current Year

Jim stood looking out the window in disinterest. It was overcast again, but it could have been raining, or snowing even, because all that mattered to him was getting the kids back.

After he sent them their supplies and they had left for Lille, he feverishly fine-tuned the transfer process and was now ready to bring them back as soon as they arrived there. It was only afterwards that he realized he needn't have been in such a panic. No matter how long he spent preparing to bring them back, it would happen as soon as they arrived in Lille. The time travel component could get confusing real quick.

His phone started ringing; eventually he withdrew his gaze from the window and pulled it out of his pocket. "Hello," he said flatly.

"Hey, Jim," said a bright voice. "This is Todd. How's it going today?"

"Oh, hey, Todd. Okay, I guess—another day of perfect Portland sunshine. How about you, man?"

"Oh, just another day in LA without *any* smog!"

They both quietly chuckled at their mutual lies.

"So, Todd, what's up?"

"Yeah, right! It's the 15th, that's what's up!"

"The 15th!" Jim groaned. He had totally forgotten the deadline for his updates on Star Commandos II.

"Todd, I'm sorry. I had a total crash of my computer system, and I've not gotten *anything* done this last month, and it's going to be a while—can't be sure how much longer. Sorry, man."

"Well, Jim, you know what this means, don't you?"

"Umm, what's that exactly?"

"It means I have to start thinking you're like all my other programmers, always missing their deadlines. It's just never happened with *you* before. It's okay, though; I'll just tell the boss that you need another six weeks or so. Will that be enough?"

"I think so. Thanks, Todd." Jim hung up and dropped the phone back in his pocket. He inhaled deeply and slowly let it out. *Funny*, he thought. *That game isn't so important anymore.*

He sat back down at his workstation, mousing over to the fine-tuning controls on his screen. He had told them it'd take about a week to get to Lille, but he knew it could be sooner, or later, when they would actually show up. Just to be safe he started looking out through the Lille funnel beginning four days after they left Amiens. He performed a slow and complete circle, searching carefully for them, but he could see nothing but trees, grass, and the city of Lille for about a block in all directions. It suddenly occurred to him how lucky it was that the Lille funnel was in the middle of a park, and not inside somebody's house—like this one.

He advanced the timer 20 minutes and looked again—nothing. He advanced the timer another 20 minutes—still nothing. He continued searching until he reached nightfall of Day Four—no sign of them. He scrolled forward to Day Five of their journey and began the process all over again, advancing his timer every 20 minutes. By now he had every tree, bush, walking path, and building within sight of the funnel memorized, but no sign of the kids.

He was already becoming familiar with the activities of the people who lived in the area as well. In the mornings vendors pulled wagons full of goods heading east on the nearby street, and in the evening they pulled empty wagons the opposite way, presumably heading home. There was an elderly couple who took a daily midafternoon walk, a young mother who brought her children to play nearby, and the constant gurgling of the small stream right next to the funnel.

He completed his survey of Day Five; still no sign of them. He knew they would show up; they *had* to. But it was tedious work carefully surveying the horizon, waiting for when he would finally see them walking towards him, whenever that might be. Burned in his memory, and his heart, was the sight of watching them walk away from the funnel near Amiens and his utter helplessness in being able to protect them on their journey. He knew he wouldn't relax until he caught sight of them again.

He scanned halfway through Day Six—June 18 according to the 1614 calendar he had printed out. *Hmm, still no sign of them.* He worried: it shouldn't take this long to get to Lille from Amiens. He scrolled back to the second day. *Who knows?* he thought. *Maybe they somehow got a ride and arrived in Lille in two days.* He surveyed every 20 minutes of Day Two and then Day Three. No sign of them.

He went back to Day Six and picked up where he left off, hungrily looking for them until there was no more daylight in their day. He leaned back in his chair and sighed. His back ached from being hunched over in front of the monitor, and he was starting to get a headache. He looked up at the clock—he had been doing this for over six hours. His stomach gurgled— *probably should eat.* He went to the kitchen and made himself a roast beef sandwich and filled a glass with water. He sat down at his dinette table and silently ate his meal, listening to his music coming from The Bridge and the steady hum of the refrigerator.

* * * * * *

The next morning he returned to his search. He had left the computers running all night—he rarely turned them off anymore since he was always running a routine of some sort or other, but he was not prepared for what was waiting for him on his monitor. It was a simple question: "Watch June 11, 1614?" It had nothing to do with the routine he had been running all night, and he couldn't recall writing a program that would generate such a question. He uneasily typed in "yes" and hit Enter.

The monitor instantly showed the familiar patch of woods in the Amiens funnel. A small tree a couple inches in diameter was slightly to the right. The video seemed distorted, like he was looking through an extremely old window pane, and there was no sound. Then suddenly the kids, and all of his equipment, appeared in midair. They didn't just fall to the ground, they were *slammed* to the ground—hard. He winced at the sight. "What?" he exclaimed. His fingers flew across the keyboard to replay the scene in slow motion. It confirmed what he feared: just a fraction of a second after impact, the small tree was uprooted and flew up out of the ground before it disappeared. Part of the tree root struck Jessi viciously under the chin, snapping her head back. *That had to have hurt bad,* he thought. He glanced towards his backyard where he had dumped the tree after it came here—*where I'm sitting!* he thought in alarm. He jumped up and stepped out of The Bridge, glancing in fear at the chair.

"Get a grip, Jim," he muttered. "The real question is how did the computer show you this in the first place?" It took most of the day before he found the routine in a hidden subdirectory within the program. It looked like his programming style, only not as sophisticated, and it reminded him of his projects when he was a rookie programmer. He knew he didn't write the routine, and the idea that the computer could have done it on its own so unnerved him he shut it down and left it off for two days.

June 18, Current Year

After breakfast he walked into The Bridge, took a deep breath, and sat down. "All right, Jim. Back at it," he said out loud, as he rubbed his hands together and hit all the power buttons to his equipment. He went back to the kitchen for his coffee, and by the time he returned, everything was up and running, including his music playlist options. He selected something upbeat and started searching through Day Seven, which was June 19 for them. By midafternoon their time, he noticed the clouds had come in, and it was starting to rain.

Now he was on Day Eight—a day of solid rain: the young mother didn't show up with her children, and the elderly couple didn't take their daily walk. Big surprise.

Day Nine was the same; it never stopped raining, and the kids didn't show up. What troubled him now was what he saw going on around him at the funnel. What had been a quiet little stream next to the funnel was now an overflowing river of muddy rainwater. Training his gaze straight down through the center of the funnel, he saw water, at least a foot deep, rushing directly below him, instead of the familiar short grass.

It occurred to him that they would have a difficult time fighting through the water to walk to the center of the funnel. He knew they would have to be positioned perfectly for the return trip, and the water rushing around their legs would make it difficult for them to be precisely where they needed to be—*the water!* He would be bringing back the water with them! He wasn't concerned about the water ruining his computers here in his house—they weren't as important as the kids—but he knew it would be impossible to properly calculate how much mass to transfer *there* to bring them back *here*, and an unknown quantity of rushing water with them, all at the same time.

He wrestled with this problem for a while, and then realized that it didn't matter. *Either they come home through the Lille funnel when it's dry or ... or they have to come home from another funnel!* A chill swept through his body. The idea of them just waiting there for the weather to change, or sending them on a journey to *another* funnel, *another* length of time where he couldn't watch over them, was more than he could stand. He jumped up and began pacing around the room, considering all the possibilities, trying to find a way to bring them home *now*.

He kept reminding himself that he just had to be creative and find the way to make it happen. "You can do it, Jim," he said to himself. He went back to the terminal and finished surveying the scene around the funnel until sunset of Day Nine, Saturday, June 21st for them—still no sign of them. *What is taking them so long?* He got up again and started wandering around his house, not paying any attention to where he was, lost in thought as to what to do next. He found himself standing in front of his open closet and saw his running outfit on the shelf in front of him.

An hour later, and after four miles around the track at the school, he finally slowed down to a walking pace. Sweat dripped down the back of his spine under his shirt as he clasped his hands on top of his head and waited to catch his wind. This felt good; he needed to blow off the energy—and tension. He felt his head clear, and a new plan started coming into focus. He jogged home, showered, grabbed his laptop, and went to the Burgerville—nothing beats a hamburger and a fresh raspberry milkshake after a long run.

When he was done with his burger, he sat staring intently at the spreadsheet on his screen. He had three columns set up: "Lille Funnel," "Horsham Funnel," and "Supplies." He had scribbled the pros and cons of the two choices, filling each column about halfway to the bottom of the screen when he realized his decision was obvious. Send them some money—he could melt down some silver and copper coins for that—and have them sit tight somewhere until the weather cleared. It was a lot safer than sending them off on another journey.

Jim grabbed the last two french fries off his plate, dipped them in barbecue sauce, and stuffed them in his mouth. He walked out of the restaurant and got into his car. Putting the laptop on the passenger seat, he then pulled out of the parking lot. He didn't go straight home—he had some shopping to do, and preparation for when they arrived in Lille.

20
Conflict

June 22, 1614

"Think about it, Ty," Jessi said. "Wouldn't Jim be giving us directions based on the funnel 'cause that's where he's looking from? So when he said south, that would mean south toward the church, right? So it's north *to* the funnel next to a big tree—and there is a big tree right over there! Just look at it!" She pointed excitedly. "That has to be the place!"

Mr. Doullens waited patiently. He couldn't understand a word they said, but he could tell they were working it out. He looked up at the sky—more rain was coming. He glanced over to the clock on the church tower—5:15; he wouldn't be leaving town tonight. He had friends with whom he could spend the night. *But not all three of us.*

He twisted around and examined their faces; they appeared to have settled their debate. "Tyler," he said as he shifted in his seat, "have you decided what you're going to do?"

"Yes sir," he answered. "We're fine now; we're ready to go."

They hopped off the back of the wagon and grabbed their backpacks. Pulling them up over their shoulders, they walked around to the front of the wagon and said good-bye to Mr. Doullens, thanking him for letting them stay at his farm and for the safe trip to Lille. With a tip of his hat, a flick of the reins, and a 'clack-clack' to the horses, the wagon jumped forward and Mr. Doullens disappeared around the corner of the church.

* * * * * *

Tyler and Jessi looked at each other and shrugged. "Well," Jessi said, "that's what I call a man of few words!"

They walked across the cobblestone street and stepped onto the grass, their feet sinking in the soft wet turf, and went straight towards the huge tree in the middle of the park. Muddy rainwater ran straight through the middle of the green space. They stood about 10 feet away from the tree and looked around, making sure they were alone.

"Jim?" Jessi called out timidly. "Ty, I feel like a three-year-old talking to my imaginary friend," she giggled self-consciously. "Jim, are you there?"

"Hello?" Tyler added in a louder voice. "I don't think he's here, Jess."

"Yes, I am! I'm here!" Jim shouted. "I hadn't turned my microphone on! I'm *so* glad to see you two. All right, so what happened to your clothes? Speak up, 'cause it's hard to hear you over the water."

Jessi smiled. "We traded them for these fancy duds: the latest in 1614 fashion!" She twirled in a circle, making her dress fan out. "What do you think? Cool, huh?"

"Very cool, Jessi," Jim replied. "But listen up. We have a problem here, and it has to do with all this water, 'cause it's flowing right through the middle of the funnel! Basically I can't bring you home from here unless it's dry in the funnel, 'cause all that water would come with you; so either you wait there for dry weather, or go to another funnel. Hang on a sec."

Jim was looking over his notes when his phone started ringing. His caller ID told him it was Todd from L.A. "Hey, I need to disconnect, I'll get right back to you ... in about twenty minutes, okay? Stay right there."

Tyler swallowed hard. His brain told him it all made sense, but the pit in his stomach hit him so hard he thought he was gonna throw up. *We're supposed to be home tonight,* he thought.

Jessi started shaking her head. "No, no, NO! What's he mean by saying 'another twenty minutes, okay?' Then click he's *gone?* No, this *isn't* okay. He's taking us home today—*NOW!*" she shouted. "*He's* not the one sleeping on the ground. *He's* not the one having to eat all these crummy energy bars." Her face was red and her fists were clenched as she paced in circles. "*He's* not having to walk all those "*leeoos*" on stupid dirt roads," she continued. "I want to sleep in my *own* bed tonight. I've had *enough* of his lame reasons for—"

She stopped as Tyler grabbed each of her arms just above the wrist. She squirmed viciously to break away, but he held on. "Let me go!" she shouted. She looked him dead in the eyes, her face flushed with rage. "Let *GO* of me!"

"No," he said firmly. "You listen to me. You gotta calm down—now!"

"Let … go … of … *ME!*" she spat out through clenched teeth.

"NO, you *have* to listen to me! We're in this together—together! We *need* each other, and I … I *need* you. But you're no good to me, or yourself, when you … you … you lose control like this."

She let out a strained shaky breath. "Tyler, let go of my arms."

The image of her giving Parker Theissen a black eye came to his mind. "Promise you won't hit me. Promise?"

She managed a meager smile. "How can I hit a guy who just told me he needs me?"

Tyler slowly released his grip, but didn't let go her hands. "Jessi, I don't like this either. But we're in this *together*, and we gotta be smart about *everything* we say and do. If we draw too much attention to ourselves, we could get in trouble here, and there's no one around to help us. It's just you and me."

"Yeah, well, you know me. Always ready to speak my mind—it's not exactly the best part of me."

"I think that's what I like the most about you, well … except for the out-of-control part."

"Really?" she asked. "You mean that?" The intensity in his bright green eyes caught her by surprise.

"Really."

Her face relaxed as she looked deep into his eyes, making Tyler's heart skip a beat. *Oh wow*, he thought.

"Ty?"

"Yeah?"

"You can let go of my hands now."

"Oh." He felt his face flush as he looked past her. "Let's take a walk," he offered. "We've got some time to kill."

They decided to get a closer look at the stained-glass windows of the church and made their way through the soggy grass to the street. Ten minutes later they had walked all the way around the church, totally impressed with the massive building, and were back where they started. They were about to step back onto the grass when they heard a familiar voice call out.

"Hey there, rat-face! Nice of you to drop by!"

Tyler froze. Sick with dread, he watched as the would-be thief approached them.

The young man was still in his long coat. He walked up to Tyler and with his left hand took a firm grip of his right arm. Tyler tried to twist away, but the older teenager was too strong for him. He tightened his right hand into a fist. "Welcome to my neighborhood," he said. "I told you I would be looking for you; maybe you should have been looking out for me!"

"Leave us alone!" Jessi yelled as she charged at him.

Hearing the unfamiliar English made him hesitate just long enough for Jessi to ram her shoulder into his side. The bully let go of Tyler as he fell to the ground, but he immediately sprang back up, his face purple with rage.

"You'll pay for that," he hollered, turning away from Tyler to take on Jessi.

The sound of horses' hooves and the rattling of wheels on the cobblestone street suddenly interrupted the fight. Mr. Doullens had returned, and all three faced the approaching wagon. He set the brake and jumped down to the street, and in three quick steps was toe-to-toe with the thief.

He looked the young man square in the eyes. "Is there a problem here?"

"No sir, not at all. They had fallen down, and I was just helping them up." He turned away from Mr. Doullens and asked, "You two okay now? Good!" As he walked away he looked at Tyler, raising his left hand to shield his face from Mr. Doullens. "I'll see you later," he said pleasantly, but with a menacing sneer.

Mr. Doullens waited until he was out of earshot. "Are you two okay?" he asked, obviously concerned.

Tyler exhaled deeply. "We are *now*, sir. Thank you."

"Did you find your friend?"

"Yes, sir." Tyler replied. "He had something to do, so he asked us to wait a little longer for him, and then that thief found us here. Thank you so much for coming back."

"Well, I thought it would be best you met up with your friend before I left for good."

Mr. Doullens waited with them on the steps of the church for another 10 minutes; all three of them keeping a sharp lookout for the bully, but they never saw any sign of him. Feeling they were no longer in any danger, and knowing their friend was returning soon, he bid them good-bye and left them sitting on the steps of the church.

He walked across the street to his wagon, released the brake, and with the familiar shake of the reins and "clack-clack" to the horses, he smiled and waved at them as he pulled away. They walked across the street towards the park, but no sooner had they reached the grass than the young man appeared from around the corner where he had been hiding. "Alright, rat-face," he yelled at Tyler. "This time you're not getting away!"

Tyler spun around and started running towards the center of the park. The young man quickly caught up with him and pushed him from behind, knocking him down to the ground, mud and grass splattering his face. The bully placed his foot on Tyler's back, pinning him to the ground. "Let the fun begin!" the thief said with a laugh.

Tyler squeezed his eyes shut, dreading what was coming next. He heard a thump, and something hit his leg as his assailant fell to the ground next to him. He looked up—Jessi was running towards him.

"I got him!" she cried. She ran up and gave the thief a vicious kick in the ribs—he didn't move. "I got him with this rock and on the first try, too!"

"Thanks, Jess. You've got a good arm. I probably would have missed!"

Jessi and Tyler stood over the thief. He had rinsed the manure off his coat, but the warm smell remained. "Phew! He stinks," Jessi sneered.

"What now?" Tyler asked.

"Leave him, I guess," Jessi answered as she placed the heel of her boot firmly on his hand as she walked away. They left him lying on the ground and hurried over to the funnel.

"What's going on, guys? Are you okay?" Jim asked.

It was *real* good to hear Jim's voice.

"Yeah, we're okay," Jessi said. "But we have to get out of here before that guy wakes up."

They told him about witnessing the attempted theft of the Laughing Boy statue and of their rescue by Mr. Doullens.

There was a pause. "Jim?"

"Yeah, I'm here. Okay, now listen up. Like I said before, I can't bring you back right now because of the water, and obviously you can't hang around there because of this guy who's chasing after you. I'm sorry, but I'm going to have to send you on another trip. You need to go to a funnel outside of London, and I'll bring you back from there. It's just too dangerous for you to stay, so you have to go, and right away!"

"Jim," Jessi pleaded, "are you sure? I'd *really* rather stay here and wait for dry weather, even if it means dealing with that moron over there."

"No. Jim's right, Jessi," Tyler put in. "It's not safe here. We gotta keep a low profile, and it could be weeks before this place dries out." He looked up as a few scattered drops of rain fell on his face.

Jim told them where the next funnel was and had them get in the water downstream from the funnel so they could catch the supplies he'd be sending them. After glancing nervously over their shoulders at the figure on the ground behind them, they plunged into the water and waited, their feet getting soaked as water seeped in through the seams in their boots.

Within moments they heard the familiar inward-blowing of air, followed by a *shuunk* as their supplies arrived. Two soccer balls sealed in duct tape appeared out of thin air and dropped into the water, floating quickly towards them. They each grabbed a ball as they came by. In the meantime there was another hiss of air and a *shuunk* as something else arrived. Long and thin, it quickly sunk down into the water. They ran forward and plunged their hands into the cold muddy water, pulling up two compound bows and a large supply of arrows.

"That's it!" Jim said. "Now get out of the water and open up the balls, get out the rope and tie that guy up. Leave him over there and then come back."

They dropped to the ground and examined the soccer balls. Silver duct tape was wrapped all the way around each ball. Jessi peeled the tape off of her ball, and it fell apart in two pieces. Inside they found sealed sandwich bags: one had a cigarette lighter and a small drawstring leather pouch; another had a tiny envelope filled with a large supply of arrowheads; the third baggie had a knife, and what looked like a garage door opener, but no rope!

After another glance at the bully, Tyler tore the tape off of his ball. His also had a lighter, an identical leather pouch, a tiny envelope, a hunting knife, a hundred feet of nylon rope, and a retractable utility knife.

Following Jim's instructions, they ran over and first tied the thief's ankles together and then his hands behind his back. When that was done, they both breathed a sigh of relief and went back to talk to Jim.

He told them again the town in England where the funnel was and how to locate it. "That's not a remote control; see the little screen? It's a homing device. I'll leave a transmitter at the next funnel that sends out a radio signal, so you can find the exact location of the funnel once you're in the general area. Okay, now bring that punk over here so I can talk to him, but don't say anything to me when you come back with him. Just put him down and then you two hit the road —pronto!"

It was a bit of a struggle, but they eventually dragged him by the feet to the edge of the water, rather enjoying getting him thoroughly covered with mud. After pausing for a moment Jessi scooped a little mud on her index finger and drew an "X" across his forehead, snapping her hand back as he began to stir. They were walking away when Tyler abruptly stopped, did an about-face, and went back. He hesitated for just a moment, and then delivered a hard kick into the bully's rib cage; he thought he heard a crack. "My turn," he said smugly. Then, grinning, he silently waved good-bye to Jim.

* * * * * *

June 19, Current Year

Jim rotated his field of view and watched them until they disappeared from sight. Seeing them walk away—again—was almost too much. *Okay, so what am I gonna do with this guy? I don't speak French.*

He spun around in his chair towards the second monitor, his fingers flying across the keyboard. Moments later his French Language database appeared. He put on headphones, took a deep breath, and pushed a special function key. His shoulders shot up as his head jerked back; a moment later he let out a deep groan, took off his headphones, and started rubbing the back of his head.

He stood up shakily. "I need some aspirin," he said in French.

A couple minutes later he was back in front of the first monitor, squinting slightly because of the throbbing in his head. With every passing minute he found himself growing angrier with this unknown troublemaker. Eventually the figure began to stir and soon was writhing in anger and frustration at finding himself tied up.

"Stop squirming, you filthy vermin," Jim snarled into the microphone. He smiled as he watched the figure turn and look to see who was speaking to him. The kid's anger became total panic when he couldn't see anyone. Jim got an idea then, and he smiled broadly. "I'm right here. I see you, but you cannot see me!"

The young man froze, wild-eyed at the unseen voice speaking to him. "Don't hurt me, spirit," he pleaded. "Please don't hurt me!" The thief had taken the bait.

"I'm not going to hurt you. It's more fun taunting you, you pathetic piece of dirt. I'm with you everywhere you go, you worm. I gave you the idea of stealing that statue—did you think you thought of that yourself?" Jim was enjoying this. "Now you just roll on home. Soon you will be hanging from a rope around your neck, and THEN I will hurt you, again and again ... forever!"

Jim laughed an evil laugh, slowly turning the volume down so it would seem like the spirit was floating away. He watched the young man bury his nose into the mud, panic-stricken and sobbing violently. Jim crossed his arms with a contented grin.

"That was *awesome!*"

21
A New Direction

June 22, 1614

Tyler and Jessi quickly moved out of the park, anxious to be out of sight of their attacker before he woke up. They paused briefly to get their bearings. The thick clouds made it difficult to be certain where the sun was, but they soon determined the direction to take, and headed north out of town.

Within 10 minutes they saw they were reaching the edge of the city; ahead of them was open farmland, and in the distance, untamed forest. After a few more minutes they came to a fork in the road; the one they were on continuing straight, the other branching sharply to the left. There were no signs to indicate which way they should go.

"What do you—oh, wait!" Jessi exclaimed. "The map Jim gave us in Amiens!"

They dropped their backpacks to the ground, and in moments had the map opened up. They had never worked with maps before, and it took them a few minutes, and a little bit of arguing, before they were certain they were looking at it properly.

Their last doubts were settled when Tyler traced his finger up to the left and pointed to a town on the edge of the English Channel. "Calais! That's the place! That's the town Jim said we should go to, to get to England."

Jessi looked at where Tyler's finger was resting. "That says, 'Calase?'"

"No, you don't pronounce the *s*."

"How do you know that?" she asked.

"I don't know. I just do," he shrugged.

Looking again at the map, they could see that Calais was actually more to the west, so they figured they should leave the road they were on and go left. Jessi folded the map and put it in her backpack.

"Let's check out everything else," Tyler said. "We were in such a hurry to get away from that guy we never looked at the other stuff Jim sent us."

They dug deeper into their backpacks and pulled out the little packages they had gotten out of the soccer balls. They each released the drawstring on the little leather pouches and poured the contents into their hands. Their palms were filled with little blobs of metal and a note from Jim. He had sent them money—sort of. He had gotten some old silver coins and copper pennies and melted them down to "trade for food or whatever you need."

After pouring the silver and copper back into the bag, Tyler pulled out his tiny envelope; it felt like it had a couple small rocks inside. Opening the flap on the end, he poured the contents into his hand. His mouth fell open as he silently looked in disbelief at what he was holding.

Meanwhile, Jessi pulled *her* envelope out, opened the flap, and looked inside. Startled, she then very gently shook out the contents into her open palm. Wide-eyed, she slowly turned towards Tyler. "Diamonds?"

Tyler never took his eyes off the two diamonds in his own hand. "Uh-huh," was all he could manage.

"Why, do you think?"

"They've gotta be worth a fortune. With these we could buy, or trade, for anything we wanted!"

"I think I know," Jessi ventured. "Jim said to get a boat to England. This way we can rent or even *buy* one!"

"We don't know how to sail a boat."

"No, but now we can hire someone to take us there!"

After looking around to see if anyone noticed what they had in their hands, they put everything away in their backpacks.

"I've never carried anything this valuable in my life!" Tyler said uneasily. "I don't know if I'm happier with the diamonds or more stressed we may be robbed."

"Let's go with happy, what d'ya say," Jessi answered nervously.

They slung their backpacks onto their shoulders, picked up their bows and arrows, and headed down the new road. Unfortunately, neither of them were able to suppress their thoughts of the ridiculous number of things that could go wrong on this next leg of their journey.

* * * * * *

Over the next couple hours very little changed around them. Mostly they saw open forest, occasionally interrupted by a farm that was sometimes nestled right up against the road, other times seen in the distance. It didn't take long at all to get accustomed to the solitude and quiet of the open road. The sounds of the city of Lille, though quite different from those of their own neighborhood, had in a way felt familiar and comfortable; but the city sounds were gone now, consumed by the surrounding trees and the distance they were putting behind them.

As they rounded a bend in the road, the setting sun shone directly in their eyes through a small break in the clouds. It was barely above the horizon, and they had to shield the rays of the sun with their hands to see clearly what was ahead.

"You know, Ty," Jessi began. "We need to find a place to spend the night. It's gonna be dark pretty soon." She pointed ahead to the right. "Maybe over there in those trees?"

With a grunt, Tyler reset his backpack on his shoulders. "Yeah, that has potential. Let's check it out."

They moved on and were soon in the relatively cool shade of the trees. It only took a couple minutes for them to locate their home for the night, about 30 yards from the road. It was an old oak tree that had cast up tall roots next to a hollow in the ground, enclosing three sides and making a small protected area just the size of a tent—that is, if they *had* a tent.

They dropped their backpacks and prepared to set up camp for the night, which didn't take long; they didn't have much gear. After rolling out his sleeping bag, Tyler pulled out his packet of arrowheads. There were eight blunt-tipped heads, and eight with razor-sharp edges sloping back from an equally sharp tip—clearly designed to kill. His stomach tightened at the sight.

All the arrowheads had threads at their base to screw into the tips of the arrows. Jessi watched silently as Tyler picked up one of the arrows that he had set on the ground and screwed in one of the sharp arrowheads. Standing up he set the arrow to the string and pulled back. The bow resisted, but as he kept pulling the resistance suddenly eased off, and he found he could hold the string back with surprisingly little effort. He lifted the bow and took aim at a large tree about 30 feet away. He let go of the string. With a speed he wasn't prepared for, the arrow was suddenly gone, a moment later embedded in the tree. It was barely an inch away from flying right by and missing it entirely.

"Nice shot, Ty," Jessi said with admiration.

"Well, not really," he said. "I was aiming at the middle of the tree, and it's a *big* one."

They walked over to the tree, and Tyler gave a tug on the arrow—it didn't budge. He pulled harder and then started wiggling it up and down. Finally, the tree released its hold, and the arrow came free in his hand.

"That was stuck in there pretty hard." He frowned.

"Maybe we should use the blunt arrowheads for target practice," Jessi offered. "And save the others for ..." She let her voice trail off.

"I've seen you doing target practice in your backyard with that set you got from Jim. Is that what you used?"

"Yeah. He also had the sharp ones, but I've never used them."

They returned to their gear and fitted all of their arrows with the blunt-tipped arrowheads. The next hour flew by as they practiced to improve their skills. They had slowly worked their way further and further from their target tree until they were consistently hitting it from about a hundred feet away. Darkness finally forced them to stop, and they returned to their campsite, flush with the excitement of a new-found sport—and the potential for fresh meat.

Tyler took the tips off his arrows. "Ya know," he said, "I was concentrating so much on the target practice, I never noticed how hungry I was."

Jessi dug into her backpack, "Here, have a couple energy bars."

They ate the last two boiled eggs given them by Mrs. Moreau first, downing them with gulps of water. Tyler peeled the wrapper off his energy bar and took a big bite; after a few seconds his chewing slowed down and then stopped. He stared ahead, frowning slightly as he slowly moved the food around in his mouth. "This energy bar is a lot saltier, and sweeter, than I remember," he said tentatively. "I think a week of Mrs. Doullens' cooking changed what my taste buds are used to."

They refilled their water bottles at a nearby stream and returned to camp. By now it was almost pitch black and getting colder, so they slipped their ponchos on over their cloaks. So much had happened—it was hard to believe they had been at the Moreau's house that morning, and just two days ago they had been at the Doullens' farm.

"Ty?" Jessi started. "What d'ya think of this hunting thing, really?"

"I don't think we have a choice. We can't just keep eating energy bars."

"I suppose," she reluctantly answered. "I just have a feeling it's gonna get us in trouble somehow."

"We'll be careful. Go to sleep, Jessi. It'll be okay."

"Yeah, I guess you're right," she replied, but she didn't sound convinced. It took a long time before she finally fell asleep.

22
A Hunting Trip

Monday, June 23, 1614

They woke up early to the sounds of birds chirping in the trees overhead, welcoming the approaching sunrise. The top of the tarp was heavy with dew, and they were glad they had figured out to put it *above* them, not under. They shed their ponchos and stood in the early morning light, rubbing their right arms.

"My arm hurts!" Tyler moaned.

"Mine too," Jessi added. "I think we used a whole bunch of new muscles with our target practice yesterday."

"You're probably right. Umm, ya wanna travel again today, or …"

"Or what?"

"Well," Tyler continued, "the only food we've got are these energy bars, and they won't last very long if that's all we have to eat. Why don't we spend a day here practicing our shot, and see if we can hunt down something to eat. If we don't have any luck, we could always go back into Lille for food. What d'ya think?"

"Wow—spend all day walking along a dusty road, or hang around and shoot arrows and maybe get some game for dinner? Hmm, let me think about that!" In the light of day her worries from the night before seemed silly. *It'll be fine*, she thought.

It only took a few minutes to warm up their sore muscles, and by midday they felt ready to go hunting. But where, and what would they hunt for?

They changed the tips on their arrows and hung them in a leather pouch from a loop on their cloaks so the arrowheads wouldn't poke them. They agreed where the sun would be setting in relationship to their campsite, so they wouldn't get lost; but, just to be safe, they made a triangle with three rocks as a marker by the side of the road.

They soon found a small trail that wound through the trees, apparently made by animals, as it wasn't wide enough to be a man-made trail. With eyes and ears wide open, they moved in single file with Jessi in the lead, doing their best to keep as quiet as possible. Almost an hour went by with no hint of game.

Rounding a small turn in the trail, Jessi froze so quickly that Tyler, looking to the left, almost ran into her. He leaned forward and lightly touched Jessi's arm. "What is it?" he whispered.

Jessi didn't turn around but kept looking forward, her eyes straining to capture even the slightest movement ahead of her, as she slowly lifted her finger and placed it in front of her pursed lips. Tyler crept up beside her and carefully searched the forest around them. Long moments later, Jessi began moving forward cautiously, scanning both sides of the trail. Suddenly, with no warning, there was a rustle in the bushes ahead and a thudding sound of hooves receding into the underbrush.

"So what was it?" Tyler asked.

"I dunno," Jessi muttered. "But it went that way."

Fifty feet ahead of them, they found evidence of the animal. "I think that's deer poop," Jessi said. "What do they call it ... uh ... scat! Yeah, they call it scat."

"Really? How do you know that?"

"I heard my dad talking about it. It seemed like a funny word for poop."

To their right they could see where it had been lying—the tall grass was pressed down in a small circle about three feet across.

"Probably lying low for the day—until we came along," Tyler muttered.

They looked around carefully, doing their best to learn whatever they could about the habits of the animal. Looking back where they had come from, Jessi felt a slight breeze cooling the beads of sweat on her forehead. Of course! They were upwind of the deer, and it probably smelled them before it heard them!

They found another trail—one that went *into* the wind, and started following it. With renewed energy and knowing there really *was* prey to be found, they began again. Time passed slowly, and quiet determination replaced their initial excitement.

Finally, seeing movement in the forest ahead of them, Jessi again stopped in her tracks. She slowly searched all the details of the forest, even as she was lifting a hand in a gesture to Tyler behind her to be as still as possible. A few moments later she spotted the animal; it *was* a deer, and she had almost been looking right at it but didn't see it until it had moved!

Jessi waited until it was looking elsewhere, and then slowly fit an arrow to the string of her bow. The deer was about a hundred feet away—nearly the same distance as their target practice.

She lifted the bow and slowly pulled back on the string. She felt the bow relax its tension, telling her the arrow was ready to release. It was then she realized she wasn't certain where to aim. Her left arm shook a little from the adrenaline sweeping through her body. The deer was standing sideways to her, presenting a perfect target.

Aiming for the neck, Jessi released the arrow. It flew straight at its target but struck the ground just two feet short of the animal. Startled, the deer sprang away and disappeared into the shadows beyond.

"Dang it!" Jessi stomped the ground. "I really thought I had it!"

They quietly went forward to retrieve the arrow. Tyler picked it up and started to hand it to Jessi, but abruptly pulled it back, bouncing it gently in his upraised palm.

"Jess," he said quietly. "I think this head is heavier than the ones we practiced with. Maybe that's why it fell short?"

"Yeah, you may be right, 'cause it sure felt good when I let it go."

They each took a drink of water, soothing their parched throats, and resumed their hunt. Ten minutes later they came across what they presumed was the same deer, but it was too far away for a shot, so they quietly crept forward.

Dropping on all fours, Jessi motioned to Tyler to come up next to her, and together they surveyed the forest around them. They decided to have Tyler move about a hundred feet to the right, and then together they would move towards the deer.

"Take your time, and good luck!" Jessi whispered quietly in Tyler's ear. "Oh, and one more thing," she hissed, "don't shoot *me*." Tyler replied with a grin and a wink as he moved away.

Jessi watched him leave, impressed with how quietly Tyler moved among the trees. When he reached his destination, they nodded to each other and slowly started moving towards the deer.

Patiently working their way forward, Jessi felt she was at the right distance to take another shot, and Tyler was out of harm's way. Lifting her bow and fitting the arrow to the string, she pulled back and took aim. Tyler stepped sideways to get behind a bush out of sight of the deer, and a dry tree limb snapped beneath his foot as his weight came down on it.

Instinctively the deer sprang forward, and Jessi stood to her feet, causing the deer to immediately see her and start running away. In desperation she released a wild shot that sailed harmlessly over the deer as the arrow silently disappeared among the trees.

"No, not again!" she clenched her teeth in frustration as Tyler rejoined her.

"I'm so sorry. I didn't see an old tree limb, and it broke as I stepped on it," Tyler explained.

"I would have gotten it this time, too!" she shouted accusingly.

Tyler blinked hard as she saw anger rising inside him. "I didn't do it on purpose! So back off!"

They stood there a few moments before Jessi let out a deep breath. "Nah, it's not your fault. Maybe I would've got it, maybe not. It's a lot easier hitting a target that isn't running away. We'll keep trying."

Tyler took a deep breath and let it slowly out. Jessi could almost feel him relax. After pausing a moment he looked in the direction the deer had run. "Let's go find your arrow," he offered.

They spent the next 20 minutes looking for her arrow without any luck. Finally, they gave up the search, and after deciding on what direction to head next, again resumed the hunt.

Another hour passed by as they continued to follow trail after trail, but they never saw another trace of the deer. When they saw the sun was low in the sky, they decided to head back to their campsite with no further delay. It took about 15 minutes for them to reach the road, where they faced a dilemma; where on the road were they? Tyler thought they had already passed by this spot, but Jessi wasn't so sure.

They sat down and scratched out in the dirt as best they could exactly in what directions they had traveled during their hunt. They decided to go right and headed west along the road. An anxious 20 minutes later, the road broke into an opening, and they saw once again in the distance the trees they had looked to for shelter the day before. Though tired and hungry, they pressed forward at a fast pace and were soon back within the friendly confines of their campsite.

They dropped their bows and arrows on the ground and looked around with disappointment. Hunger gnawed at their stomachs and discouragement ate away at their spirits. At least they had energy bars.

Safely under their camouflage tarp, they could see a small portion of the road through the trees. They knew they would never be noticed by any passing travelers, especially since they had trouble spotting their campsite even when they knew where to look. Tyler was about to open an energy bar when they both heard a commotion on the road.

Carefully crawling forward through the trees, they found a place where they could see what was going on without being seen. Slightly to their left, a wagon had broken down. The right wheel had completely pulled off its axle, and the wagon had fallen hard towards the ditch along the road. Several wooden cages were scattered on the ground, and inside two of them numerous chickens squawked loudly. One cage had broken open, the chickens had escaped, and the driver was vainly trying to recapture them.

He gave up when the chickens disappeared into the trees on the opposite side of the road from Jessi and Tyler. Returning his attention to his wagon, the driver set his efforts to the necessary repairs. Tyler and Jessi watched with amusement as he put the wheel back on the axle and secured it in place, all the while continuing a constant stream of angry conversation with himself, and to the chickens that had escaped.

Jessi didn't *really* need an interpreter, but nevertheless, she leaned close to Tyler's ear and whispered "What's he saying?"

"I'd tell you," Tyler snickered, "but I'd be grounded for a month if my parents heard me talking like that!"

They both started laughing, but knew they'd dare not make a sound, so they quietly lay on the ground, their chests silently heaving until they ached; it wasn't necessary, because the man would never have heard them over his own ranting. Eventually he threw the broken cage onto his wagon, and with a final angry glare, and rude gesture towards the trees, he spurred his horse on and quickly left the scene.

"That was more entertaining than any movie I've seen this year!" Jessi snorted.

They returned to their campsite and sat down, but Jessi abruptly jumped back up to her feet and announced, "I'm going hunting!"

Tyler looked up at her. "Ugh! Tomorrow, Jess."

"For chickens!" she said with a smile.

It didn't take long to locate the chickens: they were not bred to be silent. From 20 feet away, Jessi took aim at her target and released an arrow. It missed the chicken by barely an inch, and the chicken squawked and fluttered off, stopping a mere 30 feet further away.

Tyler took a few steps forward. "My turn this time," he muttered. He pulled his string back until the tension was relieved, took in a slight breath and held it, then released the arrow. The arrow found its target and pinned the fowl to the ground. The chicken quickly grew still.

"Way to go, Ty!" Jessi hollered. "Dinner!"

Jessi reclaimed her arrow while Tyler ran forward and reclaimed his—from the chicken. Through the trees they could hear the clucking of another chicken—another meal! Ten minutes and two shots later, Jessi brought down the second chicken off a low branch on a nearby tree. In the distance they could hear the third chicken expressing its disapproval of their hunt.

Back at the campsite, Tyler threw his chicken down on the ground. "Now what? How do we cook these things?" he asked.

"Don't you remember how Mrs. Doullens did it? She dipped it in boiling water, and then pulled off the feathers and fried it!"

"I'm sorry, have you been toting a big pot of water I don't know about? Besides, we don't have a fire on which to put the pot we don't have in the first place."

"Details! Mere details!"

By the time they had plucked all the feathers off the chickens, and they were ready for roasting, it had grown completely dark. While Jessi started a fire, Tyler skewered the chickens with long sticks to hold them over the flames.

"Oh! Don't forget the salt and 'extremely rare' pepper. I almost feel guilty that we took it," Jessi said, "though it really was nice of her!" It took a long time to roast the chickens, turning them over and over until the meat was thoroughly cooked, but they had plenty of firewood available. Their arms ached from the effort, but they both agreed it was the best chicken they had ever eaten.

By the time they were done they had almost eaten one whole chicken. They cut the second chicken into pieces with the hunting knife and placed the meat inside one of the plastic bags Jim had sent them. They cleaned their knives as best they could on some grass nearby, returned them to their sheaths, and leaned back to enjoy their fire.

"Awesome day, Jessi," Tyler murmured. "See? There was nothing to worry about!"

"Yeah, you're right," Jessi agreed, feeling foolish now for thinking that something bad was going to happen. "We're gonna do this, Ty. We're gonna get home."

Tyler held his hand up towards her, and she responded with a gentle and quiet high five. They let the fire die down, and the flames were reduced to dull orange coals before they finally drifted off to sleep, each dreaming their own version of their hunting triumph.

23
The March West

Tuesday, June 24, 1614

Jessi shivered in the cold stillness of the early morning. She reached down to pull the blankets up closer to her chin, but her hands couldn't find them. She opened her eyes and looked at the underside of the tarp, and realized where she was. Three feet away Tyler lay curled up on his side, still sleeping soundly. She thought about the prior day, smiling quietly about shooting the chicken, and having come so close to getting a deer as well.

She looked through the trees up to the sky and saw the fluffy white of early-morning clouds. It looked like after all that rain, they were going to get a second day of some decent weather.

She sat up and looked at the dead embers from last night's fire. She could make another fire, but why bother when they would be leaving anyway—and besides, in the daytime someone might see the smoke and come search them out. *We don't need that.*

The sky was steadily growing brighter, and more and more birds started waking up with the morning light—and various other creatures as well. Occasionally a squirrel would run up and down a nearby tree, chattering at some unknown foe. Then somewhere to her right she heard a familiar sound but foreign to the forest: the third chicken!

She turned her head slightly, listening intently. A minute later she heard it again; it was a long way off, but now she knew in what direction to start her hunt! As quietly as possible so as not to disturb Tyler, she picked up her bow and a couple arrows, and crept away in the direction of the noise. She left her camouflage poncho on, not certain it mattered, but figuring it couldn't hurt.

She stealthily crept towards where she last heard the chicken, and waited. A couple minutes later she heard it again, much closer, only now it was to her left. Again, she crept forward then waited. Before long she heard the chicken again, not too far ahead of her but now a bit to her right. *The hunter closes in on its prey; the animal unaware of its impending doom*, she thought.

The next time she heard the clucking, she looked towards the source and spotted the chicken as it disappeared behind a tree. She decided it would be fun to practice her stalking, so she made a game of it, seeing how close she could get to the chicken before it sensed her presence and ran off again. She totally lost track of the time as she played in the forest.

* * * * * *

Plop! Opening his eyes, Tyler watched as a nut rolled off the tarp and landed on the ground at his feet. The angry chatter of a squirrel in the tree overhead told him that it had dropped the nut onto the tarp—and wanted it back. He reached over to poke Jessi and tell her what just happened, but she wasn't there.

"Jess?" he sat up with a frown, and looked around—nothing. He shrugged, then put his hands high over his head, stretched, and gave a loud yawn. He looked towards the east hoping to get an idea as to the time, but couldn't be sure—not that it mattered.

He got up and went out to the road, pausing briefly under the cover of the trees to see if the coast was clear before he stepped out in the open. He was alone, *very* alone. Suddenly he felt vulnerable, the most since their adventure had begun, and it struck fear into his heart. He plunged back into the trees and returned to the campsite.

He stopped in front of the tarp and carefully surveyed the scene. Everything was where it should be; nothing was out of place. The nut the squirrel had dropped was gone. *Didn't waste any time*, he thought. His eyes traced up the trunk of the tree into the branches overhead. If the squirrel was up there, it wasn't making its presence known at the moment.

He looked again around the campsite, his eyes resting briefly on his bow and arrows. Jessi's bow and a couple of her arrows were gone. She must have gone hunting without him. *Lame!* He knew Jessi could be just about anywhere, so it would be useless trying to find her—and a good way to get shot, by *her.* He pulled a chicken leg out of the bag, sat down, and had some breakfast. Despite his dejected attitude, it tasted pretty good.

He waited patiently for a while, but as time went by his patience wore thin, replaced with irritation, then concern, and then bordering on panic. Every sound in the forest began to alarm him—a sudden twitter of a bird overhead, or the loud chatter of the squirrel in the tree above. Slowly, without really noticing, he had backed up under the tarp, put his back against the roots of the tree, and tucked his knees up under his chin; his hunting knife lay at his side.

* * * * * *

Hiding behind a tree, Jessi waited, listening intently to locate the chicken once again. She glanced up at the sky; the sun was well above the horizon, and she knew instinctively that she had been gone a long time. Tyler would most certainly be awake. She looked around and realized she didn't know where she was. *Idiot!* Her breathing became fast and shallow as terror overwhelmed her. All interest in the chicken disappeared as she tried to pull her scattered thoughts together.

She thought about people who had been lost in the woods, with the television news stories showing search parties scouring the terrain from a helicopter. She wouldn't have *that* kind of help here. *What was it they say lost people should do?* She couldn't remember exactly, so she sat down and leaned against the tree she had just been hiding behind. She took a deep shaky breath and exhaled slowly, looking up at the leaves overhead.

That was it! Hug a tree! Hug a tree? What was that supposed to mean? Oh yeah, stay put until someone finds you instead of wandering all over the forest. That won't work for me here either, she thought. *Tyler? No. He wouldn't look for me 'cause that'd be a good way to get shot, by me.*

She tried to breathe slowly. *Keep calm*, she thought. *Now think.* *Our camp is on the north side of the road. I didn't cross the road. The sun rises in the east. That's it!* Jessi knew which way to go! Twenty minutes later she was on the road, looking up and down in each direction, but none of it looked remotely familiar. After 10 minutes at a brisk trot along the road heading in the direction of Lille, she arrived at their campsite.

Once she was under the protection of the trees, she stopped about 10 yards short of their campsite. Tyler wasn't there. As quietly as possible she moved to the right, so she could approach their site from the side. She crept forward, paying close attention to any noise or movement in the trees and bushes around her. Nothing. Where was Tyler?

Standing right next to the tarp, she heard a snuffling sound. She peered under the tarp. Tyler was hunched down, his back against the tree, hands clenched around his shins.

Jessi let her bow and arrows fall to the ground as she dropped to her knees, overwhelmed with guilt. "I'm so sorry, Ty," she stammered. "I ... I'm so sorry. I'm stupid. I ... I pulled a Parker! I was stalking that last chicken from yesterday and lost track of time. Then, I didn't know where I *was*, and got lost ..." Tyler glanced at her, then looked away. She didn't blame him. She could hear with her own ears just how pathetic her excuses were. She stopped talking altogether and looked at him, silently pleading for him to respond. But he wouldn't acknowledge her. She thought of all the times she had called him her "first friend" and realized again how stupid that had been. Finally, he took a deep breath and let it out.

"So you know what it's like then," he said. "To be alone ... here."

"I'll never leave you alone again, Ty. I promise." She leaned forward and put her arms around him, tears filling her eyes. "Like you told me the other day in Lille," she said softly. "We *have* to stick together ... *all* the time ... until we get back home. Aw, Tyler, I'm sorry. I'm so, so sorry."

* * * * * *

With barely a word, they packed up all their belongings and headed for the road. They paused briefly before coming out of the trees, then turned right and headed west. Hours passed by as they kept pushing forward, putting mile after mile behind them. Whenever they passed anyone along the road, they kept to themselves, keeping their eyes down and going on without incident. By the end of the day, they had traveled maybe 15 miles.

Tyler split the last of the chicken between them for their evening meal. He handed Jessi her portion and took a bite of his own—and immediately spat it out.

"Eww," he grimaced. "Don't eat it, Jess! It's gone bad!" He took a swig of water, swished it around in his mouth, and spat it out. "I thought it tasted a little funny at lunch. No wonder Mom throws out the chicken in the morning when someone's left it out all night."

"Someone like you?" Jessi asked. Without waiting for an answer she unzipped her backpack and fished out a couple energy bars for each of them. "Here," she said as she handed him his dinner. "This should be okay. It says it's best if eaten sometime within the next 400 years."

"Kinda like Twinkies?" he asked.

Laughing, they sat down to eat. Relief flowed over her like a cool breeze as she realized her chicken hunt fiasco was behind them. She happily watched as he ate his energy bar.

He looked at her. "What?"

"Oh, nothing," she lied.

They sat beside each other in front of a small fire and ate their energy bars, quietly mesmerized by the flames and listening to the frogs singing their chorus. Finally, they threw some dirt on the coals and went to sleep.

* * * * * *

Wednesday, June 25, 1614

The rays of the rising sun woke them up. Refreshed from a good night's rest after the prior day's walk, they were ready for another day. They were sitting under their tarp, enjoying the warmth of the sun on their faces, when a quick movement to their right caught their attention. A small gray rabbit darted in and out of the thick grass and bushes around them, never staying in the same spot for more than five or six seconds before moving on. They quietly picked up their bows and arrows, each of them fitting an arrow on the string as they rose to their feet.

They separated from each other, putting about 50 feet between them, and then slowly advanced upon their prey. Tyler shot first and just missed the rabbit, which then ran rapidly in the direction of Jessi; upon seeing her, it made a fatal error and stopped momentarily. Jessi's arrow found its mark, and the rabbit shuddered a few times, kicking its feet before growing still. It was hard to watch. *I just killed a bunny rabbit*, she thought.

Tyler retrieved his arrow and joined Jessi next to her kill. "Nice shot," he said.

"We make a good team," she offered.

"Yeah … we do," Tyler answered with an affirming nod.

While packing up their campsite, they saw another rabbit, and then another, and within half an hour had bagged three more. They tied two rabbits to each backpack and hit the road once again, their spirits considerably higher than the previous day. Whenever a passerby would see the animals hanging off their backpacks, an approving smile would be given, making their journey even more enjoyable.

They stopped at midday, gathered up some dry wood, and made a fire. Tyler gutted and skinned two rabbits while Jessi found two branches that split into a "Y" shape, pounding them into the ground on each side of the fire. Grimacing, she skewered the rabbits on a long stick and laid the stick on the Y-shaped branches, suspending the rabbits nicely over the flames.

In less than an hour they had eaten their fill and still had some left over. They then roasted the other two rabbits.

"Ty," Jessi mused, "does rabbit last about as long as chicken before it goes bad? What d'ya think?"

"Yeah, probably. Hey! Let's smoke them. Maybe if we just put them higher over the fire, we can dry the meat out enough, and they'll last longer. What've we got to lose?"

"Just our lunch?" Jessi smirked.

The meat wasn't dried to their satisfaction until late in the afternoon, and they only got a couple hours down the road before having to stop for the night. They agreed that a larger portion of each day would have to be devoted to the hunting and cooking of their food. If they spent an entire day walking, they'd go hungry.

*****

Day by day, they made steady progress towards the English Channel. A couple of nights they earned the luxury of sleeping in a barn in exchange for milking cows the next morning; the experience at the Doullens' farm had paid off. Two full days were spent under their tarp watching it rain; they measured out their food as if they were under enemy siege.

It was midday about a week later when the road began a long slow descent to a good-sized town several miles ahead of them. Just beyond that, they caught sight of the sea, as a light breeze carrying the distinct scent of salt water beckoned to them. Ships were slowly gliding across the water, their tall sails bright in the sunshine. It was a clear day, and in the far distance across the water they could see land.

"England," Tyler said with satisfaction.

24
Calais

Wednesday, July 2, 1614

They stepped off the road and rested in the shade of a tree. This was their first glimpse of the sea and reminded them of the Oregon Coast. But *here* they saw a town nestled against the water's edge, with sailing ships quietly moving across the blue-green expanse of the English Channel. It was a scene never to be forgotten.

Jessi pulled her knees up under her chin. "You know, Ty," she said, "I've been thinking. We've been really lucky so far. We haven't lost anything or been robbed, but I think we need to be more careful, especially now that we're getting to a town. If we lost our backpacks, we'd really be sunk."

"Way to go, Jessi. Now that you said it out loud something *is* going to happen."

"You believe that?"

Tyler just shrugged.

She opened her backpack and fished around for the tiny envelope with the two diamonds inside, along with the scrap of paper on which Jim had written his note. After looking around and making sure they were alone, she took off her boots. Rolling up one of the diamonds inside the paper, she stuffed it into the toe of her boot. She pushed the envelope with the second diamond up into the toe of the other boot, and tore a handful of grass up by the roots. After shoving some of the grass up into each of the toes, she put her boots back on. "I had a little extra room in there anyway," she said. "Maybe you should too, Ty."

Moments later a cart slowly came around the bend, pulled by a huge ox. The driver had a very long, thin stick, and every once in a while would flick it on the rump of the beast. Neither man nor beast seemed to notice it, or care, as the ox maintained its same slow pace. The goods behind the driver were completely covered by a large tarp, giving no hint as to the contents. After the cart was well past them, Tyler stuffed his diamonds in his boots; they then headed down the long slope towards the town, debating the best way to get passage across the water. In the end, they decided to just ask how much it would cost to pay for a ride on a boat and see what happened.

As they approached the edge of Calais, they came upon a market. Vendors had laid out their wares: lots of vegetables and fruit, leather goods, kitchen utensils, and other crafts, much of which they had no idea for what they were used. They hadn't eaten any greens in the last week, so the vegetables looked particularly appealing.

Tyler explained to a vendor that they didn't have any money. "I don't give my food away, so move on," was the curt reply. Tyler explained that they had some silver—if that would be okay. He pulled out what was probably once a dime and handed it to the man. After examining it briefly, he accepted it as payment for two cucumbers and six dried apples. They put the apples in their backpacks and started to walk off.

"Hey there!" he called out after them. "The first of our early season apples!" He tossed each of them two fresh apples, smiled, and waved them away.

Tyler started laughing.

"What's so funny?" Jessi asked.

"Oh, I just remembered how mad my mom gets 'cause I don't like to eat my vegetables!" He put the apples in his backpack and took a huge bite out of the cucumber.

They walked straight through town toward the water's edge, where the salty air gave way to the pungency of fish. A string of wood sidewalks stretched along the water for a half mile. It was clearly the main part of town. Up and down the piers there was a constant flurry of activity: people loading boats, others unloading, shouts of laughter, arguments, raised voices. Others were leaning against buildings in the shade, calmly watching everything going on. The noise and bustle were difficult to absorb after having spent so much time in the quiet of the countryside.

Jessi and Tyler didn't know what to expect, but Tyler hoped it would be obvious where he could go to buy tickets for passage to England. He looked for a sign for "Tickets," but it wasn't to be found. Plucking up courage, he walked up to a tall, thin man who was unloading some crates off of a boat.

"Excuse me, sir?" he timidly asked.

The man didn't even look up. "What do you want, boy?"

"My friend and I need to go to England. Can you take us there?"

"What? No, not interested, no. Go away, boy. Ask someone else." He turned his back to Tyler and grabbed another crate off his boat.

Tyler swallowed hard and walked away. They passed by two more boats before he mustered up the courage to try again. A muscular, bare-chested man walked by them and jumped onto the boat, whistling a quick little tune. Tyler gave his plea for help.

"Now what do you want to go there for?" the man asked. "Do you have papers?"

"Papers? What do you mean?" Tyler asked as he shifted uneasily in front of the man.

"Papers, boy." The man pointed his thumb towards the north. "England's another *country*. You can't go back and forth between two countries without papers. Understand?"

Tyler hadn't thought of this, and apparently neither had Jim!

Looking intently at Tyler, the man hesitated and looked around. In a quieter voice he asked, "What do you want to go there for? You should stay here, in your own country."

Sensing a small opening, Tyler pressed in. "My friend here is English, and ... she got separated from her family. I'm helping her get home." Tyler hoped he sounded convincing enough.

The man looked closely at Jessi in her now-tattered dress. He felt a touch of compassion as he looked at her and said, "Miss, raise your right hand over your head."

She looked at Tyler and in barely a whisper asked, "What did he just say to me?"

"He just asked you to …"

"Never mind, boy," the man interrupted. "I believe you, but since you don't have papers, I'm not going to help you. Those blood-sucking English are particular about that kind of thing, and they would take my boat away from me."

"If you can't, sir, do you know someone who can help us?" Tyler pleaded. He hoped the man would change his mind or maybe introduce them to someone who could help them out.

"Hmm … I just might. Follow me." He stepped up out of the boat, turned, and walked along the pier, looking at the different boats, hesitating, apparently considering the possibilities, then moving on. It was clear he was trying to find the best opportunity for them.

Finally, he stopped in front of a rather large boat. A heavy man with a large beard was standing on the dock shouting orders to five other men who were trying in vain to move quickly enough to satisfy him. Their helper walked up to him and the two spoke in low voices, as twice the captain eyed them suspiciously.

A minute later he returned to them and smiling broadly said, "I think the captain here will help you. Good luck, you two."

They hesitantly walked towards the captain. He motioned them to follow him as he walked out to the end of the dock, where they could speak without being overheard. He waited until they joined him, scowling slightly at the sight of their strange backpacks.

"Take those bags off your backs and put them on the dock. I don't want them to draw anyone's attention."

They quickly set their backpacks down at their feet.

"Marcel tells me you want to go to England, but there are … complications, shall we say? I know Marcel; he is someone who does not like to take chances. Me? I think taking chances can make life interesting, especially if they pay well." He leaned forward a bit. "Can you … pay well?" he asked in a low voice.

Tyler's chest tightened. *Can we trust him?* he asked himself. Since what they wanted was illegal, this man probably *shouldn't* be trusted. If he *did* take them to England and they got caught, he'd just claim ignorance and leave them to their trouble, and there'd be no one to help them. He looked up at the smile on his greedy face, realizing they didn't have any choice.

"We can pay you," Tyler's voice quivered a little. "And very well, but not with money."

"And what would you pay me with, boy?"

Tyler looked around nervously. "May we speak privately on your boat, Captain?"

The captain led them onto the boat and into his private quarters. It smelled strongly of old smoke, leather, and fish. He sat down in a chair and put his feet up on his desk. After briefly fingering the large earring in his left ear, he lit a pipe and blew a smoke-ring at the lantern hanging overhead.

"All right, boy, enough of your fun and games—show me your payment."

Tyler quickly dropped to the floor, took off his right boot, and pulled the tiny envelope out. The captain was now leaning forward over the desk, watching him. From the expression on his face he was clearly interested.

Without a word Tyler opened the tiny envelope and gently shook out the diamond onto the desk in front of the captain.

The captain straightened up as his eyes greedily devoured the gem. He picked up the diamond and held it towards the sunlight streaming through the window. Pinching it between his thumb and forefinger, the gem scattered a spray of light and colors all across the room. A sly smile played across his face; he was obviously pleased.

"I think this will be payment enough," he said slowly, "providing whoever you stole this from isn't following you."

"Captain," Tyler replied confidently. "The gem is *not* stolen, and there is no one following us. I know it will be a great loss to my family, but I'm confident they will consider it well spent to obtain our safe return home. Beyond that, I'm sure you understand that the less we speak of this, the better. Don't you agree?"

The captain hesitated and looked up at Tyler, who crossed his arms and gave him a knowing nod.

"Hmm. Very well," the captain replied, "The outgoing tide will be at first light tomorrow morning, and I expect the winds to be favorable, as they usually are at that hour. Don't be late, or we'll leave without you." He pulled open a drawer and started to place the diamond in it.

Tyler stepped forward. "Captain? Would it not be best for us to keep our payment until we come on board?" He was afraid the boat would not be here in the morning, and the captain would have their diamond! "Or better yet ..." The captain looked up at Tyler, obviously curious as to what he would say next. "Since we have no place to stay, may we sleep on board tonight? It will give us shelter, and no one in town will see us and draw any more attention to your fine boat."

The captain appeared impressed with Tyler's offer. "Certainly, you may sleep on the floor right here in my cabin, so the young lady need not be concerned about the rest of the crew. I have an idea how to get you past the authorities on the other side. Meanwhile, to show you what a generous man I am, I'll bring you some dinner as well."

He stood up, placed the diamond in his pocket, and stepped out on deck. "A full year's earnings in my pocket for delivering them across the water. I can afford to treat these gullible children very well," he muttered to himself. "They obviously don't know the true value of the diamond."

The captain was good to his word and brought them a meal that rivaled Mrs. Doullens' farm-style cooking. While they ate with him, he laid out his plans to get them past the authorities who would demand their entry papers, and as they went to sleep later that night, they were hopeful and excited to begin their voyage the next morning.

25
𝔚ater 𝔠rossing

Thursday, July 3, 1614

They woke up to the thumping of footsteps on the deck outside the captain's quarters. To have slept in a room, even on the hard floor, had felt like a luxury after spending so many nights on the ground under their tarp. The ship had been loaded the prior afternoon, so about all the crew had to do was weigh anchor and set sail.

The captain opened the door, carrying in a basket with more food—he was obviously in a very jovial mood. "Eat up, my friends," he fairly shouted. "Then come out on deck. We weigh anchor in ten minutes!"

They pulled out of the basket a loaf of hard-crusted bread, fruit, hard-boiled eggs, and chicken. They ate about half of it, even though they could have eaten more, and put the rest in their backpacks for later; they knew the value of planning ahead.

They stepped out on deck and felt the light but steady breeze that would push them away from the pier—perfect for the trip north to England. The double-masted sailing vessel rocked gently side-to-side as final preparations were being made.

Movement to their right on the dock caught their attention, and they watched as a boy about their own age jumped on board and walked up to them. He eyed them suspiciously and demanded, "Who are you, and what are you doing here?"

Before Tyler could answer, the captain walked up and put a firm hand on the boy's shoulder. "Anton, come with me," he said as he jumped down onto the dock, motioning for the boy to follow him.

After a second glare at Tyler, Anton turned away and followed the captain. The two had a brief conversation, during which both of them occasionally glanced over at Tyler and Jessi. The captain pulled a coin out of his pocket and placed it in the boy's hand, after which he smiled, nodded, and left.

The captain jumped back on board and, ignoring his passengers, began shouting orders to his crew. Following his commands, the experienced crew had the boat free of the dock within minutes. The outgoing tide immediately created space between the boat and the dock that increased quickly, and soon they had eased well away from the dock.

"Unfurl the jib," the captain called out. Two crewmen were at the ready, and soon the opened sail in the bow bulged as it caught the gentle breeze and slowly spun the drifting boat till it was pointed due north. "Unfurl the spritsail," he ordered. The same two crewmen opened up the canvas, and with a gentle snap it filled with air, and the boat began quietly cleaving the water and quickly gained speed. Within a minute's time, the boat had left the harbor far behind.

"Barbeau! LeFevre!" the captain called out. Two other crewmen stepped forward. The captain put a hand on the cabin wall and took a long deep breath of the fresh morning salt air. "This is a very good day, yes?" he asked them. The two men stood silently before the captain, obviously shocked at his curious behavior, and uncertain how to respond.

"Spread us some canvas on the mainsail—look lively!"

"Yes, Captain!" they sang out as they spun around and ran up the rigging. They unfurled the main sails, and before dropping back onto the deck, their eyes met. Barbeau nodded imperceptibly towards the captain below, then with a shrug they began their descent to the deck below. They had never seen him in such a mood before and knew him well enough to never expect it again.

The wind filled the sails with a deep snap, and the boat accelerated forward. Soon the town of Calais was just one of many landmarks along the miles of French coastland that could now be seen. The tension on the masts by the bulging sails made the boat creak and pop under their feet, but no one paid it any attention.

The crew had made this voyage many times and needed little instruction, so the captain turned the helm over to the first mate and joined his passengers on the starboard side, where they were watching the sun lift above the water, burning away the last traces of the mist snaking along over the water's surface.

"Well my friends," the captain said. "We have a good wind, the sun is greeting us, and in just a few hours we'll be putting in at Dover. It looks like you couldn't have asked for a better day to make this crossing! In the meantime get your belongings and follow me. We must prepare to get you past my friends"—he spat overboard in disgust—"on the other side."

Tyler and Jessi followed the captain to the stern, the rising and falling of the boat in the sea swells throwing them from side to side as they made their way across the deck. More than once they lost their balance, grabbing at whatever they could to keep from falling. They noticed the crew watching them, entertained by their clumsiness. The captain pointed to a wooden box about two feet wide and four feet long. "Put your satchels, or whatever you call those things, in the box here."

They put their bows and arrows along with their backpacks in the box, and the captain threw a canvas tarp over the top and tied it down securely.

He then sat down on the edge of the box, a sober look on his face. "To get past the authorities and on your way, you will have to do exactly as I tell you, no questions asked. Do you understand?"

The captain carefully went through his plan for them one more time, adding a few details he failed to mention the night before. He made it clear to them that if they were caught, he would not be able, or even try, to help them in any way. "I will not sacrifice my boat or my livelihood for you, understand?"

When the captain left them, they made their way to the front of the boat and found a secure place in the bow where they would have an unobstructed view of their approach to the coast of England. The rising and falling of the boat felt like a rollercoaster ride as the swells would lift the bow high, and then drop it swiftly down, striking the water with a blow so hard it would send a vibrating shock throughout the craft. A spray of saltwater would fly up on opposite sides, the wind often blowing some onto the deck.

Jessi smiled, face to the wind. "Ty, this is the most amazing thing! The sun is shining and I feel like I'm drinking in the salt air, and *look* at all those sails up there! This has *got* to be the most incredible experience of my life!" As a seagull flew overhead, Jessi started to point it out to Tyler—but then she noticed Tyler was looking straight ahead. He looked sick.

"Hey, Ty. You okay?"

"Nope. Pretty sure I'm gonna hurl."

Tyler headed towards the captain's quarters. The deckhand LeFevre walked by just as he reached the door. The look on Tyler's face said it all.

"You better not go in there," he said. "You'll do better if you stay out in the fresh air, here in the middle of the ship. Besides, if you throw up in the captain's cabin, he'll pull the skin off your body one tiny piece at a time."

Tyler looked at him in apprehension. He could see from the expression on the man's face that he was kidding—at least about losing his skin. He stumbled over to the railing and looked down at the water rushing by.

LeFevre followed him, laughing. "Don't worry," he said. "Most everybody gets sick at first. You'll get used to it." He leaned closer to Tyler's ear and said in a low voice, "Even the captain was sick when he first went to sea, but he'll never admit it. He'd pull the skin off *my* body if he heard me mention it, so keep that to yourself, eh?"

He good-naturedly poked Tyler with his elbow and turned away, then paused before coming back. "You'll do better if you look at the horizon, and not down at the water."

A minute later LeFevre returned with a fistful of bread in his hand. "Nibble on this," he said. "It'll help settle your stomach."

Tyler managed a shaky smile. "Thank you," he said.

After a while Tyler's stomach started feeling better. Over the next hour Calais was reduced to a speck on the coastline, and then the coastline itself began to drop from view as they grew closer to England. He spotted what he figured was Dover and noticed that the seas were becoming calmer. To his relief, the boat had almost completely stopped heaving up and down. *Just like my stomach*, he thought.

The activity on deck suddenly picked up as the mainsails were furled, since only the spritsail was needed to gently pull them in the last few hundred yards. The crew moved from one side of the boat to the other in response to the captain's orders, and within a couple minutes ropes were thrown to waiting hands at the pier; their crossing was complete.

Jessi had watched the entire process from the bow of the boat. The giddy look on her face betrayed that she was impressed with the skill with which all hands on board, and on the pier, had worked together so efficiently to bring their boat in. She saw Tyler at the back of the boat. "Oh, shoot!" she said as she hopped to her feet and wound her way around the busy sailors to the stern where Tyler was already waiting.

No one would have known by the tone of his voice whether or not the captain was pleased with his men as he shouted out his commands. Once he saw them unloading their cargo to his satisfaction, he left them and joined his two passengers.

"All right, you two," he said sternly. "It's time to go!"

They removed and folded the canvas, and picked up the box. One in front, one in back, they followed the captain onto the pier. Tyler's legs felt wobbly and weak, yet he was grateful to be walking on a solid surface once again. What he couldn't understand was why the dock felt like it was somehow moving. As they approached the shoreline, they could see an official-looking man eyeing them suspiciously, even though they were directly behind the captain.

"Good morning, Captain," he said. "Where's Anton? Are these two with you?"

"Anton eez seek, my friend," the captain said in faltering English. "But I nevaire worree, for theez young ones are asseesting me today. I must zem go to Burliman's store for some supleez, you allow zem to pass, yes?"

"That's fine," he said. "Go on."

The captain waited till they were halfway across the street, and then called out. "Remember," he said, "It's three blocks straight ahead, then turn right for three more blocks, understand?"

"Yes, sir, Captain," Tyler replied.

They went straight up the street three blocks and then looked back. The captain was continuing to engage the official in conversation; they were not being watched. They turned *left* and went to the next street. Setting the box down on a small patch of grass, they pulled out their backpacks, bows, and arrows. They quickly threw the packs on their backs, hid the box behind a fence, and headed up the street. Walking as fast as they dared without attracting attention, they followed the street as it rose up the gentle slope away from the water's edge, nervously glancing back to see if anyone was following.

They reached the top of the hill. The road out of town went directly beside Dover Castle. Keeping their heads down, yet without appearing to be hiding from any sentries that might be on duty, they pressed on.

Ten minutes later the town of Dover was behind them, and they started entering the English countryside. They soon came to the fork in the road the captain had told them to look for; a signpost on the right read Canterbury, a sign to the left read Folkestone. Pointing to the left, Tyler said, "That's where we're going, Jess."

She looked at the sign and smiled. "It feels good to be in a country where I know the language," she said. "I feel like I'm halfway home already."

They moved on, anxious to quickly put as many miles as they could behind them. After half an hour they slowed down and then stopped under a tree alongside the road for a short break.

"They'll be looking for us by now," Jessi said nervously.

"Yeah, but the captain will tell them we're going to London through Canterbury, so they'll look down that road first."

"Well, a horse can move a lot faster than us, so let's get going," Jessi replied as she glanced anxiously back down the road.

They resumed their journey and kept up as fast a pace as they could manage. A few miles later they heard the pounding of horses behind them. They dove into the bushes and waited, hearts pounding. Less than a minute later two soldiers passed them at a fast gallop. They waited another couple minutes before cautiously getting back on the road. To follow in the direction of the soldiers seemed foolish, but they had no other choice.

By noon they arrived in Folkestone and hurriedly passed through the town, following the road to the town of Ashford.

They spent the entire day on the move, constantly looking over their shoulders and hiding in the bushes from anyone on horseback who came up the road from behind. With each passing hour they were more confident of their success, and the dread inside them subsided, but the tension was exhausting.

Finally, the setting sun was shining directly into their faces, casting long shadows along the road behind. They had no idea how far they had traveled that day and had to be content with knowing they had done the best they could.

Then, with the last bit of daylight they dove deep into the woods on the south side of the road, found a site to pitch camp, and settled in for the night. Not daring to build a fire, they huddled together under the tarp while they each ate a dried apple and the rest of the chicken the captain had given them that morning, after which they fell fast asleep.

26

𝕸𝖊𝖗𝖗𝖞 𝕺𝖑𝖉𝖊 𝕰𝖓𝖌𝖑𝖆𝖓𝖉

Friday, July 4, 1614

The chattering of a squirrel welcomed them on their first morning in England.

"Well, that's no different," Tyler said out loud. "Do *you* have a nut to throw at us too?"

With a grunt, Jessi turned over. "Who're you talking to, Ty?" she mumbled.

"Our welcoming committee!"

"Our *what?*"

"Never mind. Hey, you know what I'm thinking?"

"No, and I don't really care. I'm not done sleeping."

"Too bad. Anyway, no more translating! What a pain! No more being stuck in the middle between two other people who want to talk to each other. I'm glad that's over!"

"I'll be glad when your talking's over. I'm not done sleeping, okay?"

"Oh, don't be such a grump."

"I'm NOT grumpy," Jessi said through clenched teeth.

Later, just before they broke camp, they pulled out the map that Jim had given them in Amiens and opened it up on the ground in front of them. Jim had told them to head for the town of Horsham. They agreed between them what direction they would go for the next part of their journey and started adding up the miles.

"That's a hundred and ten miles away!" Jessi complained.

"Oh, wait. This map is in kilometers!" Tyler noticed. "So it's about, umm, seventy miles. We can way do that! We've gone further than that already, and as long as we play it smart, we'll do all right."

"What are you so perky about?" Jessi asked suspiciously.

"Well ..." Tyler hesitated, "we're making progress. We got across the English Channel, Jess! We're *so* close to getting home! How are you *not* excited?"

"I dunno. I'm just tired, I guess. I'm really ready to be home."

"We'll get there, and in the meantime we'll have a few more days to hunt game along the way!"

With that suggestion, Jessi finally smiled.

Tyler grinned. "I knew you'd go for that!"

"Hmm. So tell me, Ty. How does it feel being right all the time?"

"Oh, you get used to it."

* * * * * *

The only food they had left in their packs was a handful of energy bars along with a couple of eggs the captain had given them. They decided to each have an egg and then try their luck at hunting down some game in the area. Over the last week, as they were traveling between Lille and Calais, they had slowly but surely become better trackers, marksmen, and best of all, partners.

They spent the next two hours working their way through the forest, no longer single file along a trail, but keeping each other in sight, moving parallel to each other to improve the possibility of one spooking game out in the direction of the other. Twice they were able to convince a rabbit to move out of hiding, but neither time were they able to get a shot off before it disappeared again into the thick undergrowth. Finally they gave up and returned to break camp. They deftly untied and coiled the ropes holding the tarp and put them into Jessi's backpack. In a few quick turns they had the tarp folded cleanly and stowed in the pack along with the ropes. The whole process took barely three minutes; a far cry from the first few days of their adventure. Five minutes later their camp was far behind them.

After a couple hours, Ashford came into view. Just as they were about to enter the village, something caught Jessi's eye. "Ty, look!" Nailed to a tree was something that looked like a wanted poster.

"Reward," Jessi read. "Information regarding possible diamond smuggling from France desired ..." Her voice trailed off.

The color drained from Tyler's face. "Keep your head down, and let's *move*."

They quietly walked through the town, fearing the worst, and only began to breathe easier once they had left the village behind them. No one seemed to have paid any attention to them.

"Do you think it was us that poster was talking about?" Jessi whispered fearfully.

"I don't think so, but let's not wait to find out."

Just north of town they saw a road from the west intersecting with their path, where a crude sign on a post said simply: Tunbridge Wells.

"Just like we expected," Tyler said with a sigh of relief, as they turned onto the new road.

This road was busier than any they had ever traveled, and eventually they abandoned all effort to conceal themselves, as it was clear no one was taking any special interest in them. Without the language barrier, Jessi led the way with confidence, and established a brisk pace. Soon the sun was directly overhead, and though they were able to obtain water, their stomachs were growling.

Ahead of them, and heading their way, was a boy maybe two years younger than themselves. He was carrying some kind of animal trap from which was hanging a large, gray rabbit.

Tyler instinctively licked his lips as he watched the animal swaying back and forth in rhythm with the boy's steps. "Hi there! Been hunting?" Tyler asked.

"No, I've been trapping," he said.

Tyler set his pack on the ground and pulled out one of the slugs of copper that Jim had melted from old pennies. He held it out in front of the boy. "I'll pay you for your rabbit!"

The boy's face brightened, but then he frowned slightly. "Is that *real* money?" he asked skeptically.

"No, but it's real copper." With a flick of his thumb Tyler spun the slug up into the air and caught it in his open palm, then held it for the boy to examine.

He leaned forward and peered at the slug, taking it slowly from Tyler's hand. He looked briefly at each of them, and then took a deep breath before saying, "I accept your offer."

He handed them the rabbit and then started walking back the way he had come.

"Hey! Where're you going?" Jessi called after him.

Without turning around the boy called out, "To get more rabbits!"

They looked at each other for a split second, grinned, and ran after him. He heard them coming and quickly turned around, afraid they were going to take the copper piece back. "What do you want?" he asked nervously.

"We got bows and arrows, and we want to hunt some rabbits!" Jessi said. "Can you show us where?"

Tyler stuck his hand out. "My name is Tyler, and this is Jessi."

The boy shook his hand, "I'm Ethan." He pointed to a hill about half a mile off the road. "There's a conie-warren over there," he said. "I'll show you exactly where it is, if you give me back my rabbit as soon as you get one for yourself—deal?"

They hesitated for a moment, then realized they had one rabbit whether they bagged another one or not.

"It's a deal," Jessi said. "But what's a conie-warren?"

"You don't know what a conie-warren is?" he asked incredulously. "Well, it's a place where lots of wild rabbits live! What do *you* call such a place where you live?"

"We don't have any rabbits where we come from—at least that I know of."

Tyler and Jessi fell in line behind Ethan as he led the way among various small trails under the trees. With a quick glance at the road and the sun, Tyler and Jessi set their bearings so they could easily find the road later.

Ethan knew the area well, and within a few minutes they were spotting evidence of rabbits and then the gray animals themselves. The rabbits appeared to have no fear of their arrows and made themselves easy targets. Within an hour, all three of them had as many rabbits as they wanted. They built a fire and roasted two of them. After they had eaten their fill, they roasted and smoked two more for the next day, making sure they had enough to satisfy their increased appetites created by their long days of walking.

Their brief friendship ended as they parted ways, Jessi and Tyler heading west, Ethan going east. In addition to the food, Jessi and Tyler had picked up some valuable lessons on hunting rabbits—and skinning, gutting, and roasting them as well.

With full stomachs and food to spare, Tyler and Jessi continued their trip with little concern. The miles slipped away under their feet as they followed the course of the sun until it disappeared directly in front of them.

They found a secure place to camp for the night and set up their tarp.

"Let's collect extra firewood tonight," Tyler suggested.

Something in his tone caught Jessi's attention. "Why? What's going on?" She asked.

"You'll see," he said mysteriously.

They collected a large supply of firewood and waited for the cover of nightfall. Finally Tyler lit the fire, and loaded on the wood. Soon their biggest fire ever was blazing, lighting up the forest around them.

"All right, Ty. What's going on? I think I've waited long enough."

"Do you know what today is?" he asked as he sat down next to her. Her hesitation gave him her answer. "It's the 4th of July! I'm pretty sure that you and I are now the first people in the world to celebrate our ... our national holiday!"

"Awesome, Ty. Thanks," she murmured as she snuggled up to him.

27
Deer Hunt

Saturday, July 5, 1614

"So how much farther do you think we have?" Jessi asked.

"I dunno," Tyler answered. He leaned over and pulled the map out of his pack. They had just shared their last apple and a portion of their rabbit meat for breakfast.

He opened the map and laid it on the ground in front of them. "I think we're about here," he said, pointing with his finger. "So we're only about an hour or two away from Tunbridge Wells, and then we have … about thirty miles." By now they were both confident in the use of maps.

Tyler looked up and glanced towards the east, noting the height of the early morning sun. "I'm guessing it's somewhere between six and seven."

"It's seven-fifteen," Jessi said matter-of-factly.

Tyler shot her a puzzled look.

"What difference does it make?" she laughed. In this century, their life didn't march according to a clock but simply followed the circuit of the sun. It was time to be going, and now it was just a question of how much further they had to go. "Just yanking your chain, Ty. I don't know what time it is, and I don't care."

Tyler cleared his throat. "Well, if we don't have to spend too much time hunting today, *and* if we're lucky, we might be locating the funnel as early as tomorrow night." He looked up from the map, "Then we're home, Jess!"

She frowned slightly. "I don't think so, Ty—probably the next day." She figured Tyler was right but was afraid to get her hopes up too high, remembering her meltdown in Lille. Besides, the last few days had been awesome, and she suddenly wasn't *that* anxious to have their adventure come to an end.

They broke camp and were soon on their way, and barely an hour later confirmed that Tyler had been right about their location. As they passed through the town of Tunbridge Wells, they used some of their copper and silver to purchase some early-season fresh fruit and vegetables.

A few hours later they were uncomfortably hot, and spying a huge tree with large flat leaves, they decided to make use of its shade in the tall grass underneath. They sat there a while watching the various travelers pass by and listening to the crickets and other quiet sounds around them.

Glancing over her shoulder behind them, Jessi caught a glimpse of movement. Without a word she motioned to Tyler. His eyes looked in the direction she was pointing, and together they peered into the grayness of the shadows beneath the trees. A few moments later they both spied a small deer quietly plucking and eating leaves amid the undergrowth.

"Ya know, Jess," Tyler whispered in her ear. "It's pretty small for a deer, but that would be all the food we need for the next couple days! What d'ya think?"

She nodded in agreement, and keeping the deer in sight, they left their backpacks behind a log, safely out of sight of anyone on the road. They stalked the animal with confidence, and placing a fair distance between them to flank their prey until one of them could get a good shot, they quietly followed the deer deeper into the forest.

It was about 50 yards in front of Jessi when she looked to her right to confirm Tyler's whereabouts. Just beyond him she spotted another hunter about 30 yards farther away. Oh no! How would she get Tyler's attention without also getting the other hunter's attention? She looked around for a small rock. The deer saw the other hunter and sprang forward, disappearing into the brush beyond.

Tyler immediately stood up, drawing the attention of the stranger. He did not look pleased. Feeling it may be important to show a unified front, Jessi fitted an arrow to the string of her bow and pulled it back. Keeping the arrow pointing towards the ground in front of her, she stood up facing Tyler and the hunter—and fixed a steely gaze at the stranger, hoping he couldn't see her trembling hands. The stranger gave a friendly smile, bringing his finger up to his lips for all of them to keep silent.

Jessi reached Tyler's side as the other hunter approached. Jessi guessed he was a few years older than them, probably about 18, wearing clothing common among the peasants in the area— loose fitting browns and grays.

He smiled and extended his hand. "Hello, lad and lassie," he said. "My name's Morgan."

Jessi felt a distinct twinge of dislike for this newcomer. She knew the terms "lad" and "lassie" was a culture thing, but his tone of voice made it feel like a put-down. Besides, he was barely older than them. Even so, she took his hand and introduced herself.

"Hi, I'm Jessi, and this is Tyler," she said. "No offense," she continued, "but if you hadn't shown up just now, we would have gotten that deer."

"That's all right, lassie," he said. "We'll get him later. I know where he's gone."

"How do you know that?" Tyler asked.

The boy laughed. "Because I hunt here all the time; this is my property. I know, I know. I don't *look* like a wealthy landowner— it's my family's property, actually. I dress like this to blend in with the forest better. I tell you what," he continued, "you do what I tell you, and you'll get that deer for sure. After you do, I'll skin it and share it with you—it'll be fun!"

Morgan quietly told them the patterns of the deer trails, and the best way to come up on it unaware. Following his instructions, they found the trails just as he had described them and carefully worked their way forward, searching intently for their prey. Morgan followed behind them, clearly enjoying this new twist to his hunt.

Just as he had said, the forest ahead was coming to an end, with open grasslands beyond. The deer had stopped within the shelter of the trees, hesitant to go into the clearing. Communicating silently with their hands, Tyler and Jessi agreed that Tyler had the best shot, and moments later his arrow found its mark.

The deer leapt forward into the grassland beyond and disappeared out of sight. They ran out from under the trees into the open area and soon found it lying in the knee-high grass, as Morgan stayed behind and watched from under the cool of the trees.

Looking down at the deer, they were exhilarated with their successful hunt, despite the heaviness they felt at having taken the life of such a graceful creature. It was a young deer, still in its first year they guessed, and probably weighed less than 40 pounds. Tyler extracted his arrow, and after wiping it clean in the grass, they began dragging the deer back towards the woods.

In the distance a trumpet sounded. Far behind them where the open grass disappeared over a rise, a horseman at full gallop was heading directly their way. They stopped and waited, but the rider went right past them to the edge of the woods and turned around to face them, effectively cutting them off from returning to the trees. He then sounded the horn in two short blasts. The sound of answering horns announced the arrival of two more riders, and soon the three horsemen had formed a circle around them.

"Me name is Mr. Hurley," said the oldest of them, as he leaned forward in his saddle. "I'm Head Caretaker of Lord Kenton's entire estate. Must I remind ye that poaching is a crime, regardless of your age?"

"Poaching? What is that?" Tyler asked nervously.

"Speaking such foolishness won't protect ye!" he spat out angrily. "Hunting on Lord Kenton's property is only allowed at his behest and under his direct supervision —or those of his household, which is meself! And ye have permission from neither!"

"But we were hunting with his son, Morgan!" Jessi pleaded. "He's right here behind us!" She looked back towards the trees, but no one was there.

"Foolish words will accomplish ye nothing, poachers! Lord Kenton has no son named Morgan—ye should have been prepared with better lies than that!" He then addressed the other two men. "Seize their weapons and the deer, and bring these poachers to the stables. I'll go ahead to prepare for your arrival."

"Yes, sir," one of them answered.

Hurley drove his heels into the sides of his horse and sped off. One man dropped to the ground and picked up their bows and arrows and after an inquisitive look at the odd design of the bows, lashed them to his saddle. He tied the deer to the other man's horse and put Jessi on the saddle in front of the rider. He then put Tyler on his own horse with him and kicked his horse into a gallop.

Morgan silently watched from the shadowy protection of the trees. As the horsemen rode away with their captives, he quietly chuckled to himself and disappeared into the forest.

28
Confinement

Saturday Afternoon, July 5, 1614

The horses moved easily through the grass, unaffected by their additional burdens. Within minutes they crested the low-lying hill, and a huge building came into view. Hundreds of feet long and three stories high, it looked like something they had only seen in the movies. Two massive doors at least 15 feet high in the center of the building were flanked by scores of windows on each side. Silently declaring its strength and power, the stone mansion instilled awe and fear in anyone who dared oppose the will of its owner.

The horsemen rode around the left side of the manor and stopped at the near end of a long building that ran parallel with the manor. The men dismounted and roughly pulled Tyler and Jessi to the ground as other servants led the horses away. With a firm hand on their shoulders, the men directed them to a massive wood door. The man in front released his grip on Jessi, and with an obvious exertion of strength opened the door; they stood before a stairway leading down into darkness. With each step they could feel the warmth of the summer sun slip away, as damp cold air took its place.

At the bottom of the stairs, the man in front paused and lit a torch. He then led them down a long hallway with doors on either side, all secured with large bolts that slid into the solid rock walls. The horseman in front of them stopped at a door on the right, slid open the bolt, and putting his weight against the door, pushed it open.

The second horsemen shoved them from behind, and they stumbled forward into a small room, the door behind them swiftly closing with a loud clang. Then the long, heavy bolt scraped across the door, slipping into a groove in the rock wall with a dull thud. As the men's footsteps quietly faded away, they were left in the deepest silence they had ever experienced in their lives.

"Oh, Ty. What do we do now?" Jessi's voice was shaking.

With barely a glance he could see she was as scared as himself. He took her hand. "I don't know," he choked out.

She let go of his hand and rested her head against his shoulder. He put an arm around her and they took a little comfort in each other's touch.

"Morgan set us up," Jessi began. "I knew from the minute we met him something was wrong. I should've said something. This is all my fault." She started crying.

"This isn't your fault, Jessi. I got so caught up in the hunt I didn't think it through either." He paused. "No wonder he stayed back in the trees."

They slowly surveyed the room into which they'd been thrown. The walls were of chiseled stone that smelled of mold. The wall opposite the door had a small window about eight feet off the floor, with vertical bars placed about every four inches spanning the opening. Near the window and all across that wall the stone was damp, with a slight green color; a trace of water could be seen where the wall met the floor.

Bunk beds stood against the left wall; one folded blanket lay on each bed. There was a bucket in the corner. Besides that, there was nothing else in the room. They sat next to each other on the lower bunk.

"If they send a man to prison for stealing a loaf of bread, what do they do to someone caught poaching?" Jessi moaned.

"I don't know, Jessi. That was in France, not here. Maybe it won't be so bad."

Hours passed by as they watched the sunlight on the floor inch its way across the room, then up the wall, until it slowly faded away. A crow briefly stopped at the window ledge, its head jerking back and forth as it peered into the room. For a few moments it pecked and scratched at the stone around the bars, then abruptly flew off.

Curiosity prompted Tyler to try to look out the window. He jumped and grabbed for the bars but missed. He tried again, this time getting one hand firmly around a bar. He tried for a second bar, but lost his grip and fell back to the floor, yelling in frustration.

"You can do it, Tyler." Jessi said quietly. "Try again."

Tyler flexed his hands and eyed the bars. He took a deep breath and jumped. This time he caught two bars.

"Yes!" Jessi cried out.

Tyler pulled himself up so he could see out. Had they been welcomed visitors he would have appreciated the beauty of the manicured grass, flowering bushes, and neatly trimmed shrubs; but instead all he could see in the dusky light was that they were in a building that faced the back wall of the manor. Just 10 feet in front of him was a small birdbath where two swallows were chirping and splashing water all about them as they rapidly flapped their wings.

He let go of the bars and dropped to the floor. He cupped his hands and gave Jessi a boost so she could look outside before it became too dark. They were glad for the diversion, but it did nothing to improve their spirits.

They heard the sound of footsteps coming down the hall. They stopped outside the door. A small hatch at the bottom of the door opened up, and a tray of food and a small bucket of water with two cups were silently pushed through the opening. They eagerly jumped up and headed for the tray as the little door dropped back down, the latch slid shut, and their keeper walked away.

It was simple fare, but they happily devoured it, eating it all in less than two minutes. Sitting on the lower bunk, Jessi leaned her back against the wall and licked her fingers. "Next meal I'm eating a lot slower," she declared. "After all, it's not like I've got anything else to do."

The last bit of daylight disappeared, and not long afterwards a whisper of silver moonlight entered their cell. Looking up through the bars they couldn't see the moon itself, and had to be content with the little bit of light it provided. Covering themselves as best they could with their blankets, they finally drifted off into a fitful sleep, discouragement oppressing them more than the darkness itself.

* * * * * *

July 6, 1614

An unfamiliar sound scratched its way into Jessi's mind. Her muddled thoughts came into focus as she turned in her cot and looked at their cell door—just in time to see it close and hear the heavy bolt slide across the door once again.

Their empty food tray was gone, and more food was on a tray against the opposite wall. Jessi reached up and knocked on the cot above her.

"Tyler!" she called. "Wake up! Breakfast is served."

The cot above squeaked as Tyler shifted around a little, mumbled a low groan, and fell silent. Jessi rolled off her cot and stood on her feet, then gently shook Tyler's shoulder. "Come on, Ty. Wake up."

"Why?"

"Because ... because, I don't know why," she answered dismally. She sat back down on her cot, pulled up her blanket and faced the wall, laying her head on the crook of her arm. A few tears silently rolled down her cheek as sleep mercifully welcomed her back.

Nothing happened all day but for the delivery of their afternoon meal. They were grateful for the food but were desperate to know what was to become of them. Whoever was delivering their food ignored their pleas for conversation or information, leaving their fate to their imagination. The more they thought about it, the more terrible they imagined their punishment would be.

With nothing to do in their small cell they found it nearly impossible to simply sit still. They needed something to do, something to help them stop fidgeting and burn off some energy. They counted, then recounted, the number of stone blocks in their cell. They tried doing some exercises, but didn't really know what to do. By the end of the day, they were impossibly anxious and struggled to fall asleep.

* * * * * *

July 7, 1614

The next morning they woke up hungry, but there was no breakfast tray at the door. "A little rabbit meat would be nice, don't you think?" Tyler asked.

"I'm just thankful for anything," Jessi responded. "Besides, even the mush we've been getting tastes pretty good."

A few moments later they heard footsteps approaching. Once again, without a single word being spoken, a tray of food was delivered through the slot at the bottom of the door. Tyler sullenly picked up the tray and set it between them on the bottom bunk. When they were done, he set the empty tray next to the door and returned to the bunk. They miserably waited in silence.

It was about midday when they heard the sound of several footsteps approaching their cell.

"It's too early for dinner," Jessi whispered.

They leapt to their feet, and stood against the opposite wall, facing the door. As they waited, their hands met and their fingers intertwined. Tyler gave Jessi's hand a squeeze. "We're in this together, Jess," he whispered.

The heavy bolt slid aside, and the door opened. One of the horsemen who had brought them into the cell walked through the doorway as the other waited in the hall. Behind him entered a man they had not seen before. From his perfectly combed hair to his highly polished leather boots, he was the epitome of wealth and prestige. He silently stood and examined their faces carefully, one after the other. His face was solemn, but gave no hint of anger or cruelty—nor of compassion. After a full minute he gently coughed and cleared his throat.

"My name is Cedric Bettencourt," he began. "I am Steward to Lord Kenton. I answer to him and him only in all the affairs under his domain. Do you understand my words?"

They silently nodded their heads.

"Do you know the penalty for poaching?" he then asked.

Tyler swallowed hard. "Sir, we don't know what poaching is," he replied, his voice barely above a whisper.

"You don't ..." A look of surprise and then curiosity briefly flickered across his face as he turned to the man next to him. "You told me they were local residents," he said.

"Yes, sir. I did not know otherwise."

"They obviously are *not*. Just listen to their speech! And ..." he continued, looking them over once more, "see how they're dressed? They are unmistakably foreign." He then said sharply, "Bring me a chair—immediately!" The man hastily left the cell, ran down the hall, and soon returned with a chair.

Motioning to Tyler and Jessi to sit, he seated himself in the chair facing them. He folded his arms across his chest and studied them further before continuing. "Poaching includes the hunting of game on someone's property without their permission; even the theft of a single radish from a garden is subject to punishment. Now," he leaned forward, folded his hands, and rested his elbows on his knees as he continued, "you will tell me your story, and you *will* be honest in your words."

* * * * * *

It only took a couple minutes for the steward to realize this situation was more complex than he expected. *My other appointments can wait*, he thought. *This is proving to be most interesting.* For the next half hour he questioned them as if they were on a witness stand in a trial—a trial where their guilt had already been proven. He decided to see if he could find cause to let them go free and felt the challenge would prove rather entertaining.

They explained to him that they were traveling to Horsham where they were to meet Jim. He finally learned their journey had begun in France, as bit by bit he broke down their answers to each of his questions. Ultimately, like peeling back the layers of an onion, he came to the core of their dilemma: they had somehow been abandoned in the woods near Amiens and had slowly but surely been doing everything in their power to get home to their families.

At the end of their interrogation, the steward was certain of several things. First, that they had indeed spoken the truth. Second, they were tenacious, resourceful, and educated far beyond that of most adults, despite their simple attire and total lack of knowledge of local laws. And third, that he now had a dilemma of his own to deal with: He wished to let them go, but the final word on an offense as serious as poaching would be Lord Kenton's decision, not his. He knew well his position of influence but also knew where his authority ended.

What he did *not* know, and was totally unable to determine no matter how hard he tried, was the likely county or town they were from. English was obviously their native language, but their strange accent, vocabulary, and the manner in which they formed their sentences were unlike anything he had ever heard in his life. In addition, as their nervousness declined and their confidence returned, they addressed him with respect, but as if he were their *equal*, and not as a peasant speaking to a man of his high position. This both irritated and intrigued him.

He stood up and prepared to leave the cell. Tyler and Jessi quickly jumped to their feet and bowed awkwardly. He suppressed an urge to smile as he turned and walked out the door. *These two have no understanding of our ways and customs*, he thought to himself. *Most interesting.*

The jailor drew the heavy bolt across the door, securing them inside. The steward silently motioned for the two men to walk away, while he waited quietly outside the door, listening intently to hear whatever might be said.

"What do you think, Ty?"

He clearly perceived the quiver in her voice.

"Well, we told him the truth, and like my mom says, if you keep telling the truth, you can't get caught telling lies that don't add up. Let's just pray Mr. Bettencourt believes us and will let us go. Just think, if he does, we'll be home in only a couple of days!"

The steward smiled to himself and quietly walked away. How he would present this curious situation to Lord Kenton was coming into focus.

29
A Short Trial

Afternoon, July 7, 1641

Within the hour the door opened again, and Mr. Hurley entered their cell, a scowl on his face. "On your feet, poachers!" he said. "Ye must be presented before Lord Kenton himself within the hour. Follow me."

Without another word he abruptly spun around and left the cell. Tyler and Jessi exchanged nervous glances and then followed him out the door, as their jailor, who was waiting for them in the hall, followed behind. They retraced their steps up to the ground level and out the doors to where the horsemen had brought them two days earlier. They blinked and squinted as their eyes slowly adjusted to the bright sunshine after so long in their gloomy cell. The two men who had brought them to the manor walked up.

Mr. Hurley addressed them. "Lord Kenton demands our presence, and we must not test his patience."

With hearts pounding, Tyler and Jessi followed Mr. Hurley, with the two other men behind them, through luscious, well-kept gardens and entered a large room that jutted out from the main structure of the manor. The room just inside the door had pegs all along the two walls to their right and left, with wash basins, scrub brushes, and cleaning utensils along the exterior wall. On the wall opposite them, towards the interior of the manor, small signs were posted for the servants, with their various duties and assignments for the day written beneath.

Mr. Hurley pointed at the wash basins. "Wash your faces and hands, and make yourself as presentable as ye can. Your stench is nearly unbearable," he growled.

They quickly complied and cleaned up as best they could, while Mr. Hurley and the two men took off their work clothes and boots, and put on clean clothing that was hanging on the wall. The men sat down on the bench below the pegs and put on indoor shoes, then stood and inspected each other's clothing to ensure they were looking their best. When they deemed that they were ready, Mr. Hurley gave them a brief inspection, before turning towards the two prisoners.

"Clean your boots, poachers," he spat out. "Neither Lord Kenton, nor the cleaning maids, want any of your dirt on their floors!"

Twenty minutes passed before the house butler appeared at the doorway. He was a tall, thin man with a long, angular nose, and wiry, slicked-back hair. "Gentlemen, please follow me," he said in a flat voice that matched his sour expression. Without another word or a backwards glance, he turned and walked back through the door.

"Gentlemen? I'm not a man!" Jessi muttered.

"Sshh!" Tyler hissed.

The next room was obviously the kitchen, alive with activity. Fireplaces on opposite walls were ablaze. On one side, some kind of stew was cooking in two large pots. In the opposite fireplace, what looked like a lamb was on a spit over the open flame. A young girl was turning a crank that slowly spun the animal, as drippings fell sizzling into the fire below. The smell was intoxicating.

"Oh, Ty. That smells so good!" Jessi exclaimed.

"Silence!" Mr. Hurley shouted. "Ye shall not speak here unless first spoken to, understand?" Without waiting for an answer they kept walking.

In the middle of the kitchen two cooks were slicing various vegetables, tossing the scraps into a large bucket at one end. To one side, a woman was slicing bread and arranging rolls in a basket. Skillets and pots of all sizes and shapes hung from pegs on the kitchen wall. On each side of the fireplaces were shelves with large glass jars containing ground flour and other grains. Braided garlic and onions hung from pegs on the interior wall, along with various dried herbs and spices that Tyler and Jessi could only guess at.

The butler passed through the doorway into the manor itself, as the three men, Tyler, and Jessi followed dutifully behind. At about the center of the manor they turned right into a hall that appeared to run the length of the building. The walls were richly paneled with dark wood, ornate carvings were around each doorway, and the walls were filled with paintings of various landscapes or portraits of presumably long-deceased family members. Here and there, a niche in a wall housed a bronze or marble sculpture. The air was fresh, but there was a light scent reminiscent of fireplace smoke. Throughout the hallways candles burned to illuminate those areas lacking a contribution from the sunlight outside. The hard soles of their boots rang out on the marble floor with every step, while the soft shoes of the men around them created barely a whisper. There'd be no escaping their captors.

The butler stopped in front of a pair of doors that towered 12 feet high. He turned the handle on the left-hand door, then pushed and held it open while they silently walked past him. After entering, they waited, as he walked around in front of them to present them to Lord Kenton. "Mr. Hurley, his men, and the two children, m'lord," he said stiffly. He then left the room, closing the door behind him. Surrounded by three grown men, the steward, and Lord Kenton, they felt no less helpless in these beautiful surroundings than they had felt for the last two days in their cell. The gentle click of the door closing behind them was as oppressive as the bolt on their cell door.

In front of them, against the opposite wall, there was a large and ornate table. Small shelves on one side had numerous stacks of papers in various cubbyholes, and an oil lamp was in the opposite corner. The only other things on the table were their few possessions, laid out in an organized fashion; under the table were their backpacks and sleeping bags.

The tall and expansive windows on their left they recognized as the front of the manor. Shelves were built into the wall between each window and were filled with various books and small works of art. The inside wall to their right was lined with bookshelves from corner to corner, and ceiling to floor. Everything portrayed a sense of order and discipline.

It was in front of these bookshelves that Lord Kenton sat in a tall chair behind a large and beautiful desk. Facing the windows to their left gave him an excellent view of the courtyards and entryways leading to the front of the manor. On his desk there were some papers, an inkhorn, and a quill. In one corner was an empty glass next to a pitcher of water. Mr. Bettencourt was standing to the side of the desk, speaking quietly to the man seated in the chair. His back was to the newcomers, blocking them from seeing Lord Kenton. This further delay to see the face—and expression—of the man who controlled their fate was almost unbearable, and Jessi's lower lip began to quiver. Finally, after a few more comments, Mr. Bettencourt stepped aside, revealing the man in the chair. He watched them in silence as they were brought forward and placed before him.

They were expecting to see an old man, but instead found they were looking at a man of about 40, just a few years older than their own fathers. His dark hair was cut just below his ears but did not quite reach his shoulders. Long sideburns ended at his jawbone, and his mustache came down just to the corners of his mouth.

He made no attempt to stand as he studied each of them. His face betrayed contradictory messages of both curiosity and severity, which only increased their anxiety.

"Greetings, m'lord," Mr. Hurley said, with a slight bowing of the head.

"Hurley," Lord Kenton responded. "Are these indeed the two you caught poaching?"

"Yes, m'lord," Hurley answered as he firmly pulled them forward on either side of him, within arm's reach of the front of the desk.

"Good afternoon," Tyler meekly offered.

Hurley backhanded him across the mouth, knocking him onto his knees. "You do not speak until spoken to, and that is no way to address Lord Kenton," he spat out. Tyler tasted blood in his mouth as he slowly stood back up. Jessi stiffened as she bit her lip; her hands closed into tight fists.

"Mr. Hurley!" Lord Kenton quickly said, his deep voice rising only slightly. "Such actions are quite unnecessary. I believe they are not familiar with our customs. Escort your men to the foyer and wait there should I need you to answer any further inquiries. That will be all."

Hurley bowed his head again. "Yes, m'lord." He and the men quickly stepped outside the room and closed the door behind them. Lord Kenton turned to the steward. "Cedric, find the lad a napkin. We can't have him bleeding on the carpet, or else Lady Kenton will be certain to blame me for beating the servants!" he said with a faint smile.

Jessi slowly relaxed her hands and clasped them together in front. She quietly let out a deep breath.

The lord's smile disappeared as his gaze returned to the captives. "Mr. Hurley should have instructed you to address me as "m'lord." I believe he's being rather harsh with you because last week a poacher escaped his capture, costing him a week's pay. Mr. Bettencourt here has given to me his assessment of your situation and has recommended leniency. But first I wish to speak with you myself."

Over the next few minutes they were asked various questions that were similar to those Mr. Bettencourt had posed to them in their cell. The steward quietly listened as they confirmed and expanded the story of their travels under the questioning of the nobleman. Occasionally Lord Kenton glanced his steward's way and would receive a confirming nod. Finally, Lord Kenton got out of his chair and beckoned them to join him at the table on his right.

"Based on the information my steward gleaned from you this morning, we found these in the trees near the road. These are yours, are they not?"

"Yes," Jessi answered and hastily added, "m'lord."

It was clear Lord Kenton and the steward had carefully examined all of their belongings already. Lord Kenton picked up a pack and examined the fabric. "This material is unlike anything

I've ever seen—so light, and yet so strong! The precision of the stitches are those of a master craftsman." He picked up the rope and examined it in wonderment. "This rope is so thin despite its considerable strength, and its composition is unlike any I am familiar with: so curiously smooth. But I must tell you that I am most impressed with your bows! The wheels provide an action that is quite ingenious—it is something I've asked my bowyers, woodworkers, and blacksmiths to look into."

He then picked up one of their ponchos and examined it, curiosity and wonder in his eyes. "I also find the material of this garment foreign to me—describe its function."

"Well ... m'lord," Jessi began. "I'm not certain what the material is either, but it's waterproof and has kept us dry when it rains. May I demonstrate?" When he nodded, she put the poncho on the floor and made a depression in it with her fist. She then took the water pitcher from his desk and made a small puddle in the depression. "As you can see, m'lord, water will not soak into the fabric."

"I've neither seen nor heard any legend about a garment *completely* impervious to water," the steward muttered. "It really is quite remarkable." He pulled a handkerchief from his pocket and dropped it on the puddle. He then picked up the hunting knife and examined it admiringly. He frowned slightly as he brought the blade closer to his eyes. "What is this written on the blade," he asked. "Made in U.S.A.?"

Tyler's heart skipped a beat. "It is the name of our country, sir," he stammered. "In America. It stands for United States of America." He immediately questioned the wisdom of his response as he pictured what America must look like at that moment.

"America?" Lord Kenton exclaimed sharply. "I know much about Virginia. It is all an untamed and wild land under the dominion of our king. We know there is no great industry capable of making such as this!" Seeing them shrinking back, he softened his tone as he reached down and picked up another item and held it up in the light. "It is clear, like glass, yet it is *not* glass," he said as he tapped it with his finger, then shook it back and forth and looked at the liquid inside. "What exactly is this?"

Tyler stepped forward. "It is a lighter, m'lord. We use it to start our fires."

"Show me," Lord Kenton said.

Tyler flicked the flame on and off a few times.

"Remarkable!"

Next Lord Kenton picked up the homing beacon. "And this?" he asked.

"It's like a compass, m'lord," Jessi answered. "Only instead of pointing north, it tells us when it's pointing in the direction of where we're supposed to meet our friend."

Mr. Bettencourt reached under the table and came up with one of their sleeping bags. "This mechanism is most marvelous and closes this garment better than buttons could ever attain!"

"The mechanism is called a zipper, sir," Tyler explained.

"Zipper?"

"Yes, you'll hear it makes a sound like the word 'zip' if you move the small handle quickly back and forth."

The steward did so and began laughing. He immediately stopped and cleared his throat, as if it was improper behavior to display in their presence.

There was a long pause, and then Lord Kenton drew a deep breath. "Well, this has been a most interesting day, one which I will not soon forget! Nevertheless, by your own admission, you *are* guilty of the crime of poaching, for which I could have you hanged. That is the law of the land, and there is no recourse above me that is available to you. The decision is mine to declare, and once given, it is final."

The color drained from Tyler's and Jessi's faces as they instinctively drew close together.

"Until then …" He paused as he looked at the steward. "Mr. Bettencourt, take them to the Green Room in the east wing, and have Agnes attend to them. Give them the customary privileges. That is all for now."

The steward led them out of the room and closed the door behind them. Hurley and his two men were waiting there, and he roughly grabbed their arms to lead them back to their cell.

"Not so quick there, Mr. Hurley," the steward jumped in. "Lord Kenton wishes to have them stay in the Green Room until he declares his decision."

"The Green Room! For *poachers*?"

"Do you wish to speak to Lord Kenton himself about this?"

"Uh ... no sir."

"Very well then. You may return to your duties."

Mr. Hurley opened his mouth as if to say something more and apparently thought better of it. He led his men down the hall, shaking his head in bewilderment.

"Sir?" Jessi asked, her voice shaking. "Are we going to die?" She looked pleadingly at the steward.

"What?" he said in surprise. "Considering you are going to the Green Room, it is most unlikely. But the final decision is not mine; that belongs to Lord Kenton."

30

The Justice of Lord Kenton

Afternoon, July 7, 1641

The steward led them to the opposite end of the manor, taking them up to a room on the third floor. He opened the door but remained in the hallway. "Residents of the Green Room are considered the guests of Lord Kenton," he explained. "As such, you are permitted access to the entire east wing, going no further west than the entry in the center of the manor. You shall eat in the kitchen with the servants and have access to the courtyard between the manor and the stables behind. Your freedom does not extend to the lands around the manor. Understand that you are receiving great mercy from the lord; be careful you don't abuse it. For now, you must stay here in the room until Agnes arrives."

After the door closed behind them, they surveyed the room. It was obvious why it was called the Green Room: all the furnishings, and everything from the paint on the walls to the colors of the curtains were of various shades of green. The room itself was about half the size of their own homes, complete with a 15-foot-high ceiling. A large bed against the wall had a canopy overhead supported by four ornately hand-carved posts. The mattress was so high off the floor there was a two-step stool on each side. They could hardly believe their good fortune, especially after spending the last two days in the dungeon.

Tyler walked to the opposite window and looked out. He saw that he was looking out the back of the manor toward the stables—providing an outstanding view of the manicured gardens, water features, and artistic landscaping between the two buildings they had been viewing through the bars of their cell window.

They were still making their first pass around the room when they heard a light knocking on the door as a woman turned the latch and walked in. "Good afternoon, lad and lassie," she politely said with a slight curtsy.

They looked at her and each other, uncertain how to respond. She was obviously older than their parents, yet she was behaving as if she was their servant.

"Good afternoon, ma'am," they replied.

"Gracious! You must not call me 'ma'am', for I'm just Agnes …" She curtsied again. "… a humble servant of the household, and I have been charged to tend to your needs as long as you are our guests here. First of all …"

Agnes then began to describe a brief history of the room they were staying in, followed by a general history of the Kenton family. She then gave them a tour of the east wing of the manor and the gardens behind. They finished in the kitchen and dining area and there learned of the scheduled mealtimes. Agnes then had the household tailor take their measurements, after which they were escorted back to their room.

Hardly 15 minutes had passed before Agnes returned, knocking on the door as she walked in. They wondered why she even bothered knocking at all since she was already in the room by the time she stopped knocking.

"The tailor found these clothes for you to wear while you are our guests; these shoes are to be worn whilst inside the manor only. Your own clothes and boots will be laundered, and when returned to you, they are only to be worn outside. You already know where to change your clothing. After all, the clothes you have on are suitable for traveling, but are *not* suitable for the guests of Lord Kenton. Dinner will be ready in one hour. I don't mean to offend, but you *must* bathe first. I will have a tub and hot water brought in so you may enjoy a bath together."

"Together?" Jessi exclaimed.

Startled at Jessi's response, Agnes paused a moment. "You two *have* completed your spousals, yes?" she asked.

"Spousals? What's that?" Jessi asked.

Surprised by the question, Agnes asked again, "You *are* married, correct?"

Jessi's face turned crimson. "No! We're only fourteen!"

"That's old enough, lassie," Agnes answered matter-of-factly. "Didn't the lord or Mr. Bettencourt ask if you were married?"

"No." Tyler mumbled as he looked at the floor away from Jessi.

Agnes shook her head and rolled her eyes. "Men!"

"Well, since you are *not* married," she looked at Tyler and said, "follow me lad, if you please—don't forget your clothes."

She curtsied to Jessi and left, with an embarrassed Tyler close behind. Agnes situated him in the room next door. It was no less magnificent than Jessi's, but the room was furnished in shades of blue rather than green.

The meal that evening was certainly the best of their entire adventure; the food was prepared perfectly, and they were allowed to eat as much as they wanted—including fresh bread still warm from the oven. They ate in the kitchen with the servants, yet were treated with such warmth and hospitality that they felt like honored guests. They decided their return home could wait a few more days.

* * * * * *

July 8, 1614

The next morning began with Agnes knocking on her way through the door; she gave them notice that breakfast would be ready in 20 minutes. They had already been awake for over an hour and were together in the sitting area of the Green Room talking about how dangerously close their journey had come to ending in disaster. Outside they saw that thick clouds had rolled in during the night, and it looked as if it would be a cool and blustery day.

Because of the cool weather, the servants were tending the fires started hours earlier in fireplaces throughout the manor. As a result, the outside chill was kept at bay and a slight scent of wood smoke crept through the various halls and rooms. Tyler and Jessi entertained themselves by investigating each nook and cranny of the east wing and never went outside. By late afternoon, as the sun began to approach the horizon, it finally broke through the thinning clouds, giving all who watched a beautiful sunset with a promise of a better day to come.

* * * * * *

July 9, 1614

The following morning they were eating breakfast in the kitchen when the sour-faced butler entered. "Agnes, Lord Kenton desires to speak with our guests at ten o'clock. Be sure they are presentable and on time." Without even a glance in their direction he turned on his heels and left.

"You know, if he smiled I think his face might break," Jessi muttered out of the corner of her mouth. Agnes started to giggle but quickly masked it with a cough.

Agnes arrived 30 minutes before their appointment with freshly ironed clothes. She wetted their hair down with water and combed their hair, which hadn't seen a comb since their Sunday with the Doullens family.

"Agnes," Jessi said. "Today we saw a portrait of Lord Kenton with his family, but where are they? The only people we've seen here is the lord, the steward, and the household workers."

"Hmm, yes," Agnes acknowledged. "A couple years ago Lord Kenton invested in a tobacco venture in Virginia with John Rolfe. Then about a month ago he received word that Mister Rolfe had married an Indian princess earlier this year. April, I believe. Mister Rolfe's father at Heacham in Norfolk has thrown a celebration, even though the newly married couple is still in

Virginia. Business requires the lord to stay, but his family is at the celebration."

"Do you know the name of the Indian princess?" Tyler excitedly asked.

"Yes," she answered confidently. "Her name is Rebecca."

"That doesn't sound like an Indian name," he frowned.

"No, no. That's the name she took when she accepted Christianity. Her Indian name was Podu ... no, Pocu ..."

"Pocahontas?" Jessi blurted out.

"That's it!" Agnes exclaimed. "You have heard of her?"

"Oh, yeah," Jessi laughed. "Where we're from she's kind of a big deal."

"A big deal? What does that mean?"

"It means that she's real famous where we're from."

"Where *are* you from?" she asked as she glanced at the clock. "Oh dear, never mind, we must hurry. We must *never* be late when meeting the lord!"

* * * * * *

At two minutes to ten, she led them to Lord Kenton's study, knocked on the door, but did not open it. Mr. Bettencourt opened the door and welcomed them in with a smile. "Come in, come in," he said. "We have a few things to discuss with you. You may go, Agnes." After closing the door behind them, he seated himself in a chair in front of Lord Kenton's desk.

Their self-confidence withered when they saw Mr. Hurley standing, cap in hand, before Lord Kenton. The expression on his face gave no indication whether things were about to get better or worse. He was obviously uncomfortable as he intently studied his cap, shifting his weight from one foot to the other.

Lord Kenton sat at his desk. "Welcome," he began. "I trust the hospitality of my estate has met with your approval?"

"Yes sir, uh ... m'lord. It's been great! Thank you!" Tyler gushed, as Jessi just smiled and nodded.

"Excellent, I'm pleased to hear it," he said cheerfully. "My staff speaks fondly of you two, and your accents and manner of speech have been a great entertainment to us all. However, as you know, we *do* have some business to attend to. Mr. Hurley has some news that I believe will be of considerable interest to the two of you." He leaned back in his chair and looked towards his steward. "I called for you, Cedric, because I thought it best you hear this for yourself. Proceed, Hurley."

"Thank you, m'lord," Mr. Hurley cleared his throat. "As you know, yesterday I had the afternoon to me own doings, and as I am often wont to do, spent some time at me favorite alehouse. Whilst there, I was telling to Nancy, the woman who served me, about how I catches these two young-uns. A few minutes later, Nancy come tells me she heard a young man a few tables away telling his friends about his grand hunting adventure; how he hid himself as two young people got caught after bringing down a deer that they were tracking together. She said he was joking to his friends that he was hoping to attend a hanging."

"Joking in what way?" Mr. Bettencourt asked as he straightened up in his chair.

Without another word Hurley made a fist over his head with his thumb pointing down. He pushed his arm straight up as he jerked his neck to the side and opened his mouth.

"Well," he continued, "I didn't hear it meself from him, but I kept me eye on him and followed him after he leaves. And what do you know, but that I followed him right onto m'lord's property! His weapons in his hand tracking m'lord's game! I caught him in the act and put him in the very same cell I had put these two." He turned to Tyler and Jessi. "Beggin' your pardon, young-uns," he added.

* * * * * *

A short time later they were dressed once again in their traveling clothes as the door to the dungeon cell was opened; the jailor pushed them inside without a word. Lying on the cot and contemplating his misery, Morgan jumped up as he recognized his two cellmates. He waited until the footsteps in the hall died away.

"Well, now. Looks like we three are back together again! Been hunting any game these last few days?" he sneered.

They scowled at him. "Why didn't you tell us we were on the lands of Lord Kenton?" Jessi demanded.

"What? And spoil the fun? The risk of being caught just makes the hunt more exciting, and when Kenton's peasants,"— he paused and spat on the floor—"caught you two, there didn't seem much point in me joining your little party! Know what I mean?"

The bolt on the door slid on its brackets and the door swung open. "We know exactly what you mean, poacher! Thank you kindly for the confession," Hurley answered as he and the steward walked in. "Ye two may depart now," he added.

Morgan angrily lunged towards Tyler but was intercepted by Hurley, who threw his entire body weight into him, dropping him hard onto the stone floor. With a grunt, Morgan struggled to catch his breath as Hurley stood over him. "Give me a reason to strike you again," he said menacingly.

"I'll get you two," Morgan shouted after them as he stood up. "When I get out, I'll find you and make you wish you never met me. I'll bring you down just like that deer!"

"That is not likely," the steward said quietly. "Unless evidence is presented to the contrary, you should expect the hangman's noose around your neck—and rather soon."

Without another word the steward turned and left the cell, and as the strength in Morgan's legs gave way, he slowly crumpled back down onto the cold stone floor.

* * * * * *

July 10, 1614

After breakfast the next morning, Tyler and Jessi took a walk around the gardens behind the manor. They spotted the birdbath outside their cell and the bars of their cell window close by.

Resisting the urge to look inside for fear Morgan might still be there, they kept moving.

Since their release from that cell, Tyler and Jessi felt like they were now on a luxury vacation, but the call of the road, and home, was growing stronger. Upon hearing of their interest in leaving, the kitchen help began preparing a supply of food for them to take with them. Conversation with the servants was pleasant, but they could feel a certain tension in the air, as the staff kept glancing at the clock on the shelf.

The clock in the hallway chimed two o'clock, and the entire household abruptly set aside their tasks and filed out the rear of the manor towards the stables behind.

"You need not join us," Agnes told them. "In truth, it is best that you stay in the Green Room until I return for you."

Agnes seemed uncomfortable, and certainly unhappy, and within minutes they were entirely alone in the manor. They went up to the third floor, going into the Blue Room because it gave a slightly better view of the stables. They carefully peeked out through the windows, only to see the last of the household help disappear around the side of the stables. Tyler and Jessi went to the Green Room's sitting area to wait. Barely 10 minutes later all the help returned to their duties in the manor.

When Agnes came for them, the look of distress in her eyes was unmistakable. She seemed distracted, constantly wringing her hands, and was unable to focus on even the smallest task.

"Agnes," Jessi asked, "please tell us what happened." She reached out and gently took Agnes by the arm. Agnes looked up at Jessi, and the compassion she saw in her eyes was more than she could refuse.

"There are certain duties that Lord Kenton requires of all members of his household; today was the most difficult of them. However, to refuse means immediate dismissal, so no one dares disobey. The master believes in the quick administration of justice—today we were required to witness a hanging." She attempted to say something more, but couldn't continue. She sighed deeply and left, quietly closing the door behind her.

* * * * * *

After the evening meal, they joined Lord Kenton and the steward one last time in the nobleman's study. All their belongings had been returned to their packs, so all they had to do was collect the food from the kitchen and be on their way.

"In addition to your belongings," Mr. Bettencourt began, "this is something you ought to have with you as well." He handed Jessi a small envelope. She accepted it without a word, wondering what it was. "It is a traveling permit. Lord Kenton has been kind enough to vouch for your travels wherever they may take you until you return home. I presume you did not obtain the necessary permits when you entered the country?"

They shook their heads as Jessi put the envelope in her pack. "You mean, we need a permit to be able to walk on the roads in England?"

"Yes, my dear, you do," the steward replied.

Jessi closed the zipper on her pack, but then opened it up again. She pulled out her lighter and handed it to Lord Kenton. "For you, sir … uh … m'lord; it's *our* way of saying thank you!"

"This is a fine gift, and I thank *you*. Godspeed to both of you, wherever your travels take you." The twinkle in his eye danced in rhythm with the flame he held aloft.

31
St. Leonard's Forest

Friday, July 11, 1614

It was almost midday by the time they left the Kenton estate. Their packs were much heavier than usual thanks to the abundance of food supplied them by the staff; they had more than enough to reach their destination and return home. They headed down the driveway from the manor to the road, a half mile away, flanked on both sides by acres of grass. To one side a servant was tending a flock of a couple hundred sheep, contributing to the maintenance of the lord's estate by keeping the grass short with their grazing.

Tyler and Jessi stopped at the main road for one last look at the manicured fields and neatly pruned trees of the estate, then to their left in the direction from which they had come almost a week earlier. Six days! It seemed so much longer than that. Shading their eyes with their hands, they looked for the place where they had stepped off the road to begin their deer hunt. They saw several large trees along the way that could have been the one they stopped under for shade, but couldn't be certain of the right one—it didn't matter anyway.

They turned to the right and started walking west, the sun casting short shadows in front of their feet. They walked at an easy pace.

"Two more days," Jessi said.

"Hmm?"

"Two days from now, or maybe tomorrow afternoon if we push it, and we'll be home!"

"Gotta connect with Jim first, but yeah," Tyler added. "Look, there's the cemetery Agnes told us about."

During their stay Agnes had given them a brief description of the extent of Lord Kenton's lands and of a cemetery in the corner of his estate along the road. The graves were in disrepair—nothing like what they expected, with wood markers instead of stone.

One grave was brand new, with fresh earth mounded up in the center, in anticipation of its settling down over the course of time. A wood marker had been driven into the earth at one end; they knew it had to be the person who was hung yesterday. The tug was irresistible, and Tyler led the way as they approached the grave, curiosity driving them forward, apprehension screaming at them to turn and run away. The words carved on the marker were brutally simple, and their message was clear.

Tyler read aloud, his voice barely above a whisper. "Morgan Simpson, Poacher, 1597 to 1614."

Deep down they were not surprised, but still the shock was overwhelming. Shaking and suddenly weak, without a word to each other, they retraced their steps back to the road. They had walked a few minutes in silence when Jessi abruptly headed towards some tall grass at the side of the road. Without breaking her stride, she let her backpack drop to the ground as she lay down in the grass and welcomed the warm sweet smell as it swept around her like a blanket. Tyler did the same.

"Ty? Do you realize that could have been us?"

"But it wasn't. *We* are going home," Tyler said confidently, despite his uneasy expression.

They lay side by side and held hands, eyes closed, as they soaked in the warmth of the sun, utterly exhausted.

Hours later they woke up. The sun was rapidly dropping in the west, and a cool breeze made them shiver. They figured they had slept at least four or five hours. They got back on the road, the activity taking the chill off, and put a few more miles behind them before making camp for the night.

* * * * * *

Saturday, July 12, 1614

It was midmorning when they woke up. Their campsite was rather dark due to the heavy forest canopy above, and the rays of the sun never touched the tarp overhead.

They were refreshed from their long night's rest, and the prospect of this being their last full day of their journey lifted their spirits—matching what promised to be a beautiful day.

A couple hours later they once again found the shade of a tree alongside the road. They slipped their packs to the ground and sat down. Jessi pulled her boots off and wiggled her toes.

"I wish I had my sneakers now," she said. "These boots have been perfect for our trip, but they're a bit warm for today."

Tyler slipped his boots off as well, and leaned against the tree behind them. "Mine feel pretty good. I figure I'll wear them this summer if we go camping or take any hikes, except ..."

Jessi glanced at him. "Except what?"

"Well, if you saw someone wearing boots like these back home, wouldn't you be asking where they got 'em? What would you tell them? You got them while working at a farm in France? I don't think so."

A man walking by on the road cocked his head sideways and looked at them. "And what, pray tell, were you doing in France?" he asked as he approached them.

They looked warily at the approaching stranger. He looked to be about 10 years older than them, maybe just a little younger than Jim. Not saying a word they looked at him with skepticism as he came near; they had learned from their experience with Morgan to be more wary of strangers.

Sensing their hesitation, the stranger smiled, set his bag on the ground, and then sat down next to them. "Of course, what you were doing in France is *your* business, not mine." He smiled again as he introduced himself. "My name is Chris, Christopher Holder." He pulled off his hat and glanced up at the sun through the leaves of the tree overhead. "You don't mind sharing the shade with me, do you?"

"Help yourself," Jessi answered.

The phrase was new to Christopher, and after a moment's reflection determined it meant he was welcome. He fanned himself with his hat. "I'm heading to Petersfield," he offered. "What is your destination?"

The young man's easy manner seemed genuine, and Jessi felt her guard dropping with this stranger. "We're going to Horsham," she finally answered.

"Is that right? Then let's walk together. I always prefer to be traveling with someone instead of walking alone, don't you?"

There was no doubt at this point he really wanted to have them as traveling companions, and a quiet sense of relief buoyed up their own spirits. Not long afterwards the three travelers were back on the road and putting the miles behind them at a leisurely pace.

They passed through the town of Crawley by midafternoon, and an hour later were just a few miles from Horsham. They said their good-byes to their new friend, telling him they had to find a place among the trees to make camp for the night.

"But you're so close to home," Christopher said. "Why stay in the forest tonight?"

"Well, we're not actually going home," Tyler explained. "Tomorrow we're meeting a friend just north of Horsham, and we expect it will take a few hours to find our meeting place with him."

"I don't think that's such a good idea."

The concern in his voice was sincere, and rather curious. Puzzled, Tyler asked him, "Why not?"

Christopher stood up straight and vaguely glanced around him. "Well, I have heard tales of a strange creature in this area … around St. Leonard's Forest. It isn't safe to spend the night outdoors around here."

Jessi shifted her backpack on her shoulders. "We really don't have a choice," she informed him. "We don't have enough time to find our friend before dark."

"Then it would be better if I spent the night with you two, and we keep a bright fire burning all night, since all creatures are afraid of fire."

Tyler glanced at Jessi and mouthed, "Creatures?"

Jessi shrugged uneasily.

They found a place to make camp for the night, set up their tarp, and soon were looking for something else to do. They didn't have to wait long because a now-familiar movement in the underbrush caught Tyler's eye.

"Let's hunt rabbit," he proposed.

Jessi lay down on the ground and folding her hands behind her head, looked up at the leaves overhead. "Nah, we got all the food we need; why bother?"

"But no meat, and think about it, Jess. Once we are home we won't get to hunt for a long time. C'mon, let's do it."

Something different about Tyler's voice caught her attention. She looked up and saw he was looking intently to his left. "You saw a rabbit over there, didn't you?" she asked, eyebrows raised.

"Yup."

Jessi sighed as she sat up and looked around. All she could see were bushes and trees. Tyler had a good point, though; she knew it probably *would* be a while, if *ever*, before they hunted again. "Alright, let's do this."

Christopher shifted uncomfortably from one foot to the other. "I don't think it's wise. Around here it's better not to disturb the forest creatures."

"It'll be okay, Chris," Tyler said. "It's just a rabbit, and we won't be long. How about you get a fire started, and we'll bring back some dinner?"

"I cannot stop you, I know, but it would be wise not to go deep into this forest."

"Sure, no biggie," Tyler agreed with a shrug.

Chris watched them with obvious concern as they disappeared into the woods, then started scavenging around their camp for their firewood. Within 20 minutes he had all they would need to last them through the night.

* * * * * *

They patiently tracked the rabbit Tyler had spotted and slowly worked their way deeper into the woods. The trees around them were particularly large, some of them at least 10 feet in diameter; they reminded them of the stumps of old-growth Douglas firs they'd seen back home. It felt like they were in an ancient forest, which was both exciting, as well as a little spooky.

They continued to track the rabbit, Tyler in the lead, when more movement caught his eye, and he soon saw several more. He thought of the conie-warren Ethan had led them to last week, except here there was an odd, foul smell around the place: kind of sour, like something rotting. About 20 yards to his right, Tyler heard a large crash. Jessi must've tripped and fallen, but wasn't she behind him? When the rabbit froze at the noise, it made itself a perfect target. He quickly fitted an arrow to the string, pulled it back, took careful aim, and let it fly.

"I got it, Jess!" he shouted as he ran forward to retrieve his arrow and prey. He was just reaching for the rabbit when he heard another loud crash through the trees to his right. Dread filled him as he realized the noise wasn't Jessi at all. A cold chill passed through him as he thought of Chris's "creature," and with great effort he forced himself to face what was approaching.

32
Life ... and Death

Brushing aside a small tree as if it were a weed, a creature was heading straight for him—or did it want the rabbit? Tyler had only a moment to spare before it would be on him. He spun around to run away but took only one step before his right toe caught on a rock, and he fell flat on his face. Jumping back up and taking a quick look over his shoulder at the creature, he darted behind the trunk of a pine tree that was barely larger than himself. The creature hadn't followed him. Trembling from head to toe, he peered around the tree to get a better look.

The creature was standing over the rabbit, looking directly at Tyler, as if challenging him to compete for the food. Standing on two legs, with a head two feet long and a jaw about a foot wide, it towered over the rabbit at its feet. It then looked all around, prepared to defend its prey against any challenger. With a three-foot-long neck that raised its head 10 feet in the air, there was nothing around that could escape its notice.

Satisfied that there were no competitors for its meal, in one quick motion the creature swept its long neck to the ground and came back up with the rabbit in its mouth. The long, hard shaft of the arrow made it impossible to consume, so it angrily shook its head back and forth to dislodge it, to no avail. Finally it dropped the rabbit onto the ground, and placing one foot on the arrow it tore the rabbit off and gulped it down with ease. Then the creature stretched its long neck up and emitted a scream that sounded like a blend of a goose's honk and a lion's roar, making Tyler's knees shake. As it screamed, it kicked the arrow, which landed just beyond Tyler's reach.

He saw Jessi about 30 feet off to his right hiding behind another tree. Waiting until the creature's gaze was turned away from him, he leapt out from behind the tree, scooped up the arrow, and started sprinting towards her. This drew the creature's attention, and its screech once again filled the forest. Panic seized Tyler as he looked back and saw the creature's gaze following him. Without hesitation he jumped behind the nearest tree.

The creature charged after him and craned its long neck around the tree, snapping its massive jaws at him. Tyler was certainly no match for its strength, but at close range he was quicker. He was able to dodge the bite, and when the creature pulled back to come around the other side of the tree, Tyler was able to dodge it again. After two more failed attempts at him, the creature emitted another scream, even louder and stronger than before. Tyler sank to his knees in sheer terror as the creature pushed against the tree, which bent but didn't break.

Tyler seized this opportunity to make his escape and ran in the opposite direction from the creature. Directly in front of him he saw a two-foot rise, behind that a small clearing, and then dense underbrush where he might find a place to hide. He jumped onto the rise, but as he landed his foot got tangled with his bow, and he fell, arms and legs sprawled out. His face slammed hard into the ground and everything went dark. After a moment, he opened his eyes and unsteadily looked at a dandelion a few inches away, confused as to why he was lying down. He slowly lifted his head towards the creature he heard coming up behind him and rose to make a run for it, but he was too late.

* * * * * *

Peering around the tree, Jessi watched in disbelief; Tyler was being chased by some kind of dinosaur—perhaps a dragon that the old legends talk about heroes fighting against? If they had gone back in time millions of years she wouldn't have been so shocked at what she was seeing, but this was 1614! The six-foot-long tail was as thick as a baseball bat to the very end and was lifted off the ground, moving in perfect counterbalance with the creature's every step.

She watched as Tyler lay motionless on the ground as the dragon headed towards him. "NO!" she screamed in terror. The dragon stopped and looked in her direction as it pulled itself up to its full height. Jessi spun back behind the tree, suddenly gasping for breath as she crumpled to the ground in fear. At the thought of Tyler lying hurt out in the open and her own cowardice in hiding behind a tree, anger filled her to a level she had never thought possible. She rolled away from the tree onto her hands and knees facing the dragon and fumbled for an arrow. After what seemed an eternity, she finally got one in her hand and whipped it around as she reached for her bow. The razor-sharp arrowhead slashed across the palm of her left hand, and she instinctively clenched it into a fist as she dropped the bow to the ground. "You idiot!" she screamed at herself. Her gaze lifted just in time to see the dragon close the gap behind Tyler and jump. With predatory precision, it landed just behind him in the clearing. Jessi watched in horror as Tyler got to his knees in an attempt to run, but the dragon took one more step and placed its right foot on the back of his leg just above the knee, pinning him to the ground.

Tyler screamed as the weight of the creature pressed his leg down into the soft earth. He was powerless to do anything as the creature's center claw pierced his flesh and sunk deep into the back of his right hamstring; as it retracted, the claw dragged hard against the bone, tearing open his flesh. Even before the blood began to pour from the wound, his head snapped back in pain as if he'd been hit with a club. He screamed a second time, but it was abruptly cut off as he collapsed to the ground.

Jessi watched helplessly as he grew still under the dragon. She winced as it proudly lifted itself up—with Tyler still pinned under its massive weight—and looked over at her. It craned its neck to the sky as another screech filled the forest, and the last of the birds in the surrounding trees scattered away.

Jessi stood up and hollered at the dragon—she wouldn't let Tyler be its next meal without a fight. The reptile turned towards her, effortlessly kicking Tyler aside. With a loud hiss it pulled back its neck and, thrusting it forward, spat slime in her direction. She was far enough away that she had just enough time to spin back behind the tree as the slime landed where she had been standing. Her back against the tree, she heard a sizzle and watched as the slime quickly ate its way through the broad leaves of a plant, dripping to the ground below. *I thought dragons spat fire,* she thought. Then the putrid smell made her head swim and stomach grab; she felt like she was going to throw up.

She spun around to the other side of the tree and fitted an arrow to the string of her bow. The nausea overtook her as everything began to turn gray, and her ears started ringing. *Focus!* She ordered herself. Swallowing hard and concentrating, her head cleared, and she saw the dragon still standing tall near Tyler's still form. She lifted her bow but didn't know where to shoot! It was completely protected with scales from head to tail: black along its back, dark red underneath, and white around its neck.

Since there wasn't any obvious weak spot, she quickly took aim at the head and let the arrow go. It flew harmlessly past the dragon, easily missing its target by at least a couple feet.

The twang of the bow returned the dragon's attention to her, and after another hiss and spit, more slime flew her way. Seeing what was coming, she easily got behind the protection of the tree once again, as now the foliage on her right began to wilt under the acidic slime. She swallowed hard once again and held her breath to control her wrenching stomach. Peeking around the tree, she saw the dragon had turned its attention away from her—and back to Tyler! She fitted another arrow to her bow and positioned herself on one knee. She pulled the string back and hesitated an additional moment to take better aim.

As the dragon bent down toward Tyler, she could see a slight shift in the closely woven scales. She let go of the string, and the arrow found its mark between two rows of scales along its back, swaying back and forth as the dragon stretched to its full height and let out another piercing scream. It reached around and plucked the arrow out with its mouth, like it was nothing more than a sliver, and after effortlessly snapping it in half with its powerful jaws, let it drop to the ground. Enraged now, it left Tyler behind and started towards *her*.

Her back once again to the tree trunk, Jessi saw in front of her a tight group of small trees that might prove difficult for the dragon to move through. Careful to avoid the slime surrounding her, she raced ahead to gain what she hoped would be sufficient protection from the dragon. She made it to the trees just ahead of her predator, which stopped momentarily when she disappeared into the shade.

Looking back for a moment as she ran, she tripped on a tree root, and her bow flew out of her hands as she hit the ground, knocking the wind out of her. She coiled herself around a tree and lifted her face out of the dirt to see if the dragon was still coming after her. She tried to breathe, but her body wouldn't cooperate; everything from her throat to her gut felt like it was locked in a vise. She gulped mouthfuls of air and could tell it wasn't reaching her lungs. Panic welled up inside her as she wondered if she would die before being able to breathe again.

Hoping to distract the dragon long enough for Tyler to get away—if he could move—she picked up a rock and threw it about 10 feet away, the effort robbing her of precious oxygen. The dragon followed the sound of the rock and began swinging its neck back and forth under the low tree branches, searching for her in the shadows.

Finally, the vise around her lungs released, and she drew in a loud, raspy breath of air. The dragon swept its long neck in her direction with what sounded like a growl. Raw fear swept through her as the dragon's snout pushed through the leaves barely six feet away. She struggled to hold her breath so the dragon wouldn't hear her again; all she wanted was one full breath of air but was afraid it would be her last. She thought of the knife Jim had given her, but it was back in camp in her backpack. *Useless against the dragon anyway*, she thought in despair. In the distance, the approaching sound of barking dogs drew her back to the moment *and* the dragon's attention away from her.

Suddenly, two dogs burst into the clearing, and the dragon immediately turned to confront them. The animals paused only momentarily before lunging at the creature that towered over them, growling and snapping at its massive legs. It recoiled at the attack and struggled to reach down with its thick neck quickly enough to strike back at the whirling animals, but they were moving too fast for it to defend itself at such close range.

Jessi's strength returned just enough to enable her to weakly crawl forward into some bushes and peek through them to watch what was happening. The two dogs ran around the dragon, harassing it at every opportunity. She didn't know dogs grew that big and guessed they were some kind of mastiff. They must have been over two hundred pounds each and were relentless in their attack.

With a mighty leap, the dragon got clear of the dogs and landed 10 feet away. It immediately began to spin its massive bulk. As the dogs came forward, the tail of the dragon struck the lead dog in the side, and it tumbled away, howling in pain. Meanwhile, the second dog got underneath the dragon and was slashing at it with its strong teeth but unable to penetrate its scales. The dragon continued to spin, but the dog was too close to its belly to be struck by the tail. The first dog rejoined the fight, but was slowed by its injuries and in obvious pain.

By this time Christopher and the dogs' owner arrived, and they started shouting words of encouragement to his animals. The dogs darted back and forth under and between the legs of the dragon but were able to inflict only minor injury. Once again the dragon jumped clear and landed right next to Tyler.

"No!" Jessi screamed, still on her hands and knees, but no one heard her above the noise of the battle.

The dragon spun a second time and sent the injured dog hurtling away again, slamming it into a tree with a thud and a snap. Howling in pain, it stood up on three legs.

Despite its broken front leg, it rejoined the attack but was unable to get out of the way of the tail and for a third time was sent flying away. Whimpering in pain, it was only able to stand after a great effort. Ignoring the gnashing jaws of the dog under its feet, the dragon reared back its neck with a hiss and hurtled its poisonous slime at the injured dog. The slime coated its face and body, and it howled in pain as the venom ate through its skin. It rolled onto its side and frantically rubbed its eyes and face with its remaining good front leg but could find no relief, and within a minute the dog grew still. In the meantime, the second dog continued harassing the dragon.

Watching one of his beloved dogs savagely killed, the owner shouted angrily. He picked up a rock the size of a baseball and hurled it as hard as he could at the beast, only to watch it bounce harmlessly off its shoulder. The momentary distraction allowed the remaining dog to get a firm grip on one of the dragon's feet and it furiously clamped down on a toe. In a scream of pain the beast kicked the dog away, but it quickly regained its footing and charged underneath the dragon's belly once again.

After several more futile attempts to snatch up the dog in its mouth, the dragon once again jumped away, and then a spinning tail sent its attacker rolling. The dog recovered its balance and began to charge forward but received a spray of venomous slime full in the face. It collapsed in pain with a howl, as the dragon began to spin one last time. The blow sent the dog six feet in the air before landing upside down onto a fallen tree, instantly breaking its back; it mercifully died within seconds. At that point, the owner turned and fled in fear, cursing into the air.

The entire scene reeked of the creature's slime. Christopher and Jessi watched in horror as the dragon surveyed Tyler and the bodies of the dogs around him; there wasn't a sound to be heard, as no other man or beast dared challenge it.

Once again, it stretched its neck skyward and let loose a long screech that seemed to fill the forest and shake the trees, sending a shiver that shook Jessi from head to toe. As the strength in her arms gave way, she slowly fell to the ground, totally undone. Then, apparently satisfied with its victory, the dragon turned, and with the crack of fallen tree limbs breaking under its feet, it slowly retreated, disappearing into the depths of the forest.

33
𝕯eath … and 𝕷ife

With great effort Jessi rose to her feet, but the deadly stench around her finally took its toll, and she bent over and started dry heaving into the grass at her feet, leaving her stomach muscles burning like fire. She steadied herself and ran over to Tyler, turned him onto his back, and shook him.

"Tyler!" she screamed. "Tyler!" There was no response. "Wake up, you can't be dead! Wake up, please!" she pleaded, as tears started rolling down her face.

She picked him up by the arms and began to drag him away from the putrid stench that surrounded them, careful to avoid the slime the creature had left behind. Christopher joined her, and together they carried Tyler back to their camp, where they laid him on his sleeping bag.

Jessi dropped to her knees beside him. His eyes were closed, and his face was a sickening shade of gray. She couldn't tell if he was breathing or not. "Tyler, wake up!" she shouted desperately. "You *can't* die; you can't *do* that!" She reached out and pulled open one of his eyelids; his unresponsive eyes stared straight ahead, a pale color of gray. His eyes weren't green anymore—they were the color of death. "Noooo," she sobbed. "No, no, no, no."

Blood began to pool on the ground beneath him. They turned him over and saw that his right leg was soaked in blood. Christopher pulled out his knife and cut off Tyler's trousers to expose a six-inch long wound, blood steadily pulsing out onto the ground.

"He's alive, Jessi!" Christopher cried out.

"What? How do you know?"

"He's bleeding. Dead people don't bleed like that! Let's bind the wound and find some help. I know someone near Faygate who can help us."

Jessi tore strips of material from Tyler's trousers and tied them around his leg to close the wound, while Christopher began assembling a stretcher with which to carry him. Jessi helped lash the crosspieces to the carrying poles with the last of their rope, and together they picked Tyler up by the four corners of his sleeping bag, placing him on the stretcher.

"It's about a league away, so we should be there within an hour," Christopher offered. "Leave your belongings; we can return for them later."

"An hour!" Jessi objected. She remembered passing through Faygate the day before. It didn't seem like it was that far away yesterday as they were walking, but the idea of carrying Tyler that far sounded daunting. After about 15 minutes they stopped to rest. Jessi leaned over Tyler's face and gently stroked his cheek. "We're gonna get you some help, so hang on," she pleaded. After a few minutes' rest, they started out again.

"You there," a voice called out. Jessi and Christopher stopped. A wagon approached them from behind. When the wagon pulled alongside, the driver called out "whoa" to his donkey. Taking one look at Tyler, he offered his wagon for transport and soon they were moving as quickly as the donkey could manage.

"Thank you for coming back to help, Christopher. How did you know where we were?" Jessi asked, her eyes never leaving Tyler as the wagon bounced over the road.

"After I heard the first scream of the creature, I ran down to the road and saw the man with the two dogs. I enlisted his help and followed the noise to you, where he set his two dogs onto the serpent." He shook his head. "Until now I'd only heard rumors, but I never thought I'd actually see it. England is full of stories about these serpents; usually about how people braved the danger and killed them, oftentimes being killed themselves in the deed." He pursed his lips and winced, clearly regretting what he had just said. "I'm *not* saying Tyler will die," he quickly added. He paused for a moment and took a deep breath. "It's just that, well, it appears that there's still at least one more serpent that needs to be destroyed."

A few minutes later, Christopher told the driver to stop. They were in front of a small stone house about a quarter mile off the main road. He ran to the door and banged violently on it. "Widow Pike!" he shouted. "Open up! We need your help!"

The door opened as Jessi and the driver approached, carrying Tyler. They quickly brought him inside and laid him on her table. Brushing a few stray strands of gray hair out of her eyes, she looked closely at Tyler's face, then at his wound. She sniffed his wrapped leg.

"A serpent found him, yes?" she asked.

"A truly foul one, Widow Pike," Christopher answered gravely. "Can you help him?"

"With a thorough cleaning, the wound will heal; it's the damage to his breathing that's the most worrisome." She glanced at Jessi, "Are you with him?"

"Yes, ma'am."

Back bent with age and many years of hard work, she walked over to the opposite wall and with some difficulty took a jar off a high shelf. She pulled out some dry leaves and crushed them between her hands, dropping them into a pot of water. She then put the pot directly on the coals of the fire in her fireplace to bring it to a boil. "Come here, lass," her tremulous voice commanded.

Jessi dutifully obeyed.

"Smell this? It's called plantain. You need to get more; I'll tell you where to find some."

"Plantain?" Jessi asked. "Isn't that some kind of banana?"

"It's a different kind of plantain, lassie, and it has healing properties for this type of injury."

Minutes later, Jessi was running along a path in the woods behind the house. She was desperately searching for the plant when an animal flashed by off to one side. Thinking only of the dragon, she cried out and fell to the ground in fear, only to see a brown fox disappear behind a tree. Collecting her courage, she continued her search.

When Jessi returned with some fresh plantain, she found Tyler alone with Widow Pike. The sweet aroma of the simmering leaves filled the room. "Where's Christopher?" she asked.

"He had to leave; he said he'd return in a few days to check in on you two."

"A few *days?*"

"That's right, a few days. Come, lassie! What's your name?"

"Jessi, ma'am."

"Listen to me, Jessi," she continued tersely. "Your friend here is seriously injured and won't be going anywhere for quite a while—*if* he lives, you understand me?"

"Ye ... yes, ma'am," she stammered, taken aback. "Will he live? Because his eyes ..."

"What about his eyes?" she quickly asked.

"His eyes are gray, but usually they're a ... a beautiful green that ..."

Jessi froze in midsentence at the shock of what she had just said. The events of the last hour had been overwhelming, and now an avalanche of emotions swept through her; about Tyler, their journey, about home. She was as helpless to understand her feelings as she was useless in helping Tyler against the dragon. She slowly crumpled to the floor as an unstoppable moan found its escape.

Widow Pike kneeled beside Jessi and drew her close as the moaning gave way to sobs, and then tears. The intensity of the emotional release exhausted her. Widow Pike led her to a chair near the fire and thrust a cup of something warm into her hands. The warmth of the cup felt like fire to her left palm. Jessi winced as she opened her hand and looked at the cut.

Dried blood and dirt were so caked together that she could barely see the cut itself. Widow Pike took her to the sink and cleaned the wound, pressing her thumb into her palm to expose it to the fresh water. Pain shot up Jessi's arm and made her writhe in agony, but she couldn't pull away from the old woman's grasp.

"Hold still," she commanded. "This is *nothing* compared to your friend."

Jessi steeled herself against the pain as some silver water was poured into the cut. After bandaging the wound, she gently took Jessi's face in her hands.

"Listen," she began, looking intently into her eyes, "there's hope, there's always hope. My daughter had green eyes. During childbirth, as her pains became great, *her* eyes turned gray as well. It was dreadful and frightening to watch, to be certain. But she delivered a fine, healthy boy, and my grandson now has children of his own. So yes, there's hope; there's always hope."

Jessi looked into her clear blue eyes. "You're right. I have to be strong—for Tyler," she said determinedly.

"Yes," the old woman nodded slowly. "You *do* need to be strong and steady. Your dear friend needs you now more than ever. But, lassie, I have a couple more questions. I see that none of the serpent's venom touched him, so I must presume that his injuries are the wound to his leg and the poisonous vapors he breathed into his body. There was a stench that made you sick, yes? How close did *you* get to the serpent?"

"I was about 30 feet away."

"You should be fine, but he was right under the serpent. His life is in great danger, but the plantain will be of help to him."

She stood up and opened her back door. "Pardon me, dearie, I need some fresh air."

She lingered a long time behind her home, her eyes repeatedly being drawn to a grove of trees off to one side. With a sigh she gave in to the call and went over to the family cemetery. She looked with fondness at the gravestones of her parents, and then her husband's. The ache inside sprang anew as her eyes traced to the next marker— where they had buried her daughter shortly after giving birth to her grandson. *The young die too often*, she thought sadly. To the right she saw a spot that would be a good place to bury her young guest, if it came to that. Eventually she returned inside and found Jessi on a chair next to Tyler with her head on his shoulder, sound asleep, holding his hand in hers.

* * * * * *

Jessi never left Tyler's side the rest of the evening or the next day. She made another trip to gather plantain, and Widow Pike showed her how to keep the air in the home thick with its healing aroma. With practice, she was able to ladle spoonfuls of water down his throat without choking her unconscious friend.

Tyler lay insensible all night and the next day, motionless. The next evening, he finally began to stir. Ever vigilant at his bedside, Jessi excitedly noticed his movement and leaned in close. He slowly opened his eyes and stared blankly at the ceiling. "What happened?" he whispered hoarsely. "Where am I?" He tried to move but the throbbing pain in his leg overpowered him.

"Jessi?" he groaned weakly.

"I'm here, Ty. I'm here."

"What happened?"

"You were attacked by a dragon, but you're safe now." He nodded as he processed her words, fear briefly flickering across his face. She watched as his heavy lids began to close once more. She continued, "We're in the house of ... Ty?"

Tyler didn't respond; he had lost consciousness again.

34
Widow Pike's

July 15, 1614

Three more days passed and Tyler remained unconscious. He developed a fever, and Jessi was constantly bathing his face and head with a cool wet cloth to help manage it. Twice each day, Widow Pike would make a fresh mash of the plantain leaves and place it as a dressing over his wound. Jessi was constantly ladling spoonfuls of plantain tea down his throat to keep him hydrated, but beyond that there was little else that could be done.

On the fourth day, the morning began bright and clear, the sun burning away the few wisps of clouds as it climbed above the horizon. Jessi entered Widow Pike's house with the day's supply of plantain, and the noise of her entry caused Tyler to stir. He slowly turned his head towards her. "Jessi? Where are we?"

Jessi dropped the plantain leaves and rushed to his side. "Hey! You're awake! You've been sleeping for four days, Ty! You got one serious slice in the back of your leg but you're gonna be fine and every day I've been out collecting plantain leaves to boil in water to make a steam to help your lungs heal and Widow Pike puts the leaves right on your leg too, and—"

"Jessi?" Tyler interrupted with a weak smile. "Where are we?"

"Huh? Oh, we're in Faygate, a little village about two miles from Horsham. This is Widow Pike's house—she's the grandma of a friend of Christopher's—he brought us here after … after you got attacked."

"We're only two miles from Horsham, from going home?"

"Yeah, I guess so. I hadn't thought much about that."

257

"Wait, I was *attacked?*" Tyler asked. "I don't remember ..." his voice trailed off as his face became a picture of anxiety and confusion. "Jess, tell me what happened; I can't make sense of it in my head."

Jessi recounted the dragon's attack and described the venomous slime and the fight with the dogs. She told him how she and Christopher had brought him to Widow Pike's house and how he had been unconscious for the last three days. She described the plantain treatments and how they had saved his life.

"You should've run away, Jessi. If that slime had hit you, you'd have died."

She shook her head. "No way. Remember what I told you a couple weeks ago—you know, after I went off to hunt that stupid chicken? I'll never leave you alone again; we're sticking together, until we get home—together."

As she was talking, she had taken his hand in hers. Tyler smiled weakly and closed his eyes.

As Jessi looked down at her friend and held his hand, she realized that her hopes and prayers had been answered. "So, anyway, first you need to get healed up, and get your strength back. Then we'll ... Ty?"

Tyler didn't respond; he was unconscious once again.

During the course of the next week, Tyler continued to make steady progress. Every moment he was awake he would eat, his body craving food after four days of nothing but plantain tea. When he wasn't eating, he was sleeping. On the fifth day, Widow Pike declared he would most certainly recover, if they could prevent infection in the wound to his leg.

That first evening she had thoroughly cleaned it out with fresh water from a silver cup, a process that would have inflicted unbearable pain if Tyler had not been unconscious. Jessi had had to turn away when the old woman pressed the full length of her fingers into the wound to expose his bone and all the torn flesh to the healing properties of the silver water. Now, a week later, the stitches with which she had sewn the wound closed itched terribly, but there was no sign of infection. The resulting scar was sure to be an impressive one, though.

As Tyler continued his recovery, he was increasingly awake more and sleeping less. Jessi worked around Widow Pike's farm on whatever task was requested, while every few days Christopher would come by for an update on Tyler's condition. Two more weeks passed as Tyler continued to gain strength, and soon he had no further need of the crutches Christopher had made for him. Eventually, even his limping all but disappeared as he contributed more and more each day to the incessant demands of life on a small farm.

* * * * * *

August 21, 1614

A dark red chicken Tyler had named Ginger expectantly approached as he filled the feeding trough with the daily measure of meal. He put the bag of meal up on a shelf and then reached down to stroke the chicken's back. This particular hen had decided he was safe, but, even so, she froze and crouched down as he gently ran his hand across her back, scratching behind her wings. Before their adventure began, the only chickens he had ever touched were under shrink-wrap on white Styrofoam trays. He enjoyed the interaction with the chickens and had learned their various habits and the slight differences in their personalities. He was hoping that after getting home he could talk his parents into fencing part of their backyard and setting up a coop, thinking it'd be fun to have a half-dozen layers.

He stepped outside of the coop and pulled the kitchen scraps from last night's dinner out of a basket and tossed it around the yard—something else for the chickens to peck at. Then he went back inside the coop and filled the basket with all the eggs he could find. The early morning sun was still buried in the tree tops, and the cool morning breeze gently moved the tiniest branches at the top of the trees. This was a busy way of life, and a lot of work, but it felt good in a way he'd never experienced before. He had a new appreciation for farming and sensed a connection with the earth, plants, and animals that he had never thought likely, or even possible. He took a deep breath and exhaled slowly.

He smiled broadly when he realized he had done his morning chores without feeling *any* pain in his leg. It had now been almost six weeks since the creature attacked him, and he was ... done! He headed towards Widow Pike's house at an unusually fast pace, barely able to contain the happiness he felt inside.

As he approached the barn, one of Widow Pike's three cows came out and headed for the pasture behind him. Jessi followed with a full pail of milk in her left hand. She stopped and looked at him out of the corner of her eye.

"What's goin' on?" she asked.

"Are you ready to go home?" he blurted out.

Her face brightened a moment and quickly relaxed. "Only if *you* are," she said softly, almost reluctantly.

His heart skipped a beat as he felt a tingling in his chest. *Yowza*, he thought, struck by how pretty she looked. It was only then he considered just *how* completely she had committed to sticking with him until their return home. He felt his cheeks getting warm as he stammered, "Yeah ... YES! I'm ready. Let's go home."

35

𝕾𝖊𝖆𝖗𝖈𝖍𝖎𝖓𝖌

July 28, Current Year

Click. Full circle sweep: nothing. Click. Full circle sweep: nothing. Click. Full circle sweep: nothing. With each click of the mouse advancing the timer 20 minutes, Jim patiently scanned the entire perimeter of the landscape from the vantage point of the Horsham funnel. He was certain that it would take them at least a week to arrive there from Lille, yet he, nevertheless, started his scan from the third day—*their* third day—to be certain he would find them upon their arrival. After a few hours he had searched through five days with no results. He got up and went to the kitchen to make himself a sandwich, rubbing his hands and cramped fingers. His shoulders and neck ached from the tension of leaning towards the monitor. He was going to have to find a way to relax.

He was halfway through his tuna fish sandwich and was washing it down with some milk, when the solution popped into his mind. He quietly laughed at himself, choking a little on the milk before his last swallow went down. *Of course! Write a scanning routine, dummy!* He finished his lunch and returned to his workstation.

Half an hour later he was leaning back in his chair and watching the screen as his little program advanced the timer and did a full circle sweep of the view from the funnel. He had even superimposed a date and time stamp on the screen that showed the number of days since they had left Lille and their calendar date: now June 27, 1614. He created a data file to record the dates he had reviewed. By the end of *his* day, he had reviewed another seven of *their* days.

He looked at the screen and frowned, his eyes intently staring at the large "12" in the upper corner. *Twelve days out from Lille— that's plenty of time! They should be there by now,* he reasoned. *What could've gone wrong?* He stood up quickly, and his chair rolled back and hit the computer table behind him. He walked back to his kitchen and drew a glass of water from the tap. He downed the entire glass in one long draw and set it down with a satisfying burp. *Back at it again tomorrow,* he thought.

By the end of the next day he had reviewed another two weeks with still no sign of them. The counter now read 26 days since leaving Lille—almost a month! *What's taking them so long?*

By the end of the third day, the counter was up to 39 days— almost six weeks since they left Lille, and still nothing—nothing, of course, other than the now extremely familiar trees, bushes, flowers, and plants.

By the middle of his fourth day he was up to day 41 from Lille. It was now the first week of August for them. They had been in 1614 for almost two whole months. By now, he was expecting *not* to see them. The monotony of constantly looking at nothing in particular was taking its toll on his mind and attitude. He put on his running shoes and jogged the half mile down the street to the school. The 10 laps around the track cleared his mind as it challenged his body, and he felt better as he walked back to his house, showered and shaved, ate lunch, and returned to his workstation. By that evening he was up to day 43.

Two days later, as he was approaching midday of their day 60 out of Lille, he caught a glimpse of something that made him bolt upright in his chair. It was now the afternoon of August 21, 1614, for them. He pulled his program out of auto mode and manually worked the mouse to review the surroundings again. Sure enough, in the distance he could see two figures walking towards him—it was them! "Finally!" he shouted, pumping his fist. They were heading almost directly at him but not quite. He could see Jessi holding the tracker in her hand as they closed in on the homing beacon he had sent through the funnel to guide them.

Finally, about a hundred yards away from him—from the funnel—they stopped. He watched as they stood there for a long while looking around them in all directions. He watched them cup their hands to their mouths: it looked like they were shouting out, probably for him. But why over there? The homing beacon was right below him, at least in the Horsham funnel below him. He changed the viewpoint to look down directly at the ground where the homing beacon had been resting for almost two months now—it wasn't there!

He stared in disbelief at the grass below him. The beacon *had* been there before, he had doubled-checked that it was there and was working properly, but now it was gone! He turned the volume up as high as he could but he could not hear them calling out, nor could they hear him. He tried to come up with an alternate plan, but when nothing came to mind, panic seized him and held him in its grip. After all this time, here they were, so close and yet just a little too far away! He pounded the armrests of his chair in frustration.

36
𝔉unnel 𝔥unt

August 21, 1614

The hum of Widow Pike's spinning wheel was at a high pitch as they approached. They watched in fascination as clumps of wool twisted and became a continuous string of yarn as they passed through her skilled fingertips. They had seen her spend hours at a time in this activity, and had even tried it themselves under her guidance—with disastrous results at first.

She glanced briefly at their faces, and then back to her task. "You are wanting to go, are you not?"

They nodded their heads, "Yes ma'am."

"I thought as much. I sensed it coming for the last several days." The spinning wheel slowed down, and she gently brought it to a stop with her hands. She stood up and walked over to the stove, picked up a copper mug and dipped it in the water pot, slowly drinking all of its contents. She filled up the mug a second time and then looked at them, kindness and sadness both evident in her face.

"I must say, I've certainly enjoyed having the company of you two these last six weeks. I've led a quiet life since my own children grew up and left, and it *has* been nice having your help around the place," she added sheepishly. "I'm going to miss you, but you need to go home, of course. Perhaps you'll come visit me again sometime, yes?"

"I would like that too, ma'am, but I do not think it's likely," Tyler answered. "Thank you again—for saving my life. I'll never forget you."

"Nor I you, to be sure. Just remember that Christopher is coming this afternoon, and you should say your good-byes to him as well."

They told Widow Pike that they would be gone a couple hours to find their meeting place with Jim and then return to see Christopher and get their things. A few minutes later they were heading out the door towards Horsham. They were barely off the property when Tyler abruptly stopped.

"I'm getting my bow and arrows; I'm not going anywhere around here unarmed!"

"Arrows won't do any good against that dragon, Ty."

"Yeah, well, I'm getting them anyway."

He rejoined her a couple minutes later, and they headed back towards Horsham. After about an hour they decided they were probably close enough to the funnel for the tracker to pick up Jim's radio signal. Jessi turned it on and slowly spun in a half circle, watching the meter for a response. The meter registered a faint signal to the southwest, and they set out across the uneven woodland in that direction.

Every few minutes Jessi would check the device again, and each time the response was stronger. Finally the meter went to the maximum, so they stopped and called out into the air around them.

"Hello! Hello! ... Jim?" They felt silly talking out loud when there was no one there, at least no one they could see. Fortunately, they were alone.

Jessi walked another 10 yards and took another reading. The signal was weaker! She did another sweep of the area and the meter maxed out when she was facing Tyler. They were definitely at the funnel, but where was Jim? Remembering that Jim could only look for them in 20-minute intervals, they decided they would just have to make themselves comfortable and wait for him to spot them.

"Let's find the beacon, Ty. I'll run the meter and you go where the signal spikes."

Jessi walked in a large circle around Tyler, telling him to move in various directions based on the strength of the signal until she decided Tyler had to be standing right on top of the beacon. She turned the homing device off and shoved it in her pocket as they scoured the ground around them, but they couldn't find it. It had to be here!

"Uhh ... Jess? I think I know where it is." Tyler was pointing at a hole, about eight inches in diameter that was hidden directly under the bush he was standing next to. "I bet a raccoon or a mole or *something* took it in there."

"I'm not gonna stick my hand in there. I might get my finger bitten off!" Jessi had put her hands in her pockets without realizing it, and sheepishly pulled them out.

"Well, that would explain why Jim isn't answering us; we're not at the funnel, but we've gotta be pretty close!"

They looked around in all directions, not for the funnel, since it couldn't be seen, but maybe Jim had left some other kind of clue for them to find. The only thing they could see around them was the untouched forest that was home to the wild creatures, far from the influence of any humans.

They waited for what they figured was at least another half hour, and when they received no contact from Jim, they decided to go to Widow Pike's and make another plan. It was a discouraging walk back.

* * * * * *

August 2, Current Year

No! This can't be! Frustration and anger welled up as Jim watched them walk away. *Calm down. They'll be back*, he reassured himself. *There's no other place for them to go.* He grabbed his wallet and keys and headed to the garage. The electronics store had more beacons. All he had to do was send over another one, and they would track on the new one instead.

He backed his car out into the street and was just pulling away from his house when, with a groan, he pulled over and stopped. He had no idea what frequency their homing device was set for.

Shouldn't have thrown away the paperwork, dummy! It would do no good to send another beacon. He leaned forward and rested his forehead against the steering wheel.

* * * * * *

August 21, 1614

As expected, Christopher was there when they returned to Widow Pike's. His easy-going manner was just what they needed to lift the disappointment off their shoulders. Without totally understanding how, he had become a true friend, despite the fact that he was almost twice their age.

They had just finished telling him and Widow Pike about their failure to meet with Jim, and that they really didn't know what else to do, when Christopher's face brightened.

"Well, cheer up, my young friends. You're going to be famous!"

"What do you mean?" Tyler asked.

"Famous for what?" Jessi had a bad feeling about this.

"The news of your adventure with the serpent somehow reached London, and a man named John Trundle is going to write a story about it."

"You mean like an article in a newspaper?" Tyler asked.

"No, I understand the story will be printed in a pamphlet and distributed to warn other people to be careful when they travel in this area around St. Leonard's Forest. He will be here in a few days—on Monday—to talk with us, so I'll see you again then."

"No, I don't think so, Chris," Jessi said. "I'm sure we'll be gone by then, at least I hope so; we need to go home. Besides," she added, "I think … I think it would be better if you told the story without us being in it. We don't … belong here," she said as she waved her hand in a circle. She thought it would be better if they stayed out of the history books.

"Are you sure?"

"We're sure," Tyler agreed. "You know what happened. You can tell the story without us."

"All right," Christopher shrugged. "I'll tell him everything that happened, and just won't mention you were there. Now, as far as meeting with your friend to take you home, how can I help?"

They retrieved their backpacks and said their good-byes to Widow Pike. An hour later the three of them were back at the spot where their meter had located the beacon. Christopher was fascinated with how the tracker worked; these two were full of surprises.

They set out walking in a pattern around the beacon, spreading out further and further from each other as they would stop, call out, and listen, stop, call out, and listen ...

* * * * * *

August 2, Current Year

Jim put the clamp on the wire leads, and the *whoop-whoop* of the fire alarm in his hands pierced the air. He winced as he held it out at arm's length then dropped it on the floor. It bounced up on its side and rolled a couple of feet before falling over—silent.

Jim frowned. He did *not* want it to stop; he needed it to keep screeching after it went through the funnel and fell to the ground. He glanced briefly towards the kitchen as the oven timer dinged, telling him his pizza was done. *The pizza can wait. First I gotta get this figured out*, he thought. He pulled the cover off the alarm and looked inside. The batteries had slipped out of their clamps. After a few moments consideration, he went into his garage, sat down at his workbench, and grabbed some duct tape. *Duct tape holds the world together*, he thought determinedly.

* * * * * *

August 21, 1614

Jessi moved another 20 yards away from the others and waited. "Jim? Can you hear me?"

Suddenly she heard the muted screeching of a fire alarm off in the distance. "Tyler!" she shouted over her shoulder. "Can you hear that? It's gotta be Jim!"

Her heart raced as she quickly closed the distance, jumping over fallen tree limbs and weaving her way between the shrubs and grasses. Then her toe caught a small tree root that was sticking out of the ground, and she went down fast. Instinctively rolling as she fell, she was unhurt. She jumped back up and taking more care this time, soon found the source of the noise.

She stopped and looked straight down at the white disk at her feet. It looked like the fire alarm that was in the hallway of her house, and the whooping that usually made her ears hurt sounded like the most beautiful music she had ever heard. Written on the surface were the words: *To stop me—you gotta break me!* She picked up a rock about the size of her fist and brought it down hard on the alarm. It didn't stop.

Tyler and Christopher finally caught up with her, only to see her repeatedly banging something with a rock. Finally, silence returned to the woods.

"Jessi! What are you doing?" Tyler asked.

"Just following orders," she said with a smile, holding up the alarm for Tyler to read. She then stood up and looked around. "Jim? Are you there?"

No response.

"Jim?"

Christopher looked at her. "Who are you talking to? There's nobody here!"

They waited about five seconds before Tyler's face brightened. "It's okay, Jim. This is Christopher. He's a good friend who saved my life. You can talk to us. Jim?"

"Yeah, I'm here, guys."

Christopher took a step backwards. "How is this possible?" he asked. "I hear a voice, but I see no one. Is he a spirit only?"

"No, no!" Tyler quickly answered. "Our friend has a … a device that allows him to speak to us from a great distance. That same device will take us home."

"Thank you, Christopher," Jim said. His voice sounded like he was speaking through a drum. "I look forward to finding out how you helped them."

Christopher looked around him and then down at his feet. "Well, I just did what I could," he mumbled as he took a step backwards.

"Well, it's time to come home. Are you ready?"

"YES!" they answered in unison.

"Okay then. First, let's bring your stuff home."

They carefully piled everything in a stack according to Jim's instructions and then moved back about 10 feet. A big burst of air blew out from the midst of the funnel for a few seconds, pressing the grass outward in all directions, marking the exact center of the funnel. Then with a *soomp* their backpacks and bows and arrows disappeared.

With a muffled cry, Christopher froze, his mouth hanging open. He watched as Tyler and Jessi high-fived each other.

"All right, you two," Jim called out. "Now it's your turn, but listen closely. I've brought your gear home to me now, in early August, but I'm sending *you* back to noon on the day you left back in May. I'll be an emotional mess, and I won't be expecting you to suddenly appear in front of me—so take it easy on me, okay?"

"Ah, really? We aren't going to have our bows and arrows all summer?" Jessi grumbled good-naturedly.

Tyler approached Christopher for the last time and extended his hand. "Thank you, Chris, for everything. Don't worry; we'll be fine." They spoke quietly together in such low voices that even Jessi couldn't hear them, and then parted.

Jessi eagerly stepped into the center of the funnel and waved good-bye to Christopher. Tyler joined her, and they stood back-to-back. "We're ready!" he called out.

"Not quite. You have to be very close together."

They pressed their backs against each other and interlocked their arms at the elbow, pulling tightly together. A blast of air struck them from above and continued for at least 15 seconds.

Jessi started giggling. "Smells like pizza!"

"Nice! I'm *so* ready for that!" Tyler laughed.

Then, a moment later, the grass and trees—and Christopher, melted away as the familiar sight of Jim's living room took its place. Still laughing, they dropped a couple inches to the floor and fell in a heap.

* * * * * *

May 26, Current Year

A tiny hissing sound began, and quickly grew in intensity, reminding Jim of a pneumatic tube at a bank drive-thru. He lifted his head off of the carpet and stared into the circle, for there was no doubt where the sound was coming from. Suddenly with a *shuunk* Jessi and Tyler appeared a few inches off the floor, back-to-back, with their arms locked at the elbows. They tumbled down, laughing.

Jim jumped up and ran towards them, his mind struggling to believe what his eyes were seeing. He was happy to see them—and confused. He pulled them up off the floor and hugged them. He wasn't sure he wanted to let them go.

"Are you all right?" he yelled.

They looked around the room and then back to him.

"You don't have to shout!" Jessi mockingly shouted back at him.

"Oh, man, it's good to be home … here … now!" Tyler blurted out. "Electricity! I love it! Look, Jess!" The hall light flickered rapidly off and on as he played with the light switch. They both laughed hysterically.

Jessi then let out a deep breath. "Home, sweet home." She stopped and sniffed, a puzzled look on her face. "Where's the pizza?"

"What pizza?" Jim said.

"The air you sent our way to bring us back was full of pepperoni pizza!"

"The air I sent … *what?* Sorry, no pizza here. Don't know what to tell you."

Jim looked at them, they'd changed, and not just their clothes. They were each maybe half an inch taller, tanned, and a bit leaner, and their clothes made them look like a couple of farmhands. They were of hand-sewn fabric, tailored actually quite well to their sizes. Their leather shoes looked painful: exactly the same as each other—no left and right by shape. He was too busy looking at them to say anything else.

"Tyler, look! Just like we figured!" Jessi exclaimed. She was looking up through the perfectly cut circular hole in the ceiling. "And everything that went with us is gone!"

"Went where?" Jim asked.

"To Amiens," Tyler answered. "To France, and then after you …"

"Hold it!" Jim interrupted.

"Why?" Tyler asked, puzzled.

"I'm sorry. I know I just asked you where you went, but something tells me I shouldn't hear it just yet. You gotta give me a minute to collect my thoughts. It's been a rough morning."

* * * * * *

August 21, 1614

Christopher's legs felt a little wobbly as he looked at the spot where they had been just a moment before. The grass was pressed out from a center circle about three feet in diameter. This was something that would be hard to explain, if he dared to try. The sudden quiet pressing in on him made him feel *very* alone;

they were indeed gone. He supposed they were home now—wherever that was he wasn't certain, since every time he asked they had always been rather evasive in their response.

With a shake of his head he began to slowly walk back to Widow Pike's.

37
𝕽eturneð

May 26, Current Year

Tyler and Jessi were sitting on the sofa in Jim's living room, their hands constantly stroking the plush microfiber upholstery. He sat opposite them in a rocker. "So," Tyler began, "you're saying that in the movie, the old lady gives the young guy a music box, then he goes back in time, gives it to her when she's young, and then returns to his own time?"

"That's right," Jim answered. "She keeps it all her life until she gets old, and then she gives it to him. It makes a nice story line for a romantic movie, but leaves no place for the music box to get made in the first place. The box is in a continual loop between the two of them. That's why most people don't believe time travel is possible—it creates too many logistical problems."

"So, what are you so concerned about here?" Jessi asked. "Now that we all know we travelled through time, and got back safe, how can we mess it up?"

"I'm not sure, but I don't want to take any chances. The main thing is that you *are* back safe and sound, although you both have some explaining to do."

"Huh?"

"Well, for starters, you both look maybe half an inch taller than you were four hours ago. Therefore, I can presume you've been gone a while."

"Actually," Jessi began. "We were gone for—"

"Wait! Don't tell me! Also, you've both got great suntans, but summer has hardly begun. Not to mention, if you leave this house wearing those clothes, you'll have more questions to answer, and *not* just because of the smell. Give me a few more minutes and I'll probably think of something else you'll need to explain."

They sighed and looked at the floor. They had thought all their problems would be over as soon as they got back home. Tyler smiled as he rubbed his feet back and forth on the carpet. "Carpet feels nice, doesn't it, Jess?"

"Umm, yeah, sure. Okay, Jim, so what do we do now?"

"You can help me reassemble The Bridge, but change your clothes first, so if you have to go to the store for something, you'll not attract any attention. Plus, guys, you really *do* reek."

"Can't, my stuff went with us," Tyler answered. "It's history now—literally!"

"Har har," Jessi said with a smirk. "Yeah, I left my clothes behind too," she added. "It was just as well. We stuck out like sore thumbs, and these were better. Oh, wait! I've got some extra clothes in my backpack! You *do* still have it, right?"

"Of course I have it," Jim replied. "Remember, regardless of how long you were *there*, you left here just a few hours ago. Hmm, there's something very Narnia about all this," he muttered. Standing up, he stretched, fingertips coming just short of the ceiling. "I'll see if I can scrounge up a reasonably clean towel for you, Jessi. Grab your backpack." He headed down the hall.

"This is so *great!*" Jessi exclaimed.

"What do you mean?"

"We went back in time, were there a few months, and now we've returned right after we left!" She hopped off the couch to grab her backpack. "No one will miss us 'cause we've only been gone a few hours, and now we're gonna be here while Jim figures out how to bring us back! This is perfect! Two summers for the price of one. Yessss!" She gave Tyler a fist bump, then opened her backpack, pulled out her shirt, and inhaled deeply. "Ooh!" she giggled, "lemon fresh!"

* * * * * *

The rest of the afternoon was spent assembling all the replacement hardware, then installing and testing all of Jim's custom software, most of which he had written himself. The recovery of the database from the backup drives would take the rest of the evening.

Jim stood in front of his open fridge. "Hmm, this isn't gonna work," he said. "Can I interest you in some fast food?"

"Hamburgers sound good. It's been a long time," Tyler said.

"With ketchup," added Jessi.

"And mayonnaise."

"And fries."

"And a milkshake."

Jim looked at them. This morning they were just classmates working on a project together, clearly because they *had* to, not because they wanted to. But now they were so close they were finishing each other's sentences. "Burgerville works for me, but Tyler, you've got to get some regular clothes first," he said.

When they got to Tyler's house it was obvious no one was home. It was just as well, since it'd be tough to explain his clothes and funky smell. "Gimme ten minutes to shower and change," he said as he hopped out of Jim's SUV. He kept trying to think of where his parents could be, but it'd been so long he couldn't remember what their plans had been. Using their hidden house key, he got in through the back door, grabbed the clothes on top of the laundry basket his mom had left at his door, and hit the shower. Three minutes later he scooped up his filthy clothes, slipped into his flip-flops, and was back in the SUV. He tossed Jessi his 400-year-old clothes. "Toss these in the back, will ya?"

Jessi winced as she quickly threw the clothes over her shoulder. "Phew. Gross! *Please* tell me you used soap when you took that thirty-second shower."

Tyler didn't answer. He took a deep breath and grew silent, looking straight ahead.

Jim glanced in his direction. "You okay, Ty?"

"Yeah," he said with a sigh. "I played through my mind so many times what coming home would be like, but walking into an empty house wasn't one of them. No one even knew to miss me." He bit his lower lip and looked out the window.

"It'll be okay, Ty," Jessi said as she reached forward and lightly squeezed his shoulder. "We're home now, *together.*"

Tyler squared his shoulders and managed a tight smile. "Yeah, you're right," he said with a nod.

As Jim pulled up to a stop sign, the same nagging question hit him again. *Just how long were they gone?*

* * * * * *

The girl behind the counter smiled as they walked in. "Welcome to Burgerville, what can we get you?" Jim looked behind him. "So what'll it be? Burgers and fries?"

"Of course," they both answered.

Jim shook his head. They were so tight, they even talked in unison.

"What's the fresh seasonal shake now?" Tyler asked.

Jim looked hard at him for a moment. "It's still strawberry, same as yesterday," he quietly answered.

"Oh, yeah."

"So," Jim said as he set the food on the table. "Let's talk. Do you two remember why you came over to my house this weekend in the first place?"

They looked at each other; it'd been so long, they couldn't remember.

"I seem to recall you were researching 17th-century England and France. Do you still need access to my database for that?"

They laughed. "I think we've got plenty of stuff to write about, no researching necessary!" Jessi said.

"Yeah, and some of it people won't believe." Tyler added, his eyes looking into the distance but not focusing on anything in particular.

Puzzled, Jim looked carefully at him. He saw pain, or perhaps fear, on his face. The intensity was so apparent that Jim felt his own chest tighten.

Tyler returned his gaze to the table and looked at Jim. "Like being in a fairy tale, only it's not a fairy tale; it's *real.* Everyone will think it's just a story, but it *isn't* just a story. *It isn't!* It's something that really happened, where people and animals really got hurt, and died ..." His words stuck in his throat, and he looked down. "Four hundred years ago people wouldn't have believed what we would have to say about our modern world if we told them," he said slowly and deliberately. "Just like people now wouldn't believe us about ..." he looked back at Jim. "But it *really* happened, and people wrote about it, so it's part of ... part of our history!"

Jim leaned forward, "What is?"

Ignoring Jim's question, Jessi looked at Tyler. "Then how come it's *not* in our history books?" she asked him.

Jim glanced back and forth between them. "Hey, you gotta help me out here," he said. "*What* are you talking about?"

Jessi looked at him. "Dragons," she said.

"Dragons! You can't be serious?" Jim responded as he sat up straight in the booth.

"Dead serious." Tyler said as he looked at Jessi.

"Huh, dead is right ... no more fairy tales," Jessi quietly added without dropping her eyes from Tyler.

"Wait a minute. Are you telling me you saw dragons?"

A few seconds passed before Tyler tore his gaze away from Jessi to look at Jim. "Yeah, up close and personal."

"*How* up close and personal?"

"Well," Tyler answered slowly, as if choosing his words carefully. "Let's just say that in a Coolest Scar contest, I'd probably win." He smiled weakly, but it quickly faded into a shudder.

Jim found himself speechless as he struggled to make sense of this news. He watched as Tyler and Jessi did a slow motion fist bump over the center of the table. He knew he had a big job ahead of him, way more important than some video game, and even though he knew he'd pull it off, he felt a sense of desperation in his gut.

He rapidly slapped the table twice. "All right, you two," he began. "Keeping in mind what I told you about the 'looping' problem with time travel, I have to figure out *where* you went, *when* in time you went to, *how* I communicated with you, and *how* I got you back—and I don't think you should tell me anything to help me. I'm certain that what I need to learn to get those questions answered will be what I need to know to make it happen. No shortcuts. What's most important is we all know it's going to work out okay. For you two the adventure is over, but for me, it's just beginning!" He took a deep breath, "Okay! Let's go home."

"Wait a minute, Jim," Tyler blurted out. "Just before you brought us back you promised to let us pick out bows and arrows today to replace the ones we've been using. Don't worry! It won't make any looping problems."

"He didn't say that!"

"Well, he would have if my past self had thought to ask future Jim!" Tyler scolded sarcastically. "I don't want to lose my touch. Besides, you've *got* a bow and arrows. I don't."

"Listen, guys," Jim said with a laugh. "I'll buy you two *whatever* you want. I'm just glad you're back!"

By the time they got back to his house, the backup recovery was complete. Tyler and Jessi got to work on their history project at Jim's kitchen table and finished it in less than an hour.

Meanwhile Jim started reviewing everything that had happened in the last couple of days up to the point of their departure. He quickly reestablished the connection with the Amiens funnel, looking at the cars moving along the street. It was early morning there, and the faint smell of car exhaust again filled The Bridge. A shock of adrenaline coursed through him as he quickly disconnected. If he wasn't careful, *he'd* be the next one to be transported.

"Forget the replication, Jim," he muttered to himself. "Analyze your data." He closed his eyes and leaned back in his chair. "Think outside the box, Jim. Think outside the box."

* * * * *

Tyler turned off the television and ejected the Blu-Ray. "So what'd you think?" he asked.

"Not bad," Jessi responded. "They did pretty good with the props, but it wasn't nearly dirty enough."

"Yeah, everything was way too clean and neat."

Jim looked up at them as they approached The Bridge. "I think I know what happened!" He got up and started pacing around the living room; they just stood and waited. He stopped and looked at them. "Where'd you go anyway? What time is it?"

"We watched your copy of The Three Musketeers. We wanted to see how realistic it is."

"And is it?"

They shifted their weight back and forth as they thought about it. "Yeah, kinda," Jessi ventured. "But it's too ... neat. Everyone in the movie has clean clothes that match, with no stains or rips. Speaking of clothes, wearing clean clothes is great, but it actually feels weird wearing jeans again."

"I kinda miss the dress," Tyler teased. "Anyway, the houses in the movie didn't look very used and ... oh, I don't know, it just doesn't look like real life. But it's an okay movie." They both shrugged and looked away from him.

"Are you guys all right?"

They both let out a deep breath. Tyler frowned. "I'm totally glad to be back," he said. "But there is so much about life here that is so ..."

"Fake," finished Jessi.

"Yeah, kinda. Maybe more like extra. This feels so ... removed from the basics, you know, of food and shelter. We have so much extra everything around us. Stuff we don't *need*."

"You wanna live off the land and sleep in a pile of leaves every night?" Jim chuckled. "I think I know what you mean, though. You're right; we have a lot of comforts, and they *are* extras. We just get used to them. It's good for us to remember that most people in the world still live just like you guys did while you were gone. It's okay."

He straightened up and stretched, this time his fingers just touched the ceiling. "Oh! As I was saying, I *now* know how this all happened. It's all a matter of balance. Every one of the funnels is more or less stable, okay? Last night I started a routine to collect data, but I see now that we collected more than just data. We collected *mass*."

He could tell they weren't sure what he meant by that.

"What I'm saying is, the reason we smelled the car exhaust from the street in modern Amiens was because we were bringing in air from there to here. Remember that even air has weight—or mass, if you will. Anyway, eventually we pulled in enough mass that it blew back the other way to regain balance—and took you two along for the ride. But the transfer was too ... umm ... violent, probably from the power surge that shut down the neighborhood. Since the two of you were too *much* mass, some dirt and a tree came back here on the rebound, so to speak, and then balance was restored."

Jim wasn't talking to them anymore. He was in his zone, pacing around the room as he spoke. He stopped and looked at them. "I don't know yet why the time travel happened, but when mass travels at, or near, the speed of light, the relationships between time, mass, and energy all change. New rules seem to apply. Einstein spent his lifetime working on this issue, and even *he* admitted his research was a work-in-progress."

He stopped and looked at them again; they had no idea what he was talking about.

"Sorry, what I'm saying is that according to Einstein's Theory of Relativity, the rules all change, having to do with time and energy, when anything is traveling at or near the speed of light, which is basically how fast you were moving when you left here."

"Awesome!" Jessi whispered, as they high-fived each other.

"Anyway, I've got a lot to learn. Now that I see it's possible to send and receive mass along the space-time continuum, I have to learn how to control and manage it in such a way that ..." he looked at them, and saw he had lost them again. "Sorry, what I need is *time*," he chuckled at his use of the word. "Time to learn how to get you back."

Jim sat down at The Bridge. "This may take me five days, or five years," he said. "It won't matter to you two, because when

I'm ready, I'll just dial back to whenever you landed over there, and bring you back here. In other words, I'll move you from one funnel in the distant past to this funnel here as of noon today!"

Despite his confident words, he knew it wouldn't be that simple. Clearly some things were going to go wrong on their end. He was certain they would tell him if he asked, but he thought it best not to; it would be better to learn everything on his own.

"Oh, I talked to both your parents, and they're expecting you home in ... five minutes! I gotta get started on this right away. Good night, and welcome back." He turned back to his workstation, stretched his arms wide overhead, ran both hands through his hair, and got to work.

Without another word, they let themselves out and went home.

* * * * * *

Monday morning Tyler knocked on Jessi's front door. Her dad answered.

"Hey, Mr. Hernandez. Is Jessi ready?"

"I think so." He looked upstairs. "Jessica, you ready to go? Tyler's waiting here for you."

"He is? *Awesome*, I'll be right there."

Her tone of voice caught her dad's attention. He turned back to Tyler and looked intently at him, not saying a word.

"Uh, we had a great weekend," he offered.

"Mmm hmm."

Jessi came down the stairs. "Hey, Ty. Let's go. Bye, Dad!" She kissed him on the cheek as she blew out the front door.

Tyler waited until they were a few houses away. "That was awkward!"

"What?"

"Your dad. I got a stare down from him, like ... like I had just thrown a brush-back pitch at him."

"What did you say to him?"

"It wasn't what *I* said. It's what *you* said."

"What?"

"Well, it was more like *how* you said it."

"Tyler, what are you talking about?"

"You sounded happy to hear I was at the door."

"Well, I *was*, but wha ... oh." They walked in silence to the next intersection. "How we gonna do this, Ty?"

"Do what, exactly?"

"You and me, school, everything I guess."

"I'm not sure. Together?"

She looked at him and smiled. "I can do that."

They walked hand in hand the next few blocks. Jessi took a deep breath. "Tyler, I don't even know what classes I have this morning! It's been almost three months and ... what if I have a test today?"

"Not likely, there's only two weeks left in school, so we probably got a week to get our heads back into it, before ... you know, finals or something. Jessi, I'm having trouble with this too. It doesn't seem *right* to ... to just go back to life like nothing happened. I don't know, this isn't working out like I thought it would. I just figured everything would be like normal, but it isn't."

"I know what you mean," Jessi answered quietly. "But Tyler, we are here ... together! But *getting* here was just the first part, you know? Now the second part, getting back to our normal lives, may be the tougher part. But we can help each other do *this* too—right?" She turned and faced him.

Tyler gave a shaky smile. "Yeah, we can." The urge to kiss her was overwhelming.

They crossed the last street and entered onto school property, still holding hands, walking slowly. Parker Theissen approached from the right.

"Hey, hey! Was I right or not? It just took you a few weeks to figure it out!" he exclaimed.

Jessi sighed. "Parker, you really should think before you speak, but yeah. Hey, maybe you're psychic!"

"More like psychotic," Tyler muttered.

They both laughed as they entered the gym. The warning buzzer sounded. Three minutes to get to their seats.

38
𝕾ummer 𝕽eunion

August 2, Current Year

The phone rang three times before Jessi picked up the receiver. "Hello?"

It was Jim. "Hey, Jessi. Your stuff just got here. Grab Tyler and come over, okay?"

"Awesome! We'll be there."

Within an hour they were at Jim's front door. Tyler rang the doorbell, then excitedly said to Jessi. "I've *so* been looking forward to this day!"

"Why?" Jessi asked.

"You'll see," he said with a quick lift of his eyebrows.

The door opened and Jim welcomed them inside. "I figured you'd want to go through your stuff. There's probably something here you'll want to keep as a souvenir from your adventure."

"Oh, yeah!" Tyler quickly answered as he looked around for his backpack. It wasn't in the front room.

Jim waited until Tyler looked at him. With a slight smile he nodded his head in the direction of the kitchen. "Kitchen table."

They hustled to the back of the house, Tyler leading the way. Their packs were at the far end of the table; on the near side were the leftover pieces of the pizza Jim had eaten for lunch. Jim removed his plate to give them room to unload their packs.

"They arrived a couple hours ago. I didn't go through them yet; I wanted you two to do that, and now that your adventure is finally complete, *and* my job is done, you can tell me all about it."

By now, they'd been home for over two months and had settled back into their familiar routines. Now, as they pulled out the contents of their packs, the memories of their trip came flooding back faster than they could talk. After a couple minutes, Jim opened his laptop and started taking notes.

A strange water creature? Hauling water on a farm, milking cows? Taking care of chickens? Jim just shook his head and kept typing to keep up with the constant stream of chatter.

Reaching deep into her pack, Jessi pulled out the small leather pouch. "Here you are, Jim" she offered. "I'm sure you want *these* back; they must've cost you a fortune!" she said as she dropped her two diamonds into his open palm.

"Oh, yeah!" Tyler said. "But I just have one for you since we used one to pay for our passage across the English Channel."

"That's awesome!" he laughed. "But these aren't real diamonds. I paid forty bucks each for them—they're zircons."

"Huh? You mean like what we see at the mall?" Tyler started laughing.

"I wonder what the captain did with that 'diamond' we gave him. Did he sell it and get a new boat, or did he get in trouble for trying to sell a fake?" Jessi snickered.

"I'll never forget his greedy hands grabbing for it!"

"Or the look on his face when you first set it in front of him!"

"Well, I'm glad I thought of sending those, then," Jim added. "I figured it would be better than gold or silver, and a whole lot cheaper, too."

They then described how they slipped past the border guards in Dover, and their deer hunt with Morgan that led to their imprisonment. Jim could only shake his head. "If I'd have known all this, I would've been more worried than I already was! Of course, I knew all along that you'd be okay, since you were already back!"

Jessi thought for a moment, "Now I get it!" she shouted. "You had pizza today! *That's* why we smelled pizza when you brought us home, and you didn't know what we were talking about."

Jim closed his eyes and leaned his head back. "You're right, Jessi. I've been thinking about your pizza comment these last couple months—never did make sense to me. Maybe that's why pizza sounded good to me today. Without doing it on purpose, I actually … closed the loop, I guess you could say."

"By the way," he added. "When you first got back, you mentioned something about dragons. At the time you just weren't ready to talk about it, but hey, I really want to know what happened. What was that all about?"

They both grew silent and looked at the floor. Tyler exhaled slowly as he pulled his arms close to his chest and struggled to control his breathing.

* * * * * *

It was another half hour before Jim ran out of questions. He finally had a good handle on their entire adventure and knew he now had some serious research ahead of him. "Tyler?"

"What?"

"I wanna see that scar. Is that okay?"

"Yeah sure, but not in front of Jessi."

"I've seen it."

"You have?" Tyler blushed.

"You were unconscious. I helped Widow Pike take care of …" She turned away.

Jim pulled Tyler to the hallway, saving him from further embarrassment. "Let's take a look."

They returned to the table a minute later.

"Well?" Jessi asked.

"Looks like it healed up real well. If I didn't know it was there, I probably wouldn't have noticed it."

"Awesome," she replied, visibly relieved.

"Jim?"

"Yeah, Ty, what's up?"

"I need to connect back with Christopher—in 1614. Can I, please? I promised him I would talk to him a month after we left, to let him know that we got home and everything—okay?"

"You did?" Jessi asked.

Tyler smiled and nodded.

Jim sat down at The Bridge and dialed back to the date he retrieved them, then went forward a month. He turned on the scanning program and within 10 minutes they spotted Christopher approaching the funnel. They watched as he slowed down and stopped about 10 feet away. He sat down in the grass, apprehension on his face.

"Hi, Chris!" Tyler called out. "I'm glad you came back!"

Christopher jolted upright, startled at hearing Tyler's voice, even though he was expecting it. "Hello, Tyler, my young friend. How *are* you?" he said as his eyes glanced around, as if hoping to see him.

"I'm good. Glad to be home."

Christopher reached into his bag and pulled out a small booklet. He held it up and smiled towards the empty space in front of him. "I have it! You can see this—right? The printer from London wrote our story! He got a little carried away, saying the serpent itself was slimy and smelly, but other than that, it is properly written. This copy is for you."

He gingerly stepped forward and placed it on the ground in front of him, more or less where he thought they had been standing when they disappeared last month. He quickly stepped back, getting in the spot itself made him a little nervous. Jim had him move it about a foot to the right, and put a small rock on top so it wouldn't blow away. After that a rushing wind blew briefly, and then with a *soomp* the rock and the fluttering pages of the pamphlet disappeared. Christopher took another step back.

Tyler picked the pamphlet up off the floor, tossed the rock aside, and read the title: *"True and wonderfull. A discourse relating a strange and monstrous serpent (or dragon) lately discovered... "* He stopped reading the lengthy title and looked towards the monitor. "Thanks, Chris! I got it."

They chatted for a few more minutes before reluctantly saying their final good-byes. As Christopher turned around to go, Tyler called out, "Chris! Wait!"

He ran to the kitchen table and grabbed his lighter. He placed it on the floor and turned to Jim. "Send that to him, okay, Jim?"

"Sure thing," he replied, as his fingers flew across the keyboard. He paused for a moment and then hit a special function key. There was a whoosh of air. The lighter disappeared and the faint scent of grass spread through the room.

"That's for you, Chris. As long as there's liquid in the tube, it'll make fires real easy to start."

Christopher picked the lighter up and smiled. "Thank you, my young friend, and Godspeed." He then quickly walked away, never looking back.

"Good-bye, friend," Tyler whispered to himself.

Jim sat quietly in his chair thinking of Christopher with that lighter in his hand. Something was bothering him, but he wasn't quite sure why. "That's it!" he finally blurted out.

"What's it?" Jessi asked.

"That cigarette lighter we gave to Christopher didn't invert! Remember at the funnel in Amiens, how the stuff that went back and forth between here and there got twisted inside out? Well, that lighter went back and forth to the funnel in Horsham—but it didn't invert! I have no idea why, but I'm going to find out. Great. One *more* item on my 'To-Do' list."

"Hey, look at this!" Jessi called out. "I just googled 'true and wonderfull' ... and here it is! The pamphlet became part of the 'Harleian Miscellany,' whatever that is."

Jim spun around in his chair and looked at what Jessi had discovered. He soon found the answer. "'... in the 1780s, Lord Harley assembled a large collection of written works into a compilation that came to be called the Harleian Miscellany.' Interesting. That'll be fun to read through later."

Tyler stepped into the kitchen, and returned a few moments later. He was holding something in his hand, an odd smile on his face.

Jim looked up at Tyler. "What've you got there?"

"My Laughing Boy," he said, breaking into a wide grin.

39
𝔄 𝔐𝔞𝔶𝔬𝔯'𝔰 𝔖𝔭𝔢𝔢𝔠𝔥

August 14, Current Year

"Would you like any more pancakes, Jessica?"

"No, thanks, Mrs. D. I'm stuffed."

"Tyler, how about you?"

"No thanks, Mom. I'm done too."

They were having a great summer. The weatherman was saying that yesterday had almost set a new record, coming within 2° of the record high set over 40 years before. They had been in 1614 for about two and a half months, back to school for just two weeks, and now only a few weeks were left in their summer. It *was* like having back-to-back summer vacations.

Tyler took his dishes to the sink and rinsed them off. "Mom, we're heading over to Jim's; we should be back around noon."

"What for?"

"Remember, I told you last night while you were watching TV."

"Oh ... right. So, tell me again what you want to do there?"

"Well, that history project we did at the end of the school year has me wondering about some stuff that only his computer can tell me."

"Oh, okay. Have fun!"

The crisp early morning air had already given way to another bright and hot day as they made their way down the street. The rhythmic snap of their flip-flops were in perfect cadence with each other as they eased into a comfortable pace—a result of their months of trekking over two hundred miles together across northern France and England ... about four hundred years earlier.

They rang Jim's doorbell and waited, then rang again. After waiting another minute they opened the door themselves and cautiously stepped across the threshold.

"Jim ... you here? Hellooo?"

He was right in front of them, not saying a word, yet software code was appearing on the monitor as if the computer was reading his thoughts. He was in his zone again and didn't hear the doorbell that was just over his head.

"Typical," Jessi smirked as she glanced around the room. Jim leaned forward and raised his arm straight over his head, his index finger extended, then slowly and deliberately he dropped his arm down and hit the enter key.

"Yes!" he exclaimed, as he jumped up and started a happy dance, swaying side-to-side as he slowly spun in a circle—until he saw them at his front door watching him. He cleared his throat. "Oh, hey there. I just finished all my upgrades to Star Commandos—Version Two, and it is *outstanding!*"

"Didn't you start that months ago?" Tyler asked.

"Yeah, but I had to put it on hold until I got a couple of people home from a hiking trip," Jim said mockingly. "Have I *not* mentioned that before?" he added with a grin.

"Rrrright. Speaking of which, can you let me look through the Lille funnel? I've been wondering lately what it looks like now—you know, see if it's changed much over the last four hundred years since we were there." Tyler realized he sounded like his grandpa telling another tall tale, complete with his usual exaggerations.

"Sure, Ty! Here you go."

Jessi and Tyler sat down in front of the monitor as Jim entered the coordinates. "Don't worry," he said with a smile. "It's in 'safe mode'; you will *not* be going there!"

They were looking directly towards the church. The only obvious difference was that the street was now asphalt instead of cobblestone, and there was a concrete sidewalk around the park. Tyler grabbed the mouse. "How do I rotate the view?"

"Just move it sideways."

"Oh, okay." The view shifted to the left towards the stream, but Tyler stopped before getting that far. They were both staring hard, their mouths hanging open.

"What's wrong?" Jim asked.

"The statue!" Jessi yelled.

"Ow!" Tyler winced, "You yelled right in my ear!"

"Oh, sorry. Anyway, it's the 'Laughing Boy', the statue that moron tried to steal— at least it looks like it's the same one. It's kinda hard to be sure 'cause it's up on that … what do you call it?"

"Pedestal?"

"Yeah, pedestal."

Jessi squinted her eyes and leaned closer to the screen. "What's that plaque there under the statue say? Can you zoom in closer?"

"Push the mouse forward, Ty," Jim offered.

"Great, now I can see the words, but I don't know French," Jessi grumbled. "What's it say, Ty?"

"It says, 'Laughing Boy, presented to the people of Lille by the honorable Marcel Dubois, Mayor of Lille, September 12, 1669'."

Jim's eyes narrowed as he thought for a moment. "You know what?" he asked. "We can watch what happened on the twelfth of September. What d'ya think?"

"Yeah, of course!" Tyler responded.

"Sure!" Jessi added. "But first …" she stopped and took a deep breath. "I've been thinking about this for a long time now … I'm not looking forward to the headache, but I really want to know French—with your machine's help, I mean. Then, I can watch and understand what's going on with both of you. Okay?"

Jim spun out of his chair and started walking down the hall. "You're gonna want some aspirin," he said in French.

Jessi leaned over to Tyler. "What'd he say?" she whispered.

"I don't know," he answered. "He said you're gonna want *something*, but I'm not sure what it was."

A minute later he was back.

"Jim?" Tyler asked. "What did you just say you needed? You were speaking French, but I didn't know the word you used."

"Aspirin. I needed to get some aspirin for Jessi."

"Why didn't I know that word?"

"Huh, I'm not sure."

"Well, you know I got French pounded into my brain on the way there. But I don't know any modern words, like airplane or … light bulb … or aspirin."

"You probably learned 17th-century French, not the modern language. That's why."

Fifteen minutes later, Jessi rolled off the couch onto the floor, resting on her hands and knees.

"Feeling better, Jess?" Tyler gently asked.

"My head is still pounding, but the aspirin is helping." Tyler helped her up and walked her to The Bridge where Jim had a seat waiting for her.

"Are you sure you're ready for this?" Jim asked.

"Yeah, I'm ready," she said in French.

"All right, let's do this," Jim replied as he hit the enter key. In front of them they could see what they knew was the statue, but now it was covered by a giant tarp. A small platform was in front of the statue, and a good-sized crowd of people were gathered together, right through and around the funnel itself. Jim had moved the viewpoint for them about seven feet above the ground so they could see what was happening from above the heads of the people. They saw that the stream had been rerouted to the left of where the statue now was.

The crowd cheered as a white-haired elderly man made his way up the stairs onto the podium. He waved his hand and they quieted down as he began to speak.

"My fellow citizens, I will do my best to be brief …" he hesitated with a smile as soft laughter rippled among the people. "Fifty-five years ago a young man in our fair city was on the road to destruction; angry and frustrated, he actually took pleasure in his destructive actions, with little regard for the suffering and pain that others received from his hand. When his conscience would prick his heart, he would excuse away, or justify, his actions. But one day, something happened at this exact spot that forced him to examine his deplorable condition, and it changed him forever."

The old man paused, all eyes were fixed intently on him, and the only sound to be heard was a bird chirping from a high branch in a tree overhead. "This young man was myself!" Several people gasped in disbelief; someone said, "surely not!" as the old man looked straight ahead, lost in thought, reliving once again his actions so many years earlier.

"Yes, I was not always so kind and gentle!" The twinkle in his eye and the smirk on his face brought another ripple of laughter from the crowd. "On this very spot I beat and threatened a young man barely half my age—a total stranger—who earlier had prevented my theft of a statue, the very statue which is now hidden under the canvas behind me."

"Hey! No way!" Tyler shouted, jumping out of his chair. "That's not fair! He ended up becoming rich and famous—that is *so* not fair!" he whined.

"Shut up, Ty!" Jessi said as she thumped him on the back of his head. "I want to hear what he's saying, and it's tough enough with this pounding in my head."

"But you're not the one he beat up, Jess."

"I know, but I want to hear what he's saying, so shut up!" With a loud sigh Tyler flopped back down in his chair. The old man was still talking.

"... and frightened beyond words to describe, I sought counsel from Father Morel, now with our Lord for over twenty years, and forgiveness from God Almighty. With Father Morel's help, I was reconciled with the talented artist who crafted the statue, becoming his employee, and actually assisted in placing it in the flower garden of its eventual owner, where it has stood, or should I say, leaned, for over fifty years! Now, having secured its purchase, I happily give it to be enjoyed by all the people of our city, to serve as a reminder that there is hope for even the darkest of scoundrels in our midst."

Cheers erupted from the crowd, and a few wiped tears from their eyes as the canvas was pulled off the statue revealing the "Laughing Boy." The old man turned away from the people and looked intently at the statue, steadying himself with his cane. He then stepped forward, leaned over, and kissed the laughing boy's hand. After that, he left the podium amid the cheers of the crowd.

The cheering and clapping of the people stopped as Jim shut off the connection, and the screen returned to its usual background: an artistic rendition of Jim's Star Commandos video game. No one said anything for a few moments until Jim muttered under his breath, "Who'd a thought?"

"What?" they both asked in unison.

Jim folded his hands across the top of his head. "I was angry with him for treating you two like he did, and since I couldn't hurt him—and I would have if I could—I could only frighten him, and believe me, it wasn't meant to make him reform! But now it looks like it worked out in a good way, beyond anything I would have thought of, or wanted."

* * * * * *

Tyler and Jessi spent the next three hours playing Jim's new version of Star Commandos. Then, they gave him their opinions of the story line and new features.

"So, is there any one thing that makes it stand out, you know, that could really 'sell it' to all the gamers?" Jim asked.

"Oh, yeah," Tyler quickly answered. "The best part was getting to watch the spaceships break apart from the perspective of the enemy—and always different based on where I hit them with the lasers."

"And getting to watch it in slo-mo is really cool," Jessi added. "And also the way the air and stuff gets sucked out into space."

Jim just looked at them, not saying a word. After a few seconds they felt like they must have said something wrong and didn't know how to fix it, whatever "it" was.

"Umm, let's go out front for a sec," he finally said.

After he closed the front door behind them, he walked with them out to his mailbox at the curb. "Do you two know much about 'artificial intelligence'?" he asked.

They both shook their heads.

"It's the idea that machines get so smart they start thinking; they … start *creating* on their own, not just following the steps in a program."

"Like we see in the movies?"

"Right. I didn't write the enemy-perspective-destruction thing," he said. "I remember briefly thinking about what it might be like, but that's all. I think the computer took it from there and provided the option."

"Do you think the computer is alive?" Jessi asked, wide-eyed.

"No, at least not like how we define 'alive' for people. You see, the computer did this for me a couple months ago. It wrote a simple program to show me how you landed when you were transported to Amiens. Then I ran it in slo-mo, which is now an option the computer put into the game. I didn't do that! It's clearly getting smarter. It makes me wonder if you went back in time because … because it was, at that point, an 'infant' developmentally. You were looking at ancient documents, and it was confused by the power surge."

Tyler and Jessi were having trouble keeping up with his logic, since all they could think of was that the computer might be coming alive.

"Well, anyway," Jim continued, "tell you what I'm going to do; I'm gonna make sure you two are credited as part of the development team for Star Commandos Two. Sound good?"

They both nodded.

"Jim?" Jessi asked. "Are we out here 'cause you didn't want the computer to hear what we're talking about?"

"Umm … yeah," he said sheepishly. "Hey, I'm sure it's fine. I'm just being a little paranoid. Don't worry about it. I'll see ya later." He nervously cleared his throat as he turned and headed for the house.

* * * * * *

The long summer day finally ended, and it had been dark barely half an hour when Tyler went to bed. Spending the day at

Jim's and recounting their adventure had triggered a flood of memories and emotions that continued to invade his mind all through the evening. He smiled as he thought about collecting eggs in the chicken coop at the Moreau farm, and Ginger, the chicken at Widow Pike's. He winced and pressed his head back into the pillow as he thought of the dragon shoving him down into the ground.

After a few minutes, the rising moon cast its silvery light through his window onto the shelf above the foot of his bed. His miniature Laughing Boy could clearly be seen, bringing back once again the memory of the sculptor grabbing him by the shoulders and kissing him on each cheek. Finally, with an occasional whisper of the warm summer breeze coming through the open window, and the sounds of a laughing child echoing through his mind, he fell asleep.